THE LADY'S LOVER

DEB MARLOWE

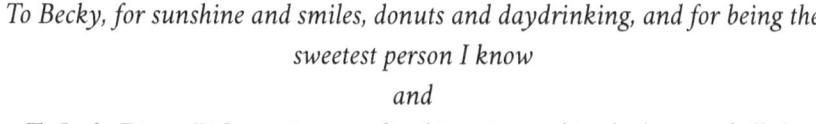

To Becky, for sunshine and smiles, donuts and daydrinking, and for being the sweetest person I know
and
To Lady Diane DeLuna, immortalized in print and in the hearts of all the Debutantes.

THE HALF MOON HOUSE SERIES

HALF MOON HOUSE

CARLTON HOUSE

LONDON, ENGLAND

I thank you for coming so far with me, gentle reader. I thank you for listening to my story, told in my own words. I beg your indulgence, for I know I have not offered the titillation you hoped for—and I fear that I am about to disappoint you further . . .
—from the Journal of the Infamous Miss Hestia Wright

"This feud of yours . . ." The Prince Regent of England stood at a window in the private audience chamber in his home, shaking his head and not looking at her while he spoke. "This battle between you and Marstoke, it has gone on quite long enough."

Hestia Wright had both training and practice at hiding her emotions. Not even the impatience and exasperation the Prince Regent inspired could furrow her brow. She had learned from the best. Her mask sat firmly in place. "You will find no argument from me on that score, Your Highness."

"What I would like to find is an end to it." He gave a half turn she knew was meant to showcase his grey silk coat and navy waistcoat against the blue curtains behind him.

"No more than I would, sir."

"Oh, a great deal more, I suspect," he snapped.

Not for nothing had Hestia been named Queen of Courtesans in Great Britain and Beyond. Those days might be long behind her, but she still dealt with men of power and influence. And royal blood, too. She straightened her spine and raised her chin. "I do hope you have not called me here only to berate me, Your Highness. If you will recall, it was my people and their work that led to Marstoke's capture not so long ago. And he was in the Crown's custody when he escaped from Newgate."

"Damn him!" The Prince Regent whirled from the window, the color rising across his fleshy cheeks. "Damn his defiant, insolent, impudent—"

He choked on his own words and didn't continue.

Hestia waited while he coughed and wheezed and regained his composure. "Yes. Marstoke is all that and far worse besides," she said, using her most conciliatory tone. "And with all due respect, sir, I am not the only one involved in a feud with the man, am I?" She held up her hand, ticking off her nemesis's evil deeds on her fingers. "He planned to publically attack and embarrass your wife before all the foreign dignitaries visiting England—while placing the blame on you. He planned worse for your daughter—for who knows what he might have done to her reputation—or her person—with a look-a-like ready and waiting? And this latest attempt to kidnap Miss—"

"Yes, yes!" The Regent cut her off before she could state out loud the woman's name—the woman she knew was likely the secret daughter of his first, unrecognized marriage to Maria Fitzherbert. Interesting, that. It told her that someone was listening. But someone who did not know the particulars of that state secret?

Unlikely.

"There is no need to reiterate all of the villain's misdeeds," he grumped. "I am well aware of them."

"I rather suspect there are a few more that I am unaware of," said Hestia wryly. "What is important is the pattern here. Marstoke is repeatedly trying to use the women in your life to harm you. Granted, most of his . . . transgressions are against women, but these acts appear to be deliberate and focused on you. If I knew the reason behind his animosity, I might anticipate—"

"Reason! Reason?" The Prince Regent was breathing heavily again. "There is naught of reason in that man! He is quite mad! I should think that was obvious."

"It has been obvious to me for quite a long time," she said shortly. "Which is why I have devoted so much of my time and so many of my resources to thwarting him."

"But not enough, clearly! For he is still out there, is he not? Scheming and manipulating and generally acting a great, noisome nuisance."

She closed her eyes. Nuisance? The man who had stolen her innocence, abused her body and mind and ruined her life—and countless others, too? The man who tempted well-bred young gentlemen into wickedness and treachery? Who had maimed and injured dozens and left no small number dead in his violent wake? Ask any of them and they would name him far more than a *nuisance*.

"Well, I will not have it," the Prince Regent declared. "Not any longer. Do you know how many burdens I must bear? The wars, and my infinitely troublesome wife, and my stubborn daughter who will not look at the Prince of Orange with the consideration he deserves. And now rioting in London's streets!" He waved his hands above his head, and light sparkled from the jewels on his pudgy fingers.

Hestia raised a brow. "Well, the price of bread is—"

"Yes, yes, I know it! I didn't bring you here to debate the Corn Laws, Miss Wright."

She sighed. "Why have you brought me here, sir?"

He drew himself up. "I brought you here to tell you that I want this business with Marstoke taken care of once and for all. Imprisoned or dead or transported, I do not care, as long as his plotting is put to an end. And since you have not managed the job on your own, you will be working with some of my people to see it done."

"I see." She drew a deep and bracing breath. "There might be a problem with that plan, Your Highness."

That pulled him up short. "Indeed?" One word, but it emerged as frosty as an ice from Gunter's.

The growing ire she hid so expertly kept her warm in the face of it. "Yes. How many people know the name of Miss—" She stopped herself. "The name of the lady I so recently brought to you, sir?" She raised a brow. "Very few, I suspect, and fewer still who understand her significance. And every one of them are likely in your inner circle, are they not?"

"For the most part," he acknowledged. "What do you mean to say, Miss Wright?"

"You've a cat amongst your pigeons, sir," she said baldly. "A turncoat."

All of the bluster went out of him. He leaned heavily on the desk in the midst of the room, then sank down into the padded chair. "Yes. I have feared so, and it has weighed upon me, too. Who has betrayed me, I wonder?" He sighed. "Another burden." He shook his head and looked at her with mournful eyes. "It is hard to go through life not knowing whom to trust, my dear."

Harder still to know whom one *should* trust—and find them wanting. But she was wise enough not to bring up the betrayal of family to this particular royal. She kept the thought to herself and displayed the sympathy that the Prince Regent clearly craved.

"It's why I had you brought here, to Carlton House, and kept the meeting quiet. Only a select few will know of this project and you will be working with one of my most trusted advisors."

She had a hunch she knew who that might be. "Thank you, sir, but that won't be necessary. The fewer who know of this, the better, and I can manage quite on my own."

"No, ma'am." The Regent's gaze had gone hard. He looked suddenly like the man who held a nation in his hands—and had fought to get it. "I've suffered this particular thorn in my side for too long. I want it plucked out and crushed underfoot. Perhaps doused in oil and burnt too, for good measure."

He leaned toward her. "I know you do a great deal of good work, my dear. Do not think I am unaware or unappreciative of the care you take of some of my most unfortunate subjects. But I ask you to put all of that aside now, or give it into someone else's hands. I want all of your concentration and focus on working with my agent and finally putting a stop to Marstoke and his ceaseless machinations."

Give it into someone else's hands. Easy enough to say, perhaps, when one was the acting king. When one was surrounded by lackeys. When one spent more hours endlessly redecorating than on state business and spent the nation's money on chandeliers and overwrought gilding and that Rembrandt on the wall.

She wanted to scream her defiance. Sneer at his dismissal of the endless work awaiting her.

None of it showed.

It never did.

The mask was in place.

She nodded. Stood.

He pushed himself to his feet. The door into the antechamber, where she'd waited earlier, opened. A footman bowed and held the door open for her.

"Your Highness." She curtsied low.

"I look forward to hearing of your progress, my dear."

She did not reply, only walked out and through the endless opulence of his home. It was a relief to leave the oppressively quiet and rich atmosphere for the bustle and noise of Pall Mall. She stood for a moment, undecided, then set off, heading east toward Cockspur Street.

John Everett, the Earl of Stoneacre, allowed his feet to drag as he made his way through Hanover Square, to his father's home. He might have delayed a few moments longer, had the door not swung instantly open.

"Hello, Sommes." He handed the butler his hat and glanced at the magnificent arrangement of hothouse flowers in the entry hall. "Only one?" he asked. "Are we economizing this week?"

"We are, sir. I am afraid there is only one choice each of savory and sweet on the tea tray today."

"Horrors. How provincial. My mother must be vexed, indeed." They shared a grin. "I suppose we shall muddle on, though."

"The muddling has begun without you, sir."

"Oh, very well." Stoneacre sighed. "Let's have at it, then."

Sommes opened the parlor door. "The Earl of Stoneacre has arrived, my lady."

His mother brightened as he stepped over the threshold, and beckoned him in. "There you are, dear. Come in. I'd hoped you'd arrive earlier, but never mind." She stood to greet him with a kiss and then turned, presenting the other ladies with a wave of her hand. "Allow me to introduce you to Mrs. Chisholm and her lovely daughter, Miss Chisholm."

Stoneacre made his bow and bent over his mother's hand as she sat, raising a brow at her as he did so. He took the seat she indicated and held up a hand to demure a cup of tea. "I was under the impression that you had an urgent errand for me, Mother."

"I do. But it can wait long enough for you to sit a moment." The marchioness passed a plate of savories. "We were just discussing the heat. It comes early this year and seems to have driven a large number of people out of London."

"Traffic does seem thinner," he agreed. "Are you thinking of heading back to Wiltshire, soon?"

"In time. It is easier to bear the heat at home, but there are some pleasures that just cannot be found in the country. Don't you agree, Miss Chisholm?"

"I do, Lady Woodbury. I would stay in Town straight though to the end of the year, if I could."

"Are you finishing your first Season, Miss Chisholm?" Stoneacre asked politely.

"I am. It has been wonderful," the girl said with satisfaction.

He didn't doubt she'd been a success. She was lovely—all prim blonde locks and pale cheeks and the sort of slim tidiness that showed her simple day gown to the best advantage.

"Will you return to the country with your family, my lord?" She turned innocent blue eyes on him.

"I don't believe so. My work keeps me busy, just now."

"That must be why we have not met before now," she remarked.

"Stoneacre's work with the Privy Council can be quite demanding," his mother interjected. "When he marries, his wife will have to learn to be flexible."

"Or perhaps just busy in her own sphere," Mrs. Chisholm suggested. "There are any number of activities for a young matron these days. Charity has found much to occupy her in Town, beyond the Season's festivities and the usual tourist destinations. She has joined several ladies' societies and discovered a couple of causes well worth her time."

"Very laudable, I'm sure," his mother said with a nod.

"There are so many things to learn, as well," the girl added. "I very much enjoyed the lecture on the ancient Greek buildings that Mrs. Montague sponsored last week." She looked at him through her lashes. "Does your work for the Prince Regent lead to much travel, my lord?"

"It does, now and again."

"My son returned from France, months past, and I've barely seen him since," his mother complained.

"I was in Brittany, Mother," he corrected her.

"It's all the same, isn't it?" his mother asked with a toss of her head.

"Oh, I don't think I'd like to go to France," Miss Chisholm said with a shudder. "Not even after the Duke of Wellington put Napoleon in his place. I don't care for the color green at all."

Stoneacre glanced at his mother, hoping for an explanation, but she was wearing an expression that echoed his befuddlement. Even the girl's mother looked puzzled.

Miss Chisholm looked around, clearly sensing the confusion in the air, but not understanding it.

"Green, dear? Do you reference the uniforms of the French soldiers? I believe they wear a good deal of blue."

"No, I meant their skin," she explained.

At the continued silence, she looked around again. "Their green-tinged skin? Lawrence explained it when I asked why the French are so often referred to as frogs."

Stoneacre ruthlessly suppressed a laugh. Not for the world would he bruise the girl's feelings. His mother coughed and turned her head. The girl's mother, however, rolled her eyes.

"Really, Charity. I should think that you'd learn not to be so gullible where your brother is concerned."

Color rushed into her face. She darted a quick glance his way, then lowered her gaze to her twisting hands.

"Do not fret, Miss Chisholm." He gave her a smile. "Such a misunderstanding casts no shame in your direction. Only your brother should feel badly over it."

"Oh, he won't. Not a bit." She breathed deeply and met his gaze directly again. "Thank you, my lord. You are very kind."

"Not at all." He stood. "Forgive me, Mother. As you are in no hurry to share your errand, I'll return later to address it. For now, the Prince Regent has a task for me that he does consider urgent." He bowed to the room. "Ladies, I bid you good day."

He made his escape, shaking his head at his mother's machinations. Yes, she'd been pestering him lately about his age, his duty and the integrity of his bloodline, but he hadn't expected her to push so hard, and so quickly.

He sighed. He knew his mother was right on all counts, but it wasn't her nagging that made him admit it. It was his own . . . loneliness. The dawning realization that his work was not enough anymore. The ache and the sense of something missing that haunted his quiet moments of late.

He probably should be looking for a possible countess. Miss Chisholm was a perfectly lovely girl, but she was not the one to fill his emptiness. Nor any girl like her. He was too old to chase after Society's fresh-faced debutantes. He wanted a woman of wit and intelligence and humor and heart. He'd found one, too, damn it. But she'd made her indifference plain. And the Prince Regent was likely right now grinding to dust any slim chance he'd ever had with her.

With a sigh, he set off for Carlton House, to see how much damage had been done.

CHAPTER 2

You've heard, now, about the beginning, about the stupid mistake I made, the terrible misjudgment of character that forever changed my life. You wait with bated breath, I am sure, for the details regarding the relationships that followed. The details about the men who bid for me, once my new life as a courtesan was underway. I know many want to know the identities of the men who fought and bought their way into the honor of my company . . .
--from the Journal of the Infamous Miss Hestia Wright

Stoneacre arrived at the Prince Regent's residence and entered through a private door. Making his way through the maze of servant's corridors, he arrived outside the receiving rooms, where the Regent's secretary informed him that Hestia Wright's audience was already under way. With a nod, the earl slipped to a small room nearby, took a seat and slid a hidden panel to one side. Leaning in, he listened intently.

He bit back a grin. Hestia was giving as good as she got. But the interview ended rather abruptly and he had to hurry to extract himself—before the Regent could realize he was there, and call for him—and before she could get away.

She moved fast and he burst out onto the street just in time to catch a glimpse of her retreating back. Unexpected pain stabbed him at the sight. Damnation. He admired this woman more than any other, yet she was always moving away from him. Even when she stood in place right before him.

She was angry. Even from here he could see she was all tight shoulders and stiff spine and purposeful steps. He'd expected that. The Regent might just be the only man alive who could dictate to Hestia Wright. Unfortunately, Stoneacre would likely bear the brunt of her resentment.

With a sigh, he set out after her and after a few minutes, he realized she was not heading for Craven Street and Half Moon House. He wasn't sure she had any destination in mind at all. She headed for the crowds at Charing Cross, where she hailed a hack. He got one too, and followed as she rode over the Westminster Bridge and into Southwark. Let her have time to brood. After that interview, she deserved it.

The conditions they drove through deteriorated. If she paid attention, his presence behind her would rapidly become obvious. Eventually, they reached a neighborhood through which the hack would not travel. She climbed down and kept walking. Stoneacre did the same. He kept close enough to intervene, should occasion arise—but he should have known better. Hestia, dressed in an elegant gown fit for her royal audience, made her way into some of the most crowded, foul and dangerous neighborhoods in the city—and she was perfectly safe. Those few who did not recognize her on sight were pulled back from the folly of menacing her, with a quick grab and a shake of the head—and they thanked their friends for the intervention once they understood.

Hestia Wright was untouchable. She had friends, allies and devotees everywhere, from the lowest hovel to the highest courts, from the ballrooms of England to the royal courts of Europe. She had money, influence and power—and she used it to help those who needed it most.

She was as at home here as she was in Carlton House—and the squalor around them did not slow her step at all. Stepping nimbly, she dodged rats and feral dogs and street children gone nearly as wild. Once in a while an urchin would approach her and she would crouch to listen and exchange a few words. Once she stopped and spoke with a wan, tired woman standing in a doorway. Always, though, she moved on, moving adroitly around noxious puddles and sprawled drunkards, nodding to those brave enough to meet her eye.

Finally she stopped at a lane that ended at a rusty, iron fence. She stood, gazing out at the small plot of land beyond it for several long minutes.

Stoneacre watched her. He leaned against a dirty timber wall and did a bit of his own brooding. There was one place Hestia Wright wouldn't be welcome—and that was his mother's drawing room. There were plenty of people in Society who respected her and the incredible work she did, but the high sticklers would never accept a former courtesan into their ranks.

The hypocrisy of it sickened him. His parents of all people should know better than to hold past mistakes against anyone. But it didn't stop them. Nor did their inevitable disapproval keep him from dreaming of Hestia Wright.

Honestly, it made no sense, neither the intensity with which he was drawn to her, nor the fact that his feelings thrived in the face of her indifference. Surely her polite detachment should wither his enthusiasm. But, no. Even facing away from him, her slim elegance and silent strength called to him.

Abruptly, he answered. Pushing away from the dirty wall, he approached her.

"I guessed it would be you," she said without turning around. "When the Regent said he wanted me to work with an agent, I knew he meant you."

"Yes. I suppose I should have known better."

She glanced askance at him. "Better?"

"Better than to wish for a chance to work closely with you. Now the fates have answered with the one position sure to annoy you beyond redemption."

She didn't answer for a moment, then her mouth curved. "We'll see." Turning away, she contemplated the modestly marked burial plots beyond.

Stoneacre glanced at the small sign on the gate. "Cross Bones?"

"Indeed. Are you familiar with the Bishop of Winchester's geese?"

"I don't believe so."

"Well, there they lie." She waved a hand. "For hundreds of years the Bishops collected rents from the many brothels they owned here in Southwark. They made fortunes from these prostitutes, but when the women died, they would not allow them burial in the churchyard. So they were laid to rest here, out of the way and in unconsecrated soil."

His lips pressed together. "I wish I could say I am astounded by such hypocrisy."

"I'm sure you see the like every day, working with the Prince Regent and so many high government officials." She said it completely without irony. "We'll encounter worse, trying to complete this mission."

"I've no doubt about that."

She raised a brow in question and he took a moment to drink her in. She had skin like moonlight on water, pale and alight with its own glow. Blue eyes, deeply colored and slightly slanted at the ends. So knowing—but how could they not be, when she'd seen so much of the world's darkness and so many of mankind's secret flaws? And yet, her eyes were not cynical. The tiny, upturned lines at the edges showed that she could still find laughter and ease—and he rejoiced and marveled at it.

"No doubt about either," he answered her unspoken question. "I know we'll encounter plenty of hypocrisy in this mission. And I know that we'll finish Marstoke once and for all."

Silence reigned for a few minutes.

"We haven't seen much of you since the night we captured Marstoke in that basement." It was not quite an accusation. "I was surprised to find you at the wedding last week."

"Of course I attended. I was thrilled to be invited."

"It was Francis's doing. And Callie's. They are fond of you."

"As I am of them." Was it a first strike? Her failure to mention any of her own feelings for him? She would find that he refused to war with her. Neither would he importune or push in where he was not wanted. He swallowed a sigh. Nothing about this was going to be easy. "Did you think I had given up after Marstoke's escape from Newgate?" He shook his head. "On the contrary."

"Oh?"

"I've been working my way through the piles of papers your Duchess of Aldmere found in Marstoke's secret office." *Most* of the documents. According to the duchess, formerly Miss Brynne Wilmott, a sack full of the most interesting evidence had disappeared that night, when the marquess had made his first move against the Prince Regent. Stoneacre had his suspicions about where it had gone.

Something darkened behind her eyes. "That cannot be pleasant."

"No. I've been finding a path through the tangle of his polluted business dealings." He shook his head. "So many accounts of blackmail and bribery, so much corruption. He's built an empire on fear and hate, through cheating and outright theft. He uses multiple names and identities and nothing seems beneath him." He couldn't hold back the harshness that crept into his tone. "I have enjoyed the process of dismantling it all, brick by brick. Piece by piece. I've spoken to so many—his victims, those who stood against him, the subordinates who disappointed him. Broken men, all. And ever so slowly, I've begun cutting him off from his various streams of revenue. He may have escaped Newgate, but he should be finding it a different, smaller world."

He glanced over and froze at what he saw, unguarded for just a moment, in her face.

Like the strike of a match out of the dark, she was lit with surprise and relief, with blazing approval and with . . . more. With something that looked both fervent and . . . breathless.

"I . . ." He couldn't find words for a moment. She'd never shown more than a hint of emotion in his presence and now her expression blazed with a host of them and he could not turn away.

She blinked, summoning a shutter that slammed down over it all, and she turned away.

"I . . . There are so many of them, devastated by his cruelty," he continued haltingly. "It makes me feel sure we will find someone willing to help us, to lead us to him."

She looked out over the burial plots again, brow furrowed.

"Are any of your people in there?" he asked after a moment. "The women you tried to help?"

"No. I have my own place for them. Private. Quiet. Pretty." She tilted her head and closed her eyes as if reaching for that image of peace.

Ah, hell. Her profile was perfection. Her mouth was sweet and wide and made for the press of a kiss. He wanted to touch her lips, trace them with his thumb and coax them open—just for him.

He imagined her reaction. No slow, swelling sweetness or soft, quick shivers of passion from this one. Not even a bite. He'd likely end up with a knife in his ribs.

He was in a world of trouble. This mission was going to be the death of him, one way or another.

"No."

"No?" He hadn't been fool enough to say any of that out loud, had he?

"We won't find anyone willing to betray him. Marstoke chooses wisely and acts thoroughly. He never makes a move without guarantee of his victim's full capitulation." She breathed deeply. "But you've been blocking the flow of his funds?"

He nodded.

"I saw a few signs of it, in Kendal," she mused. "When I went to the aid of the Prince Regent's . . . of young Miss Smythe. There were too few men involved, considering that last gambit was a move against both the Regent and me. And Rhys reported a good bit of bickering among them. Not what I'm used to seeing amongst the marquess's well-compensated and eager game players. Usually they act as disciplined and regular as a machine."

"Yes. And I assume you've heard that more than a few recalcitrant second sons have found their way home over the last few weeks?" he asked. "When we raided the estate Marstoke been hiding in with his recruits, they had all gone. But it appears a few of them have quit Marstoke's grand game and returned home."

"I did hear. And a few of the names surprised me." Her gaze unfocused a little. "There are always surprises with Marstoke, but I think it's time we hit him with one of our own."

He nodded grimly. "We are overdue."

She gave him a crooked, conspiratorial smile that set his heartbeat to sputtering. "Not all of his business dealings are in his ledgers, Lord Stoneacre. Like the Bishops of Winchester past, the marquess makes a pretty sum off of many of the city's prostitutes. If he's short of funds, he'll be looking to these hidden streams more heavily. And I know of a major source."

"Oh? Where will we find such a place?"

"Meet me at Half Moon House tonight, after sunset, and I'll show you. And wear black, please." She turned her head toward the graveyard again. "But for now, if you will allow me to say my goodbyes, then perhaps we can walk back to a spot where we can find a hack?"

He nodded and walked away. Glancing back, he was arrested at the sight of her once more. Grace and beauty and steel and intelligence and kindness—all set against that sad backdrop. He sighed heavily and knew he'd carry that image away with him.

LATER THAT EVENING, Hestia sat at her vanity table and carefully checked the lay of her false hair. She'd become a redhead tonight, which always made her feel a little bolder. A bit saucier, in general.

Perhaps not a wise choice.

Too late to worry over it now. She turned her head this way and that, but all sat tight and neat. She added the two clips that accessorized this particular outfit. The large one, long, heavy and elaborately carved, she anchored at the back of her elegant red chignon. The smaller, obviously paste and cheaply made, she tucked away beneath a swath of hair so that it could scarcely be seen.

From below echoed a chorus of laughter and mostly good-natured squabbling. Listening, she closed her eyes and dropped her head into her hands for a moment.

That sound was a balm to her soul. It meant safety and warmth and a hope for a better life—for at least the too-small number of girls she could fit within these walls.

At the same time, it made her restless, for there was still so much work to be done, so many other women who needed attention, opportunity or just someone to care.

Give it into someone else's hands. The echo of it still infuriated her. What did the Prince Regent think she'd been doing? She'd been fighting Marstoke since she was fifteen years old and recruiting others—to help women like those who came to Half Moon House, as well as to help curb the wicked marquess—for nearly as long.

Now she had help—and an ultimatum. The thought of life without the worry of Marstoke hanging over her beckoned, a shining dream. And though she didn't like how the Prince Regent gave orders without sharing likely vital information, she was grateful to have his men and resources behind her—if only they didn't come with Stoneacre at the helm.

Stoneacre. He was going to be a distraction.

A big man, the earl was. Like a Viking, the girls downstairs would likely whisper—and they would be right. A man's man, she would label him, tall and broad, but not bulky, with dark hair that somehow threw off light, like the shine in a raven's wing. Dark eyes, almost black when he was displeased. A solid, strong blade of a nose and skin like a sailor's—burnished by time spent in sun and wind so that it was another color altogether from most of the English peerage.

Different from them in other ways, too. The earl had made his interest plain, almost from the moment of their first meeting—much like a large percentage of the men she encountered. Unlike the others, however, he hadn't acted as if his attentions were a favor to her. And he hadn't pushed when she didn't respond. No pouting, no annoyed disbelief, no angry attempts at domination. Instead, he'd stepped back when she let his interest pass unnoticed, although it was still there, apparent when they met, and it grew increasingly harder not to indulge her own . . . curiosity.

That's all it was, surely. Clinical interest in a man who possessed both the looks and charisma of a predator, and the honor of a true gentleman. Not carnal temptation. Such things belonged in her past, burned out of her by hate and callous necessity. Never mind that his easy smile and open gaze stirred up—

She straightened abruptly as the door latch rattled and Isaac stepped in even as he knocked. He paused as he noticed her outfit.

"Oh. It's to be a night like that, is it?" He started to back out. "Let me arrange to have another footman or two on duty tonight and I'll be ready in a trice."

"No. No need." She beckoned him back. "I've arranged for another escort tonight."

Isaac looked disgruntled. "Is that why Stoneacre just showed up downstairs?"

"It is." She stood and fetched a gossamer shawl from a chair. "I need you to stay here tonight. Stay alert. And message all of our eyes in Town. If Marstoke is in London, then I want to know about it."

"In Town?" Isaac looked startled. "With all the world still looking for him? Would he be so brazen?"

Hestia checked her reflection in the mirror. "The end grows near, old friend. The game is winding down. At this point, we need to assume that Marstoke is capable of anything."

Isaac stilled for a moment, his bulk filling the doorway, his eyes narrowed and focused. He would have been a warrior in an ancient time, proud and strong and willing to throw his heart into righteous battle. "I'll start those messages. And I'll call in a few extra guards to put into the rotation around here." He set off for the servant's stairs at the back of the house.

Hestia went on silent feet down the front stairs, her mind

replaying the scene that so often came to her when Stoneacre's name was mentioned.

It had happened the night that they'd captured Marstoke. She and Stoneacre and Callie and Tru had been riding high on triumph when Marstoke and his top couple of lackeys were hauled away from the damp cellar that night, but one of the Wicked Marquess's lieutenants had thought to ease his own punishment by giving up some of his compatriots. Even before he'd been bundled into the back of a horse van, he'd told them of a handful of others, waiting for Marstoke nearby.

Stoneacre had gathered the soldiers he'd brought and they had all set out for the place. They'd split into two groups and Stoneacre had taken his men to the back, to flush the villains out. But the henchmen were desperate and turned as vicious as Marstoke himself. They fought back. Tru and his group of soldiers had rushed them. Two lackeys had fallen before the rest saw the wisdom of surrender.

Except for one. A dirty brute of a man, who rushed out of hiding. He'd lifted a pistol and pointed it at Tru. He couldn't miss from that distance.

She stepped forward, opened her mouth to scream a warning. But Stoneacre came out of the darkness behind the thug. Large as he was, he reached right over the man's shoulder, grabbed him by the wrist like a recalcitrant child and pulled up. The shot fired into the ceiling, perilously close to Stoneacre's ear, but he just grinned and braced his feet apart and held the man slightly off the ground—and barely drew a deep breath doing it.

He was hailed a hero—but shrugged it off—and if he spoke a little too loudly for the rest of the evening, no one mentioned it.

That scene came to her sometimes, when she was slipping off to sleep, or working on her ledgers, or sliding down into the bath. Physical prowess. Casual heroism. It gave her a thrill every time she thought about it. It made her shiver a little. And it calmed her somehow, made her feel good about the fact that such a man existed out there in the world.

She pushed the image away now, as she reached the bottom of the stairs. The noise from the parlor had changed. The girls had an audience. She paused to listen and peek around the corner.

Isaac would have left Stoneacre in the formal parlor, but the earl hadn't stayed there, of course. He'd wandered across the wide entry hall to the similarly sized room on the other side—a spot far more cluttered and perpetually busy. *The project parlor*, Hestia called it in her own mind.

Tonight Jesse had pushed two tables together to form a makeshift counter. The girl had lost a beau recently, when the butcher's son turned out to be a traitorous lout who'd succumbed to Marstoke's bribery, but now Jesse had more than made up for the loss. The owner of the notions shop just a few streets away had begun courting her. Jesse was coaching the girls on sales techniques, hoping to bring at least one along as a shop girl when she married.

"You'll have gentlemen customers, will you not?" Stoneacre asked her as she presided over her stock of gathered and borrowed items.

"Certainly, sir."

"Then allow me to help, won't you? I'll be the customer and you can take turns waiting upon me."

Jesse looked uncertain, but Molly pushed forward. "What have you come looking for, sir?" The girl's tone had gone husky and Hestia sighed.

He scanned the items. "Stockings," he said decisively.

A round of giggles went through the room. Cook, sitting and knitting in the corner, snorted.

"Well, then." Molly sashayed around to face him across the counter and picked up the pair of woolen stockings, letting them drape all along her arm. "Can I help you, my lord? Perhaps you need the item modeled?"

"Molly!" Jesse protested. "You cannot talk to customers like that!"

"I think I know how to make a sale," Molly sniffed.

"It's a notions shop, not Mother Sally's!"

"She's right," Stoneacre told the girl. "You must think about your customer. Here I am, a gentleman come to purchase ladies stockings. It's not a gift I would take home to my mother or sister, is it?"

"I wouldn't think so, but you never know about the quality," Molly said with a frown.

Still lurking on the stairs and peering around the corner at them, Hestia bit back laughter.

"Well, *I* would not do so," he said and she heard the amusement in his voice, too. "And if that is the case, then I must have come into the shop with a woman already on my mind. Trying to tempt me with your charms isn't the best idea, then, is it?"

Molly looked ready to argue the case.

"It's not good form," Stoneacre hastened to add. "Even though your own charms are considerable, I'm sure."

She giggled.

"So. I'll be the shop girl now," he declared, taking up the stockings and spreading them out along the table. "Use this," he said, reaching across and tapping her temple. "Think about why the gentleman is here."

He waited a moment and all of the girls grew quiet. He smiled, then, at Molly and ran a finger along the length of the stockings. "This pair is made from some of the finest silk to be found in the city, sir, and it goes on so softly against the skin. The embroidered primroses are popular, too, and if you are interested, we have the matching garters to tie them with. So dainty and feminine, are they not? Such a pretty picture altogether." He gave the girl a crooked smile. "And it does make a girl happy to wear something fine and special beneath her skirts, even if she's the only one to know it is there."

"Your lordship!" Jesse gasped, sounding scandalized.

He laughed. "Yes, it was a tad naughty, wasn't it? But I was thinking of the gentleman who might be making this purchase and painting the sort of picture he would want to see."

"It worked a treat," Molly said, fanning herself.

"It hardly seems fair," another girl said.

Stoneacre pursed his lips. "Tell me, ladies . . . Have you heard much of me? Gossip? Tittle-tattle?"

A chorus of nods and agreements was his answer.

"What have you heard?"

The answers rang out. "That you brought down a Cornish smuggling ring all by yourself."

"That you can shoot a pig's eye at fifty paces."

"That you can charm the warts right off a toad."

He laughed at the variety of attributes offered up, but pointed at Peggy, who had mentioned the toads. "Yes, although I am unacquainted with any specific toads, I am reputed to be charming, or so my mother informs me. Would you all like to know the secret to charm?"

Her girls were nothing but enthusiastic, Hestia thought, when they all loudly agreed that they would, indeed, like to know the secret.

"It's easy—but it must be real. True." He placed a fist on his chest. "Heartfelt." He looked at each one of them. "You must get to know another person. Even if it's just a little, it has to come from true interest and caring. You cannot fake it just for your own gain. Insincerity is obvious and unattractive." He shrugged. "Just show a bit of real interest. Put yourself in someone else's shoes. Say something to brighten their day."

"I doubt it is that easy," Jesse said sourly.

"It is. I swear it. Use your head. Engage your heart. It works in the ballroom. It will work in the shop." He lifted a ribbon and leaned in to hold it next to Jesse's face. "Oh, you need something to hold your bonnet, Miss Smith? Not the pink. This ribbon will do the trick—and the lavender color will bring out the green in your eyes so that every gentleman in Hyde Park will take notice."

He stepped over to bow before Cook. "It will work in the market place, too. I've heard your sweet buns are known far and wide, madam. These currants are so fresh and plump and fine, they can only add to your reputation." He stepped back. "Now, you try."

The girls started to chatter and Hestia leaned her head back against the stairway wall. *Why? Why? Why?* She banged her head gently with each reiteration.

Lingering thoughts about the earl's big hands, powerful thighs and changeable eyes were one thing. But why must he act so kindly and generously toward her charges? That was the sort of thing bound to crawl under her skin and emerge at the most inconvenient time.

Laughter rang out again and she straightened. Time to get to business. She rounded the last step, pulling on gloves as she went. "Good evening, everyone." She looked around at the happy girls. "Stay in tonight, my dears, and watch carefully. Keep each other safe." She cocked her head at the earl. "Lord Stoneacre, I believe we have some work to do?"

CHAPTER 3

But, no. Here is where I diverge from your expectations. I am going to tell you a different story entirely. A story about a monster, more than a man. Or rather, many stories. The unspoken tales of those who have suffered at his hand.
--from the Journal of the Infamous Miss Hestia Wright

S toneacre stared. None of the young women blinked an eye, but the change in Hestia Wright's appearance struck him sharp, an elbow to the gut. She still looked beautiful, of course. And with her fair skin, she absolutely convinced as a redhead. But she'd lost some of that famous, ethereal, blonde aloofness, somehow. She looked more human. More approachable.

Earthy.

Exactly the wrong thought to strike upon as he handed her into the carriage. Even through gloves he felt a *frisson* of excitement at her touch. And though she might look different, she still smelled the same —and how did a woman contrive to smell like . . . *spring*, in any case? Not floral, not exactly. But yes, floral. And fresh and sweet and faintly herbal. And just like a passing breeze of spring air, the scent filled him with eagerness and anticipation and . . . craving.

He continued to stare as the carriage set off, taking advantage of the streetlights as they turned onto the Strand. "I know there are very many fine wigs available, of course, but I confess—I'm wildly curious to know what you've done with your eyebrows."

Hestia gave a little laugh, but she didn't reach up and touch her brows as one might expect. Her hands stayed very correctly folded in her lap. "Oh, it's just a bit of powder with clay dust mixed in. It washes right out, but it does look convincing, does it not?"

"Utterly." He couldn't look away, even on those stretches when he could scarcely see her. "Are you often a redhead?"

"I play whatever role is necessary to get the work done, sir. As you do yourself, or so I hear."

He grinned. "It's true. I've acted a sea captain and a housebreaker, an art thief, an auctioneer, and an attaché to the Duke of Wellington. My work for the Privy Council is interesting and varied."

"And all done for the good of England."

"So far," he said with satisfaction. "As is yours. Speaking of which, I hope I didn't overstep my bounds with the young women tonight."

In the light of a passing street lamp, he saw her face soften. "Not at all. Anyone who advises them to use their heads and their hearts can only earn my gratitude. So, I thank you."

He didn't want her gratitude, damn it. He wanted . . . a bit of *her*. The real woman behind all of the polite calm. He knew there were deep waters below that placid surface. Fathoms of wit and energy and intelligence. He wanted to see it, experience it all.

And he damned well wanted her to see him, too. As flesh and blood and someone with more than a little of his own wit and insight. As a man. Not just another weapon to aim at Marstoke.

But pushing her was a damned sure way to *not* get either of those things. So he ignored how those red eyebrows and the faint smell of rosemary and . . . something that made his skin feel too tight . . . and he opened his mouth to change the subject.

She beat him to it.

"Were you listening to my interview with the Prince Regent?"

"I came in at the end," he confessed—and he couldn't hide his amusement. "The things you said to him! I could tell they were surpassed only by the things you wanted to say."

Was that a twitch at the corner of her mouth? "You heard the things I didn't say, did you?"

"I did." He leaned forward suddenly. "And so did he, you may rest assured. Our Prince Regent is vain and self-indulgent, but he's not stupid."

"Good. Then he will have the wisdom to heed my warnings. You know I am right—about someone in his inner circle talking to Marstoke?"

He sighed. "I assume you spoke to Miss Smythe, then?"

"We were thrust together for days of travel which nearly ended in captivity. Did you think I would not get her whole story? She's always known the truth about her parentage, and she's always understood what it would mean to the monarchy if the truth came out. She's kept their secret. She doesn't use any of the names that might allow others to track her down and use her as a weapon. Nor does she ask for special treatment. But she's been alone for years now. At the last, she was out of funds and short on opportunities. She needed help. She sent the Regent a letter asking for it—the first time she'd done so, I might add. Not long after, men showed up, asking questions about her. She was smart enough to realize they were not the Prince's men —and that's when she hid away and sent for me."

Outside, the street lamps were no more, as they traveled through the outskirts of the city. Out of the darkness, he heard her tone grow tense. "They were Marstoke's men and obviously the marquess has somehow infiltrated the Prince's inner circle. Do you have any idea who the culprit might be?"

"I have suspicions."

"Might it be a man under your charge?"

He stiffened. "Absolutely not. I have only a handful of men working directly with me—and I trust them all with my life."

Even in the dim light, he could see her nod of approval. "It is the same with me. But there is another possibility to consider. Marstoke found Miss Smythe and me, after I went to fetch her, because he bribed the butcher's boy who was courting one of the girls at Half Moon House. The boy had access to the house and somehow managed to discover Isaac's arrangements for us." She shook her head. "Today I saw the considerable work still ongoing at Carlton House. With all of that endless renovation, the marquess could easily bribe a plasterer or a carpenter—or disguise one of his own men to look like one. It could be anyone, do you see?"

He did. "Damn."

"Yes. It makes our work infinitely harder if we do not know where Marstoke is getting his information. I propose, then, that we keep this mission close. Between you and me, when we can. Enlisting our trusted few when we must."

"If we do not, there's a good chance he'll always be one step ahead of us."

"Precisely. You agree, then? We'll keep most of this enterprise between the two of us?"

"Yes." He'd only been dreaming of something perilously close to that notion for months. "Of course. But Hestia?"

"Yes?"

"I assume this means we will be working together. A partnership. Sharing information and ideas?"

"Of course." Her tone was at its coolest and most civil.

"Then perhaps you might tell me just where the devil we are going right now?"

"Oh!" A surprised laugh burst out of her. "Yes. Apologies. We are not going far." She leaned toward the window, straining to see ahead. "In fact, see for yourself."

She sat back and he took her place, ignoring the soft scent that still lingered. They were at the outlying bits of the city now, and it was difficult to see much, but ahead lay a blazing beacon of light.

"What is it?" He could see a big structure, brightly lit and surrounded by a contrasting sea of darkness.

"It's a brothel. A particularly vile one. It is also one that pays a tithe to Marstoke."

"And how, exactly, do you know that?"

Out of the darkness came the sudden gleam of her smile. "Never ask a woman to reveal her secrets, Stoneacre."

He sat back. "I can't stop myself. I'm all wrought up at the thought of learning your secrets, Hestia."

She did not reply. But he could almost hear the metaphorical slam as she closed herself off again.

"I'm not talking about the secrets of your past." He waved a hand, even though she likely couldn't see it. "Keep them. Sell them to the newspapers. Forget them entirely, whatever you wish. I want to know the interesting things about you." He leaned in again. "What is your favorite color? The food that you miss from your childhood? What song runs through your head as you brush your hair or work on your accounts? What do you hate that everyone else loves? Love that everyone hates?" He shrugged and gave a little laugh. "You know. The really important things."

For several long moments, she didn't respond at all. Then she cleared her throat. "Perhaps you'll learn some of those things. Perhaps not." Her tone grew stern. "But I will tell you that there are fewer of those brothels making payments to Marstoke than there used to be."

His interest sharpened. "How have you managed that?"

"Very carefully. I do not have the heft of the government behind me as I work," she said ruefully. "It's best if these things are not attributed to me. But you take a house like Mother Sally's. A horrible place, where the girls were mistreated and the men who frequented the place were routinely fleeced and occasionally drugged and black-mailed. I shut it down with a quiet word to the papers about the latter and a few delicately placed rumors of pox amongst her girls."

"Well done," he said, all admiration.

"It doesn't stick, though," she said with a sigh. "Sally has already reinvented herself and opened Molly Beck's."

"Like insects," he murmured. "Step on one and find ten more."

"Or a hydra," she agreed. "The best thing we can do is to strike at the top and work our way down."

"We have to *find* Marstoke first," he sighed.

"And so we will. And here is where we start." She looked out at the inky night. "Let me do the talking when we arrive. You must trust me. Go along with whatever I say—even if it seems outrageous, or if it changes." She gripped his arm as the coach slowed. "Can you do that?"

He deliberately did not look at her hand, even though her touch sent a shiver through him, as sharp and taut as the plucked string of a harp. "I *can*," he said, deliberately provoking her.

Her grip tightened.

"And I will," he relented. "I trust you, Hestia. Can you trust me?" His word choice was deliberate.

They were drawing near to the big house. A bit of light came in the window, illuminating her determined expression. "I'll do my best."

A SERVANT MET their coach a little distance before the house, forcing them to walk in the dark along a crumbly pavement for a few feet before they reached the stairs. Stoneacre had to admit, it was damned good strategy, forcing the customer to climb from the Stygian dark up to the big, white, brightly lit building. If making a chap feel like he was rising from the depths of hell to the shining gate of heaven was the effect they were going for, then they'd done a grand job of it.

A footman in livery met them at the door, enforcing Stoneacre's impression that this was an establishment that catered to the wealthy, higher end of Society. The servant's slack-jawed surprise at seeing Hestia step into the marble entry hall told him they were not expected.

Stoneacre kept a step behind Hestia, as she'd instructed. The footman shot him a glance of obvious dismay.

"Ah, excuse me, madam . . . but, but, I do not think—"

"I'm sure you do not," Hestia interrupted. She ran an appraising eye over the tall, well-formed man. "But then again, I doubt that is why Mrs. Ledger hired you."

The footman returned the scrutiny and for the first time, Stoneacre looked past Hestia's changed hair to her gown. She wore a black pelisse over fawn colored skirts with some sort of shimmery, gauzy overlay. Unusual. Not the sort of thing normally worn by fashionable women—but the quality was evident and he seriously doubted the footman would know the difference.

"I have an appointment," she informed the servant. "Please show me to your employer's office."

The footman gaped. "But the *Madame* is not here!"

Hestia drew back, looking appalled. "Not here? Mrs. Ledger? She is not here to meet with Lord Marstoke's appointed courier?"

"I . . . I . . ." Clearly the man had no idea how to respond.

"A message was sent! The time appointed! Have you people ignored his lordship's wishes?"

The footman stood frozen.

"Mrs. Ledger. Where is she?" Hestia demanded.

"I'm sure I don't know!" the footman gasped.

"I'm sure someone should!" Hestia pursed her lips. She turned away and took a few steps around the entry hall. Somewhere above a door opened and music and laughter drifted down. When the door closed and the noise stopped, Hestia turned on her heel. "Do you know what will happen to your *Madame* if she does not pay her tithe to Marstoke?"

The footman swallowed, looking frightened to death.

"Surely there is someone here who can tell me where she's gone? They may very well save her, in doing so."

"I . . . Well . . ."

"Yes?"

"Mr. Reimer likely knows."

"Well, then. Take me to him at once!"

"He's . . . ah . . . occupied at the moment."

Hestia sighed and closed her eyes. "Yes, I see. Your employer steps out and the help decides to sample the wares." She frowned fero-ciously. "You can be sure I will report all of this to Lord Marstoke."

"I'm sorry, ma'am—"

"Never mind. Show me to Mrs. Ledger's office. I'll wait for her lackey to finish his . . . business." She clapped her hands. The footman jumped as the sound echoed against the marble. "Let's go, then!" She beckoned to Stoneacre. "Come along."

"Yes, ma'am." Stoneacre bit back a grin and ambled after them. The grin faded, however, as the footman led them up a short flight of stairs and into a large, crowded and dimly lit room. Rich, cluttered and sumptuous, it might have graced any home in Mayfair. Card tables were scattered across the center of the parlor. Gentlemen indulged, while the ladies of the house draped themselves over laps and shoul-ders. Low couches and chairs lined the edges of the room, occupied by couples and groups in various states of entanglement. A pair of scantily clad girls sang a naughty song atop a small dais in one corner.

Stoneacre wondered briefly if Hestia suffered the same sort of anger as he did, walking through the sordid opulence. What would they do, all of these men of wealth and good standing, if he marched to the middle of the room and shouted the truth—that their money was going to support a traitor, a violent, virulent plague upon the good people of England?

"Don't gawk," Hestia snapped at him. "And keep up."

He scurried after her. The frustration must be worse for her. To be sure, she'd never worked in a low situation like this, but he knew she had shut plenty of them down, and must have witnessed every sort of abuse the girls at these places suffered, from both the customers and their masters.

She showed no sign of it, though. Keeping her head high, she followed the path set by the footman. He led them away from the room and down a candlelit corridor graced with a plush carpet and scrolled wall sconces. He opened a door near the end and they all entered.

The office was well appointed and tastefully done up in shades of blue. Hestia avoided the large desk at the center of the room, heading instead for the tray of decanters sitting atop a side table. "Fetch your Mr. Rinner—"

"Mr. Reimer," the footman corrected automatically.

She raised a brow and Stoneacre laughed inwardly as the fellow squirmed. She had him completely cowed.

"Yes. Him. Fetch him straightaway." She poured a glass of brandy. "We'll wait here."

"Yes, ma'am." The footman bowed and began to back out, as if she was the queen and he daren't turn his back to her.

"Don't dawdle," she warned.

"No, ma'am."

The door closed and Stoneacre immediately moved to the desk. "Can you listen at the door?" he asked. "Tell me if someone comes." He quickly rifled through all of the accessible drawers, before kneeling in front of the locked one.

Hestia made a small sound of agreement. She was at the door, peering out. Stoneacre turned his attention to the small, thin packet that he pulled from his coat pocket. He examined the lock, then let his fingers hover over his favorite set of lock picks.

"Any information we can use won't be in the locked drawer. Check for false bottoms in the others."

Hestia's voice sounded muffled. He looked up and found that she'd closed the door and removed her wig and her pelisse. She was bent over, trying to untie the gauzy overlay from her skirts.

Was she right? Well, he couldn't leave any stone unturned. Stoneacre pursed his lips and went to work. Only a couple of minutes passed before he felt the last click and slid the drawer open.

He suppressed a groan. She was right. Inside lay a tangled dragon's hoard of jewelry. A mix of trumpery and the occasional real jewel, if he was any judge of those pearls and a set of ruby earrings. He reached in and the whole mess came out in one piece, proving there was nothing else of real interest in the drawer.

He paused for half a moment to laugh a little. How did she know?

Without looking at Hestia, he dumped the glittering knot back in and returned to the unlocked drawers. He found the false bottom in the middle right drawer and yanked it open.

"Here it is!" He frowned down at the sheaf of papers. "Monthly incomes and expenses, a list of gentlemen's names, marked 'special' . . ." He whistled. "Including a couple of MPs."

"No surprise there," Hestia said with a sigh.

"There's a list of girls 'sent on', and here we are—a list of payments made to Marstoke." He whistled. "And a substantial one to be made the day after tomorrow."

"The day after tomorrow?" Hestia sounded dismayed.

He looked up—and blinked. It might have been yet another altogether different woman standing over there. Her blonde curls were loose and messed. Her fawn-colored bodice was gone. A forest green one must have been lain underneath. It was markedly smaller—and she was fashioning the gauzy overskirt into a not-very-effective, clavicle-skimming fichu, fastening it in place with a cheap-looking clasp she took from her hair.

She didn't look like quality any longer. Her skirts, without the extra shimmer, appeared sturdy and plain. Even as he watched, she folded the wig into the pelisse and used a long, ornamental clasp to close it. Reaching up, she attached it to a loop on the underside of her skirts.

"Good heavens, Hestia. You've turned yourself into a doxy."

He said it blandly, but his heart gave a great thump—and then stalled. He sank down into the desk chair, brought low by a savage stab of unbridled lust and sheer admiration.

For she was indeed utterly changed, once again. Flushed, and slightly mussed, like she'd just crawled out of someone's bed.

And he nearly dropped the papers as anger surged, sudden and violent, from his gut.

Damn the fates. Damn Prinny. And damn her too. It was colossally unfair. That such a woman should exist—gorgeous, determined, principled, wily and resourceful—and that he should be expected to satisfy himself instead with a child—some sweet, simple girl bred to go uncomplaining from the schoolroom, to the ballroom, to the bedroom.

He pushed back against the rage, shoving it down, deep inside, where she wouldn't find any evidence of it. And he summoned a grin. "Just like that," he said lightly. "Well done."

"Indeed," she returned. "Thank you." She smoothed her skirts down. "Mrs. Ledger must be meeting Marstoke some distance away if the payment is set for the day after tomorrow and she's left already. Will he meet her himself? Perhaps he'll send one of his lieutenants. Does it say where the meeting is to take place?"

With a start he recalled the papers in his hand. He scanned them. "No."

She cursed under her breath. "Well then, Stoneacre. You will need to transform too." She waved a hand. "Just like that. Change your coat so it is inside out, as if you've done it for good luck in the gaming."

"Ah." He stood and hurried to do as she bid. "Are we going eavesdropping, then?"

Her brows raised in surprise—and approval. "Mr. Reimer has already been caught out once tonight."

"He'll be defensive. And suspicious."

"Yes. It's unlikely he'll voluntarily tell us anything useful."

He shrugged back into his turned-about jacket and tucked the papers into his waistband at the back. "Then let's not give him the choice in the matter."

Nodding in approval, she cracked open the door and peered out. "Wait."

A pair of giggling women hurried by.

"Now." She slipped out and took his hand, pulling him along with her. "The footman went this way." They hurried around a corner. When the new passage came to a crossing, she paused and held up a hand for silence.

It wasn't something that he'd ever done before—listening closely inside a brothel. For good reason, it turned out. Laughter and talk drifted from the parlor at the front of the house. From somewhere nearby came the vigorous squeaking of bedsprings. And from behind the door at his elbow came the sound of a man reciting his nines.

"Two nines are eighteen. Three nines are eight and twenty."

Thwap!

"Seven and twenty, I meant to say!"

Stoneacre grinned and looked to Hestia, but she had her head tilted, listening. He slid in close behind her and waited.

HESTIA LISTENED and tried not to wonder what that look had been about. Stoneacre had appeared to be delighted at her disguise—and then . . . something else had flashed behind his eyes. Anger?

It puzzled her. She'd been thinking how easy he was to work with, how quick to size up the situation and react. And now . . . now she had to try to rein in her fluttering heart.

It wouldn't listen. It had been entirely thrown by the feel of the earl pressed close behind her. The size of him. The heat he pumped out, like a warming brazier. And the comforting smell of bay with a slight tang of citrus.

It had been a long time since so much glorious masculinity had hovered so close. She told herself that was why her skin prickled and her heart tripped along, unsteadier than a Thoroughbred stuffed with opium balls before a race.

She sighed, forcing herself to focus instead on the soft, incessant knocking on the door around the corner. There was work to be done —and no time for anything else.

The knocking stopped.

"Have you lost hold of your senses?" A masculine voice, full of annoyance and threat. "I told you to leave me be!"

"It's an urgent matter, sir. I don't think it can wait longer. I would not have disturbed you, otherwise."

She held her breath. They were so close. Stoneacre crowded even closer behind her. They both stood quiet while the footman spoke low and at length.

"What other message?" the other man demanded. Mr. Reimer, she presumed. There was nothing of panic or worry in his tone. Only outrage and impatience to get back to his . . . activities. "We received *a* message. *The* message. The one that bid the *Madame* to travel to make the payment."

Travel where? She pressed herself against the wall, willing the man to say it out loud.

But the footman was muttering again and Reimer continued to scoff. "I daresay someone is playing you for a fool. Now leave . . ." A silent pause. "Unless . . ."

The footman and Hestia and Stoneacre waited. "Marstoke's other houses all received the same message," Reimer mused. "There was enough griping about it. Did they all get the second message as well? Did ours go astray?"

"I could send a boy to one of the other—"

"No. We must be . . . careful. What if this is a ploy? One of the others could be trying to trick old Ledger into missing the drop. She'd be discredited with Marstoke then, right enough."

Hestia heard the man suck in a breath. "Wouldn't it be just like that Madame Noir? *Noir!*" he scoffed. "As if we don't all know that she's plain Ann Jenkins from Ipswich!"

The footman made a sound like a squeak. Had Reimer grabbed him?

"Here now, what's this tart look like? Marstoke's supposed envoy?"

The footman took a moment to answer. "She's pretty. Fair skinned and red-headed. Irish, maybe? Though she didn't sound it."

"Irish? They do say that old Molly Beck has a couple of new Irish girls."

"She's dashed odd," the footman continued. "She looks like she's got money, but no idea what to do with it. No idea of fashion."

Hestia glanced back at Stoneacre, her mouth quirking. The footman saw more than she'd expected. Perhaps she would consider hiring him away.

"She's hard, though. Like Marstoke," the footman added. "Likely she's got a mean streak, too."

That killed her smile. Hard? Yes. By all that was holy, she was hard. She had a knife's edge honed by years of tense self-reliance, of sorrow and sacrifice. Years of dealing with Marstoke and with a great many other evils wrought by man. Hard, yes. But like Marstoke?

No. Not in a thousand years.

"Here's what we'll do. You go and distract them," Reimer ordered. "I'll send young Charlie to Molly Beck's house to ask about a second message. He's fast."

"Distract them? How?"

"I don't know. Send in a girl. Or a boy. Whatever. Or offer them a stake in one of the games in the parlor. Just keep them busy for a bit."

"I can't offer them a girl!" The footman sounded aghast. "Besides, she don't seem the sort to be easily swayed from her mission."

"Dammit, man! Just find a way! We need to find out if this is a trick before we send word to recall the *Madame*."

Hestia started as the door slammed. Immediately, she turned and pressed up against Stoneacre, hiding her face in the crook of his neck. "Now, sir," she cooed. "You know that some things are best done in private. The cost of a room ain't much—and what better use for all them winnings?"

Stoneacre, bless him, caught on right away. He wrapped his arms around her, bent low and buried his face in her hair.

She felt the footman come around the corner, in the change in the air and in the sudden tension in the earl's frame. Letting loose a soft, sultry chuckle, she arched her body into Stoneacre's.

The footman passed. She watched him over the earl's shoulder. He was moving fast, but he slowed as he reached the end of the passage. Instead of turning the corner to return to the office, he stopped and began to spin slowly on his heel.

She stood on her toes and pressed a kiss to the earl's mouth.

He stiffened. His hands clenched at her lower back. Opened and clenched again.

She listened for the footman's step. Nothing. He hadn't moved—either closer or away. Was he watching?

Stoneacre must have reached that conclusion. Without warning, he bent his head further and kissed her back.

Really kissed her. Deeply and fully. She forgot to watch the footman as his lips pressed hard and hungry, as if all of him was starved for the taste of her. His tongue plundered her mouth, exploring thoroughly and demanding an answer in kind.

She gave it to him. It was to be expected. She played the role.

But the clear, logical flow of her thoughts, the concise *observe, react, adapt,* that always clicked into place during a mission like this—it all slowed. Snarled. Curled in on itself, entwining until it became as jumbled and disorderly as a carting accident in the Strand.

She'd been kissed a hundred times. More. She'd been kissed to convey possession, as pleading, as punishment. And this kiss was masterful. But it wasn't controlling. It wasn't a weapon, a question or a command. It wasn't like any of the others.

She tried. Tried to retreat. To take a step back and watch. Stay calm. Evaluate. Plan.

She couldn't. He kissed her slowly, with a lovely, maddening rhythm that called her. She answered—but the shocking thing was that she *wanted* to answer. Heat poured off of him and she burrowed into it, against that broad, solid wall of a chest. She kissed him back. He was gentle. She was thorough. Their tongues moved in a languid dance that crept beneath her skin and shivered through her veins.

Hidden away, at her core, sheltered a small orb. Tucked away. Safe. Untouched. The music of his kiss wrapped around it, knocked with soft throbbing beats against the hard shell.

No. *That* wasn't part of the role. Nor was the sudden, nearly irre-sistible urge to grasp him hard and pull him tighter against her.

She didn't think it was play-acting either, when he gave a nearly imperceptible growl and his breath brushed hot and fast over her cheek.

Alarm had her shaking. Stunned, she stared up at him.

She was going to be the death of him.

The shock of that kiss still bounded within him, ricocheting from one nerve ending to the next.

She'd meant it to be a lie. A means to an end.

Instead, in the end, it had turned out to be . . . *true.*

And his entire being was still caught in a flood of ancient reflex. A storm of primal urges that all coalesced into one, thrumming thought.

There she is. The whisper came from his soul. *At last.*

It shook him. She pulled away to stare over his shoulder and he let her go.

Frowning, she looked again. "He's gone," she whispered. "The footman. When? How long since he left?"

Stoneacre shook his head, more than a little disgusted with himself. He hadn't noticed. He'd been completely caught up in that kiss.

"Let's go," she breathed, turning away—and the shout went up.

"Here, now! Where are they? Find them!"

Footsteps. Opening doors. Questioning voices.

"Here! Here now!" The footman's shouts sounded frantic. "They must be found!"

"This way." Stoneacre pushed her in the direction that the footman had gone, but stopped before a baize door in the middle of the corridor. "Servant's door. Let's go." He pushed her in and pulled the door shut behind them.

A stairwell, narrow and dimly lit. From below came the murmur of voices and the clink of dishes.

She nodded. "Out through the kitchen."

The moved quickly and quietly, stepping carefully past another door on the landing below. Their eyes met as a shout sounded behind it, too, but they didn't stop. They both slowed, however, as they neared the bottom of the stairs. It emptied just at the entrance to the servant's dining hall. Several footmen and a couple of maids sat there, laughing over a card game.

"Steady," Stoneacre said, low. "No hurry. We've all the time in the world."

They rounded the last stairs and passed the kitchens on their left. Ahead lay a long passage with a door at the end. "The door to the yard, presumably?" he whispered. "Let's go."

They were halfway there when the door opened on the landing they'd just passed.

"Malcolm! Georgie! Come up! We've lost some toffs!"

Groans from the dining hall.

"Malcolm! Georgie! Now!"

A door popped open just ahead of them. A woman in black peered out. "Who is shouting?" She eyed him and frowned at Hestia. "Who are you?"

"I'm the milkmaid." Hestia shot her a grin as she grabbed his hand. "He's the squire. He means to toss my skirts up over the fence post."

The woman rolled her eyes.

They kept going.

"Wait!" the woman called suddenly. "We've got no fence posts out there!"

"We'll make do!" Stoneacre answered, and then they'd reached the door and they were out, racing past the privy and a small kitchen garden to the mews.

"To the left!" Hestia insisted. At a jog, she led them through a maze of back alleys until they emerged onto a main thoroughfare. A coach sat just ahead, silent and waiting.

"Yours?" Stoneacre said, and marveled at her confirmation. "Well done!"

"We're not finished, though. We need to find out where those payments are to be made," she answered, ignoring the driver, who had climbed down to hold open the door. "There's a mount hitched to the back."

He pulled up short, then just laughed. "You never cease to amaze." Unfortunately, there was no time to contemplate her brilliance. He moved to the back and began to unhitch the animal. "Where is Molly Beck's? I'll see if I can beat young Charlie."

She gave him directions. "Shall we meet back at Half Moon House once we've found something?" she asked.

"Yes." He mounted up, both reluctant to leave her and anxious for a moment away, so he could gather his thoughts. "You'll be all right?"

She laughed. "Yes. I'll be fine. You be careful. Molly has some wicked brutes in her employ."

"Good," he said grimly. "I'll see you soon." He set off, feeling as if a bit of violence would not come amiss. Perhaps Molly Beck's brutes would let him work off some of this . . . heat.

HESTIA STOOD FOR A LONG MOMENT, staring into the dark, after he left.

Trouble. This was going to lead to trouble.

"Come on out," she said, eventually.

A young boy slipped silently from inside the coach. "You know Mrs. Ledger's grooms?" she asked him. "Her coachmen?"

"Aye." He yawned. "I'll watch and listen. Find out where she's gone."

"I'll wait at the Spotted Dog," she told him. "Go in the back when you've something to report. I'll see that it's worth your while."

"Aye." The urchin grinned. "Ye always do."

He melted into the shadows and with a sigh, she climbed into the coach.

CHAPTER 4

Many of you have heard the rumors about Lord M—. Heard the whispers
of cruelty, of bribery and threats, even of treason. They are all true. You
may be surprised, dear reader, to know that they are the least of his sins.
—from the Journal of the Infamous Miss Hestia Wright

Stoneacre yawned as he left his set of apartments. He hadn't
rested yet. Not truly—as he refused to count the ten minutes he'd
fallen asleep in the tub. But he'd scrubbed the blood away—Molly
Beck's bullies had indeed proved useful at allowing him to release
some tension—and now he had to face Hestia and tell her that no one
at that seedy brothel had known where their employer had gone to
meet Marstoke.

He struck out onto Piccadilly, cursing the wicked marquess for
scaring his subordinates into such unshakable secrecy and wondering
if he was going to be able to find a hack this early in the day. And
mostly, dreading delivering bad news to Hestia.

He wouldn't shirk his duty. Would never lie to cover his failure to
find the information they needed. But he meant to do better. *Had to*

do better. Bad enough that she wasn't interested in him as a romantic partner. At the very least, he meant to dazzle her with his abilities in their mission. She'd certainly dazzled him. She'd planned brilliantly last night, seen to every detail, anticipated every snag—except perhaps . . . he rather thought she hadn't predicted that kiss.

That kiss. He still felt stirrings in places that should have long gone quiet. Likely because he kept reliving it. Couldn't get the shock of it out of his head. In fact, he'd—

He'd just started to cross Bond Street when he heard someone call his name. Stopping, he craned his neck. To his shock, he saw his mother hanging from the window of her carriage, beckoning him. Every pleasant, lingering, carnal recollection promptly gave up the ghost and popped out of existence. Fighting off a wave of annoyance, he went to meet her as the coach pulled to the side of Bond Street.

"How fortunate that we were passing at the right time," his mother called as he drew near.

He paused. *We?* Cautiously, he approached.

"Good morning, Stoneacre." His mother spoke casually, as if she conversed out of the carriage window on a daily basis. "We are just heading to an appointment with Madame Dumont. I am in dire need of a sturdy bonnet before we set out for Wiltshire."

"We? Surely you have not dragged Father out to your milliner's? And so early."

"Don't be absurd. Your father has not emerged from behind his newspapers. Miss Chisholm is accompanying me."

So he could see, as his mother leaned back. The girl leaned forward in her turn and smiled brightly. "Good morning, sir."

"Good morning to you both, ladies. I had no idea that milliners opened so early."

"Of course they do," his mother said with a wave of her hand. "What else should they do, lay abed all morning?" She lowered her tone, as if someone might hear. "It is always best to get in early. One arrives before the rest of the ladies and I do like to have the Madame's full attention."

"Well, do not let me delay you." He touched his hat with a nod.

"Not so fast, sir." His mother pointed to the door latch. "Would you be so good as to hand me down? I would speak privately with you, for just a moment. That errand we discussed, don't you know."

Stoneacre sighed, but did as he was bid. "Do excuse us," he said to the girl. "We won't be but a moment."

"Of course. I will be content enough, right here."

"Such an accommodating girl," his mother said as he tucked her hand into the crook of his elbow and walked a few paces away.

"Really, Mother? Have you resorted to lying in wait for me in the streets?"

"Don't be absurd." She rolled her eyes. "I merely arranged to be here at such a time as when you might be passing." Pointing a finger, she chided, "I would not have to resort to such tricks if you would only come to call on me more often."

"I would perhaps call on you more often, if I could see you alone," he countered.

"Yes, well, I must make hay while the sun shines with you, sir."

He laughed. "How bucolic of you, Mother."

"How aggravating of you, sir, to force me to such tricks."

"Why don't we throw caution to the wind, then, and just come right out and say what we mean?"

She gaped at him. "Have you spent too much time abroad in service to the Prince? That is not the English way."

"Humor me, Mother. I prefer not to play games with those that I care for."

That softened her. A bit.

"Very well. There isn't truly an errand."

He raised a brow. "You shock me."

She drew to a stop and pierced him with a sharp look. "I wish for you to come to dinner tomorrow."

"I'm sorry." He frowned. "I fully expect I'll be out of Town by then. My work is becoming—"

"No." She glared. "Your work can go to the devil. It is time you addressed your duty to the family."

Mothers were to be given leeway. Every man knew it. Mothers

worried. They fretted. Evidently, they plotted. But they also knew how to wound. And even knowing it didn't stop the bitter rush of indignation and anger that rose up and tightened his throat. "I think I've more than proved my loyalty and devotion to the family, ma'am."

"You have." Her tone did not gentle. "But you are not done."

"Nor am I done with the work that came out of the whole fiasco. The Prince Regent has given me orders."

"And what is he thinking, to send you off on dangerous quests when your succession is not secured? Really, he should be attending to his own affairs in that department and leave you to yours."

"I don't disagree, Mother. But I must obey." He cast a sardonic glance back at the coach. "You will have to content yourself with Miss Chisholm's company. No doubt her invitation has already been extended."

"And what if it has? You should look closely at her, sir. She is young and pretty and quick-witted. Still malleable, too. And her sister has borne Pollonsby four sons already."

"Good breeding stock," he murmured.

"Yes. Not only an heir but insurance in the way of three more sons," his mother said approvingly.

Unbidden, an image of his friend Lord Truitt rose up in his head—a picture of how Tru looked when he entered a room and found his wife there before him. He bore a mixed-up, nearly foolish look of joy and lust and intense satisfaction and utter relief, every time.

Every time.

Just like that, craving and a fierce, heated *want* powered up Stoneacre's spine. That, *that* was marriage. Not malleable young misses with good, wide hips.

"And don't you think to scorn such a consideration. Nor should you be ignorant of the fact that one of Miss Chisholm's best qualities is the fact that she has not written you off as a marriage candidate."

"Good of her." He managed not to sigh, but he did turn them back toward the carriage.

"Others have, you know. It's been said that you are too old, too pre-occupied and unlikely to show a wife the right sort of attention and appreciation."

"Should I choose the right sort of wife, then none of that should be a worry."

"Well, it is a worry, and to some of the most appropriate of the girls," she fretted.

"Then perhaps I shall turn an eye to some inappropriate candidates." He almost winced. What had made him say such a thing? He knew. He knew *exactly*.

"John!" He'd shocked his mother into using his first name. "How could you say such a thing?"

"Don't worry overmuch, Mother." He kissed her hand and helped her to retake her seat in the carriage before he leaned in close. "The inappropriate women aren't interested, either."

He slapped a hand to the side of the coach. "Walk on," he called to the driver.

"Good day to you, my lord!" Miss Chisholm called.

"Good day, ladies." He lifted his hat and turned on his heel and headed off toward Craven Street.

"She p . . .p . . . put a l . . . log on the fir." The woman paused. "Fire. She put a log on the fire." She looked up at Hestia, shining with triumph.

"Very nice, Beth. I can tell you've been working hard." Hestia smiled at the woman's delight and suppressed a sigh as she bent back over her book.

All mask, that smile. In truth, Hestia was tired. She'd come home when it was still dark this morning, as the farm carts began to roll into the city, and she'd found Beth wandering the halls, clutching her primer. As she'd just sent a note summoning Stoneacre, she'd offered to help Beth with her reading until he arrived.

They'd settled at the desk in her office. Or, to be precise, Beth had done so. Hestia was feeling decidedly *unsettled*.

Because of that kiss. That encounter. Unwise, the whole of it. No matter that it had been necessary. Successful. It had been foolish.

Her eyes closed. It had been a pleasure, if she was to be honest. The heat. The softness of his lips. The touch of his hands—large, elegant, but rougher than an earl's should be.

The real danger, though, had been the chaos he had set off in her brain. The tempting little melody that had touched her too deeply.

For years she had held tightly to her calm. She was no longer accustomed to chaos. Not used to being rattled.

"Li . . . li . . . What is this word?" Beth asked with a frown.

Hestia leaned forward. "Light." She glanced toward the window. "Light—like the sun is bringing us now."

She jumped a little as Isaac knocked and stuck his head in. "He's here," he warned.

She nodded, feeling nettled. Jumping at a simple knock—in her own home! Rattled, indeed.

"Ask him to grant me a moment?" She smiled at the woman seated across from her. "One more sentence, Beth, than I must get to business."

"Get to business," Beth echoed.

Hestia nodded and smiled at her.

"The light ch . . . ch . . . cher . . ." Sudden understanding lit up her face. "The light cheered her."

The door opened. Isaac stood there, but Stoneacre hovered close behind him. Beth, getting to her feet, caught a glimpse of them. She made a strangled sound of fear and dropped the book. Backing up, she hit the desk. She didn't turn. She never took her eyes off of the men at the door, but inched over and then moved back until she came up against the wall.

Hestia held up a hand to prevent Stoneacre from coming further.

"Beth, you know Isaac. Isaac is your friend. And behind him is my friend, Lord Stoneacre. Can you greet him?"

The girl had put her chin down and glued her gaze to her feet. She stayed pressed to the wall, but managed a credible curtsy. "Good day, my lord," she whispered.

"Lord Stoneacre is a friend, Beth," Hestia repeated. "He is here to help. He is going to come in and sit at my desk, just as you did." She gave the earl a significant look. "When he's seated, then why don't you run along to the kitchen and see what cook is putting together for breakfast?"

The girl nodded. Stoneacre, thankfully, did as he was bid, moving carefully, and once he reached the chair she'd just left, Beth darted past both men and out into the passageway.

Shaking his head, Isaac withdrew and closed the door.

"I apologize." Stoneacre reached down and picked up the primer, setting it on the desk. "I should have stayed back. I had an idea and only wished to share it."

"No need for apologies. Beth is skittish. Honestly, that was a mild reaction." Hestia took the book and filed it on a shelf before she sat down to face him.

"Is she new to the house?" he asked delicately.

"No." Hestia raised her chin. "To the contrary. Beth was one of the first to come to us after we opened our doors."

He didn't bother to hide his surprise. "I didn't think you kept the girls so long. I thought you found them new places, new starts."

"We do, whenever we can."

"I've been in and out for a while now," he mused. "I've seen the girls change, noticed that some stay a bit longer. Molly stands out," he said with a grin.

"That she does," Hestia laughed. "She keeps us laughing."

"But in all that time, I've never noticed Beth."

"You wouldn't. Like a mouse, our Beth hides in the corners and shadows. Only when all lies calm and quiet does she venture out."

"So, not often," he said wryly.

"Exactly." Pursing her lips, Hestia gazed at him for a long moment. "Beth's story is quite entangled with my own," she said abruptly.

She immediately regretted it. Cursed herself silently and thoroughly in her head. What did she mean, blurting something like that out?

"Ah." Stoneacre merely leaned back in his seat and wisely said no more.

Her mind was racing. "I'm not sure why I said that," she admitted.

"Your story is your own," he said easily. "You may share if you wish. Or choose to keep it to yourself." He speared her with a direct look. "You can be sure, of course, that whatever you tell me will be kept in the strictest of confidence."

"Will it?"

His expression darkened. "Do you doubt me? Still?"

Hestia heaved a sigh. "No. I don't believe I do."

And that might be part of her problem.

He sat, silently waiting for her to decide. Exactly as she might have wished, had she foreseen this conversation.

Damn him.

SHE CONSIDERED IT. He could see it. And in the end, she compromised.

"I will tell you this much—it was Marstoke who left Beth outside Half Moon House. It was a move meant to show me for a fraud. To bring me down a peg or two or a hundred. He fully expected that I would not take her in—and in rejecting her, I would prove to myself and to the world, that I could not live up to the promises I made."

"The promises this house stands for," he said.

She nodded.

"But you did take her in."

"Yes. I had to. It wasn't easy. But truly, I have often thought I should thank Marstoke. He tested my convictions at the start, and I haven't wavered since."

Stoneacre nodded. Clearly there were painful depths behind that scanty outline, but he considered it fair progress to have heard any of it at all.

And then . . . he paused, on that thought.

Running a measuring eye over her, he considered. Had she been any other woman, he would have counted this a victory. A crack in the armor that wrapped so tightly and thoroughly around her that every man in London and beyond knew it to be impenetrable.

But this was Hestia Wright. She sat there, practically glowing in the morning light. She'd changed out of last night's odd wardrobe, but she'd forgotten her eyebrows. They stood out, still red, a bold signal calling to him from an innocent frame. In a light pink morning dress embroidered with long, vertical tendrils of flowering vines, she looked ethereal again. Otherworldly.

And yet, he knew with a sudden certainty that what she was, was . . .

"Ruthless," he announced.

"Excuse me?"

"It is what you are. Ruthless." He sat straight up in his chair. "I'm willing to believe that it was happenstance that you found that poor girl abroad in the house when you returned home, but it wasn't a coincidence that she stayed in your office this morning, was it?"

"I don't know what you mean." She was at her most regal.

"Oh, yes, you do. What was the message that little scene was meant to convey? Was it a reminder that you might have been that girl? Had you been less strong? Less determined?"

Anger flared behind her eyes.

"Or was it just a general reminder of the darkness of Marstoke's soul?" He gripped the edge of her desk. "Did you think I needed a refresher? Because I'm the sort of man to forget what that villain has done?" She started to speak, but he didn't allow it. "*No one* knows the extent of his evil like you. No one. But I'm not new to this fight. I've already committed to it—and last night I committed to this partnership. As did you. Yet you continually question me. You throw that girl's misery at me like some sort of test? Why, Hestia? Why do you continue to doubt my veracity?"

She glared at him.

"Let's have it out," he demanded. "All of it. Now."

"Very well." Her chin lifted.

He waited.

"That kiss."

"Ah. I should have known. Yes. That kiss. Let me remind you that *you* kissed *me*."

"I did. As part of the role."

Still, he waited.

"You *enjoyed* it!" It was an accusation.

He laughed a little and threw back his head. "Yes. I am a man. I enjoyed it. Quite thoroughly."

"So I noticed," she said sourly.

"So did you," he tossed back at her. He closed his eyes. "I admit. I did deepen the kiss. In part because that wretched porter was watching, and it fit the parts we were playing." He opened his eyes, then, and gazed directly and openly at her. "But honestly, no red-blooded man could keep his equilibrium in the face of . . ." He gestured. "You."

She pressed her lips together. "It's been clear for some time—"

"Yes. I made my interest clear, when we first met. But you made your feelings clear too. And I have abided by your . . . *coldness, avoidance* . . . disinterest." Sighing, he rifled his hands through his hair. "I apologize if I offended you with my enthusiasm. But you should know by now that I know how to act like a gentleman. There will be no need for regular reminders. In fact, I find myself insulted by the notion."

Standing, he went to look out the window for a moment before spinning on his heel to face her again. "In fact, why don't we just address the issue right now?"

"Haven't we just?"

"I'll take it a bit further, if you don't mind." He spoke carefully, silently urging her to accept his sincerity. "Hestia, you are a beautiful woman, but that is not a tenth of what draws me to you. I *like* you. I like that you are smart and shrewd. I like that you act fearlessly, even though you know more than most how much there is to fear. I like that you are willing to get up to any damned thing if it gets you closer to your goal." He sighed. "We're already partners in this mission. Would it be such a stretch to count each other as friends?"

Her gaze ran over him, searching his features. "Friends?"

"Yes. I know a very few have been chosen for that honor. I'd like to be counted among them."

She sighed. "Because of the nature of this work," she gestured around her, "many of the people in my life are . . . transient. We might have intense moments together, but most move on. With my encouragement, of course, and hopefully to a better situation than they've had before. My friends . . . my *real* friends, are the ones that stay, in some fashion or another."

"I'm not going anywhere," he declared.

She was reserving judgment. He could see it. But he wasn't going to give up.

"Very well. We will be friends." She sounded as if she was testing the notion.

"Yes, and as a token of our friendship, I'll freely admit that I failed in my aim last night. I wasn't able to discover where Molly Becks went to meet Marstoke. None of her people seem to know. But I did have an idea on the way over here. It came to me because of something my mother said, believe it or not." He grinned and shrugged. "She mentioned insurance, and it made me remember a business associate of Marstoke's. Someone I found through his papers. Someone he still works with, occasionally, from what I can tell. He might have gone to him for money. If we approach him—"

She held up a hand. "No need for confessions, or for chasing down Marstoke's associates."

He waited, brow raised questioningly.

"I know where they are going." She didn't look happy about it. "I know where Marstoke is meeting them."

CHAPTER 5

*Within these pages you've read of my own faked marriage. This is a
favorite gambol of Lord M—'s. As he did at my own erstwhile wedding,
he often masquerades as the vicar, performing an invalid ceremony—and
taking the place of the groom at the wedding night.*
--from the Journal of the Infamous Miss Hestia Wright

S aints and angels and sweet baby cherubs, but she was tired.
Perhaps it was because she was growing older. Perhaps she
just did not have the stamina, any longer, to direct a devious night's
work, to skip sleep and still carry on with all that must be done.

More likely it was because of the shock she felt at being so thoroughly *seen*. How had Stoneacre done that? Spotted so clearly what
she'd only half-admitted to herself? When was the last time a man had
seen past the surface of her intentions? How hard was she going to
have to work, while they were entangled in this process, to keep her
mask firmly in place?

The mere thought of it exhausted her. Right now she longed for a
bit of peace. For a few moments to drop the masquerade entirely, to

eat something hot and sweet and starchy and just lie back and let all of her cares go for an hour or two.

She wasn't going to get any of that until Stoneacre had gone. And they both needed to make ready for this next part of their hunt.

That thought exhausted her more than any other.

"What have you discovered?" he asked quietly.

"I sent one of our boys into Mrs. Ledger's stables. Most of her people there were as woefully ignorant as Molly Beck's. But one groom had been sent to hire the carriage for the *madame's* trip." She dropped her gaze to the desk. "A carriage to take her to Somerset."

"So far?" His surprise showed and his lips pursed as he absorbed the implications. "Very well," he said after a few moments. "I will scour the papers from his office. Surely there will be a link—"

"No need," she repeated, interrupting him. She drew a deep,, bracing breath. "If Marstoke is in Somerset, then I know where he will be." She did not look at him. Instead she drew out a sheet of paper and poised her quill above it.

"Hestia." He spoke softly. She glanced up to find his gaze fixed on her quill.

She'd forgotten to ink it.

"Oh." She laughed a little. "Lists. I'll have to makes lists and arrangements aplenty, but I can be ready by late this afternoon."

"Perhaps I should—"

"No." It emerged more harshly than she'd intended, so she gentled her tone. "No. We are partners in this. We will both go."

She looked up. He loomed there, so large and capable. He'd changed this morning, too, into the buff breeched and blue-coated ideal of English masculinity. Except—he wore a look of kind concern instead of the sneer so often directed her way. She could smell that faint bay scent—and it brought on a sudden desperate wish to burrow into it, to let him wrap her in against that strong, broad chest while she closed her eyes, just for a moment. . .

She snapped to sudden attention, aghast. Good heavens, clearly she was overtired.

"Can you be ready?" she asked briskly.

"Of course."

"Good." She stood. "Well, then, I have preparations to make, as I'm sure you do."

"Hestia," he began again.

But a knock sounded at the door and Isaac poked his head into the room. "I'm sorry to interrupt, but something's happened."

The old, familiar alarm wrenched her gut. Mercilessly, she pushed it aside and stood. "What is it?" She held on to her studied calm with an iron grip.

"Somebody tried to snatch Molly. Tried to grab her and stuff her in a carriage."

Hestia immediately stepped from behind her desk, heading for the door. "Is she all right?"

Isaac moved out of her path. "Yes. She got away. Just."

Hestia moved quickly and knew Stoneacre followed. She could hear the commotion coming from the entry hall. She stepped out into the space and found Molly there, surrounded by a gaggle of concerned, angry and frightened girls. Some of the staff mingled there too, offering comfort and exchanging solemn looks. Molly, in the middle and talking fast, caught sight of her and abruptly burst into tears.

Hestia went and gathered her in her arms. She held her tight and let her cry. "There, now. You are safe. You are home," she said as the sobs began to subside. She looked over Molly's head to where Stoneacre lingered at the edge of the crowd. "Perhaps we could delay our departure until tomorrow?"

He nodded. "Of course."

"Early?" she asked.

With another nod and a sympathetic look, he slipped away.

STONEACRE MARCHED straight to Carlton House. It was still early and he knew it would be best that he make his report directly to the Prince Regent. He found him just awakened. While His Royal Highness made ready for the day, Stoneacre answered a multitude of questions, endured another rant on Marstoke's perfidy and fended off the insistence that they should take a brigade of soldiers with them. As soon as possible, he took his leave and went to the cramped office he'd been granted in Whitehall.

He sent off a courier with a note for Hestia, and once he received her reply, he spent time making arrangements for their departure and journey. For a bit, the flurry of traffic in and out of his office held steady, but at last the plans were set and he was left alone, his thoughts far away as he sat holding Hestia's note and enjoying the faint scent of her drifting from the paper.

Abruptly, he shook himself back to matters at hand. He dragged out his files and for hours he pored over the stacks of Marstoke's confiscated papers. Though he scoured his notes and searched everywhere he could think of, he could find only a couple of mentions related to Somersetshire. A card for the Red Fox Inn in Bath and a name; Mr. Denton Coombs.

On a hunch, he also searched for anything significant located in the surrounding counties, but only turned up a rope-maker's address outside Bristol.

The sun hung low when he finished and the shadows deepened as he walked home. Why Somerset? What mischief was Marstoke brewing there? He still wracked his brain as he entered the courtyard outside his building. As his key turned in the lock, he tensed. A step sounded close behind him. His hand crept toward the knife in his boot as he turned.

"No need, lad. It's just me."

"Father?" Stoneacre relaxed, but only for a moment. He must have truly upset his mother for her to set his father upon him.

"Damned porter would not allow me to wait in your rooms," the Marquess of Woodbury complained.

"Yes, the rules are strict here, sir. You'll have to alert me in advance, I'm afraid, for you to enter without me."

"Advanced notice? From your own father? From *me*?"

Stoneacre shrugged and let his father pass into his darkened rooms before him. "Security is necessary, I'm afraid. The Privy Council insists upon it. Wait here a moment, sir, and I'll light the lamps."

"Why don't you have servants for that?" his father fretted. "You are an earl, for God's sake."

"Yes, but I'm an earl with an utterly erratic schedule, which tends to drive servants a bit mad."

His father sniffed.

"I make do with a man who comes in to tidy up a couple of times a week. He takes care of my wardrobe as well, and otherwise, I'm fine looking after myself."

"I was inclined to think your mother was exaggerating, but now I begin to wonder." The marquess poured a drink and sat in the seat before the empty fire. "What have you done this time, to set her off in such a tizzy? She's wailing about your work and I cannot decide if she thinks the Prince Regent is driving you too hard or if she thinks he's become an unhealthy influence on you."

"She believes both, I'm sure." He poured his own brandy and took up a stance at the mantle.

"What's set her off this time?"

"My refusal to consider the latest candidate for child-bride."

His father said nothing, and merely took another drink.

"What?" Stoneacre gaped. "Now you are in league with her?"

The marquess shrugged. "I've met the Chisholm girl. I suppose I thought you might be interested."

"She's barely out of the schoolroom."

"Yes, she's young, but pretty. I detect a hint of intelligence there, too, so that she might eventually become interested in things beyond her next ball gown or tea party."

"Just in time to become obsessed with getting her offspring married off, perhaps?"

"I give her, perhaps, a little more credit than you do."

"Do you?" Icy shards of irritation roughened his tone. "Well, I'd tell you to have a run at her, but you already have a wife with whom you have nothing in common."

Strictly, that was not true. His parents did have a certain level of artifice in common. A concern with appearance that did not extend to actual substance. But he could not throw such a truth at his father.

Yet, neither would he bend himself into a shape that would reflect their idea of perfection.

"Don't be vulgar," the marquess chided. "Your mother is right about one thing. It's time you thought about your duty to the title."

"The title is in no danger. My cousin Edwin is a perfect heir presumptive. A fine, upstanding gentleman of good character and a nursery already filling with boys."

"It's your birthright, son. You cannot just hand it off to a cadet branch of the family."

Stoneacre said nothing. He merely met his father's imploring gaze with a steady one of his own.

His father blinked, then groaned. "Damnation, but she's right. This work has ruined you. And it is all my fault." He covered his eyes and slumped in his chair.

Stoneacre sighed. He felt the pull of it, the old desire to conform, to please his parents and win the approbation of Society. But he'd learned long ago how hollow it all was. How shallow and unfulfilling.

"The work has nothing to do with it."

"But if I had not . . . If you had not had to go to all of that trouble . . . the Privy Council would never have tagged you for these sort of undertakings."

"You know I already felt differently about things before all of that, Father. If I hadn't been tapped by the Prince Regent, I'd likely be abroad now. And wouldn't Mother have hated that?" The corner of his mouth twisted. "I might have brought home a foreign bride and where would she be, then?"

"A foreign girl of good family and noble birth? At least one of your mother's worries would be assuaged."

Anger reared fast and ugly from his core. So, his comment had his mother running scared, did it? Good. He set his glass aside and gestured toward the door. "I am leaving London in a matter of hours, sir, and I need to pack. But you may tell my mother that I will choose my own bride and I will be looking for a woman of true character and substance—for we all know how deceiving appearances can be."

His father stood. "I deserved that. I know it. But you will remember your duty, son. I know you will." He gave a nod and departed.

Stoneacre stared after him. Closing his eyes, reminded himself of the truth that he'd learned the hard way. His father's need for perfection was a well that would never be filled.

Eventually he turned away to drag out a portmanteau.

CHAPTER 6

Pretending to be the vicar is not Lord M—'s only wedding trick. Using a
false identity is another. He has enacted entire courtships under a fake
name, tricking young ladies and their families thoroughly. Some of these
unfortunate girls are abandoned after their wedding nights. Several
have disappeared—and have yet to be found.
--from the Journal of the Infamous Miss Hestia Wright

Hestia took the warm loaf of bread from the baker's hand and breathed deeply. "Mmm." Everyone at Half Moon House missed Callie's rosemary bread. This wasn't the same, but a bit of fresh, warm bread for breakfast would cheer them all. "I'll have half a dozen," she told the flour-speckled man.

She walked back to Craven Street in the rising light of dawn. She loved doing a bit of marketing at this hour. The streets were never so peaceful as at this moment. Everyone up to trouble and mischief had slunk back to their holes and the vendors and shopkeepers were still mostly optimistic about the new day and not yet tired, cranky or disappointed. She stopped at a farm cart and filled the spaces between loaves with fresh eggs. She was just leaving the Strand when a young girl approached her.

She didn't know this one. In her dirt smeared hand she held out a straggly bouquet of wildflowers. "These are for you, mum," the girl said. "From the gentleman across the way."

Hestia looked, but she knew the man wouldn't be there any longer. Gently, she took the flowers. Nestled in the midst of them was a chess piece. A king's piece, with an intricately carved crown. A note curled around the length of it.

You will never see it coming. The final blow approaches.

She sighed. Marstoke did like his games. Every so often he sent one of his lackeys with a note like this, hoping to intimidate her, or just to infuriate her. He should know by now it would not deter her. She rather thought he counted on it.

Ripping the note into pieces, she handed the chess piece over to the girl. "Take this to Mr. Song's shop. Do you know it?"

The girl clutched the piece and nodded.

"He'll give you a few coins for it."

The urchin blinked and then she was gone. Hestia made a note to look for that one again, in the same area, then she handed the flowers to the egg girl and headed home.

It wasn't long after that she settled before the low fire in her rooms with a cup of tea, a sausage and a slice of that fresh bread. Just a bit of peace before a very long day ahead, that's all she hoped for. She'd barely taken her first sip when Isaac announced an unexpected visitor.

Unexpected visitors were *de rigueur* around here, of course, but this one managed to surprise her. Her tea had long grown cold by the time the woman stopped talking long enough to sob into her kerchief.

"I know I should have told you!" Lady Diane sobbed. "I don't blame you for being terribly angry."

"I'm not at all angry," Hestia reassured her. "Just surprised." Lady Diane was one of the regular volunteers here at Half Moon House and had been for at least a year of two. "I'd noticed that you've established a friendly relationship with several of the girls here. Molly clearly looks up to you. But I would never have guessed—"

"No one knows!" The countess wiped her eyes, but tears still flowed. "I confessed to my husband before we were married—at least, I told him that I was not . . . chaste. I did not tell him of the little girl I had borne. My mother knew, of course, but she passed long ago."

"Your daughter's father knows, presumably, if you suspect him of trying to abduct her."

"I know it was him," Lady Diane said fiercely.

"We suspected it was one of Marstoke's people who tried to grab Molly. Your . . . her father . . . he is not . . ?"

"Marstoke?" The countess gasped in horror. "No! Certainly not! Her father is a wastrel, to be sure. A man of good family and a horrible penchant for gambling, but nothing like the sort of villainy Marstoke gets up to."

"He appears to be climbing the ladder of villainy if he's moved up to abduction."

"He must owe a huge sum. He approached me at the start of the Season and tried to blackmail me, threatening to tell the world about my sins. I knew I could not give in or it would never end."

"Very true," Hestia said with approval.

"So, I lied. I told him my husband knew everything and would have him thrashed within an inch of his life if he uttered even a whisper. Or if he came near me again."

"You did exactly right," she said warmly.

"I don't know why I was so foolish as to want him to begin with." Lady Diane dropped her head in her hands. "I was young. Headstrong. And he seized my mind. Stole all of my focus. It was the same as when I was eleven and the local boys teased me, told me that I was *just a girl* and would never get to the top of the chestnut at the edge of our park. So, of course, I became obsessed with climbing it. I went back again and again until I climbed that tree."

Hestia suppressed a smile. "So, someone told you that the young man was not for you?"

"Oh, yes. It was exactly the same with that handsome rogue that I was not supposed to turn my eye to. I could think of nothing else. I flirted relentlessly and was determined to conquer him, just like that tree."

Her words conjured an image of Stoneacre—tall, solid, imposing—and forbidden. "Yes," she sighed. "We've all had men we'd like to climb like a tree, haven't we?"

"Except that this time, they were right. He conquered me, in the end. He refused to offer for me, and my mother took me abroad to hide the consequences." She lifted her chin, suddenly fierce. "I won't have Molly suffer further for my folly. The girl has been through enough." Her shoulders slumped again. "Oh, but he must want her for proof. Surely he's gone and tracked her down. If I was able to do it, he must have been, too."

"And how did you?" Hestia asked. "You must know I took the girl out of a bad situation in a bawdy house."

Lady Diane sniffed again. "I do. You must not think the worst of me! I promise you, Hestia, I placed her with a kind couple. They were tenants of my sister's husband, childless, and so happy to take her in. I sent money and help when I could, with my sister's aid. But the influenza went through the village. It took the couple and laid my sister low for months. By the time I found out and got there, Molly had been sent to the poor house, and they had immediately shipped her off to the mills in Manchester. When I found the place—she'd already run away."

Hestia straightened as a memory blossomed. "You were the one who brought the news of the girls being siphoned from the mills to work in the brothels."

"Yes, I . . ." She dipped her head. "Oh, please do not tell my husband!"

"I will never betray your secrets, my dear."

"I pawned some jewelry to pay an investigator when I could not find her in Manchester. He found the place she'd gone. His report was . . . sickening. I didn't know what to do, but I knew you would help if you learned of it."

"I'm very glad you came to us. Molly was only one of the girls who needed to be liberated from that place."

"And you've been wonderful, knowing just how to help them recover from such a terrible ordeal. Molly has grown so, has she not? She's funny and eager and a kind girl—thanks to you."

Hestia held still when Lady Diane reached out to grip her forearm. "I owe you so very much. And now I must place another burden on you and ask you to keep her safe."

"It is no burden. Molly is one of our own. As are you, my lady. We will not allow anything to happen to that girl, and will do our best to help you, as well. Now that we know where the threat is coming from, we can combat it."

"Oh, can you? Could you?"

"We can," Hestia assured her. She waited a moment, wondering if the countess would share the name of her tormentor, but the woman seemed wrapped up in her thoughts and after a moment's reflection, Hestia thought it might be best if the gentlewoman knew nothing of what might come next. Instead, she asked softly, "What will you tell Molly, if anything, now?"

"Oh, I don't know! There are so many things I wish I could say to her. Things I wish I could do for her."

Hestia stood. "I would advise you to spend a bit of time with her, Lady Diane. Say nothing now, but she has been a bit low-spirited since the attack and I know she would relish the kindness. Listen to her thoughts and fears and hopes." She pressed the countess's hand. "I know guilt and fear must weigh heavy upon you, but you must remember that your goal should be to do what's best for Molly. It deserves careful consideration."

Lady Diane nodded. "I will not rush into anything, despite the temptation. I promise, Hestia."

She guided the countess to the door. "I am leaving Town for a few days, but I will speak to Isaac. May I be allowed to tell him the truth? There is no better man to keep your secret—and your girl—safe."

Lady Diane slumped a bit, but then stiffened her spine. "Yes, of course." She faced the door and rallied herself. Sunlight streamed in the window, finding glints in her blonde hair and making her skin shine like pearl against her navy gown. She was a fine woman. Hestia suspected she would do more than right by Molly. "Thank you, Hestia," the countess said fervently. "I trust you know I am deeply in your debt. I will do whatever necessary to repay you."

"You do so much good work here, my lady, I beg only that you will continue."

"Always," the countess vowed.

She took her leave and Hestia went in search of Isaac. She shared everything pertinent and he only nodded in understanding, as always betraying not the slightest bit of surprise or judgment.

"It should be no hard matter to ask around the clubs and hells and find who is scurrying about so desperately under a large debt," she said thoughtfully.

"I should think we can find him in a matter of days," Isaac agreed.

"We have so many friends. Surely we can find someone to whisper in the blackguard's ear. Someone to remind him of the folly of threatening our people?"

"Consider it done," Isaac said with determination. Nothing stirred his ire like someone using their power to threaten those less fortunate.

"Thank you, Isaac." She allowed all of her gratitude, for this and for so many other reasons, too, to infuse the simple words.

Her merely nodded and went to work. Hestia drifted back towards her rooms, hoping she could finish her cold breakfast before Stoneacre arrived.

Stoneacre. His name caused a flutter in her belly she barely had the chance to push away.

"Ma'am?" Beth floated out of the shadows in the passage.

Hestia stopped. Beth called her ma'am only when she was upset. "Yes, Beth? Good morning, my dear."

"You're leavin', ma'am?"

"I am. But I will return. I always do, Beth. You know that."

Beth clutched her arm, which was highly unusual. "Please don't. Stay behind this time, ma'am."

The woman looked truly fearful.

"I cannot, Beth," she said gently. "But you are not to worry. You will always be safe here. Always."

Pressing her lips together, Beth gazed at Hestia a long moment, then whirled and disappeared around a corner.

Hestia stared after her, then turned and continued on her way, hoping that was the last surprise she'd have to face this morning.

THE PAVEMENT before Half Moon House was filled to overflowing when the carriage pulled up. Stoneacre descended to find a communal farewell taking place, with Hestia the recipient of many hugs and admonishments to take care. He supervised the loading of her luggage and received a few shy farewells of his own—and one long, meaningful glance from Isaac.

And then they were off. They both sat quietly as the city rolled by, each lost in their own thoughts. The traffic still lay thick about them when they passed the Kensington tollgate and still Hestia did not speak. Stoneacre grew impatient. It was too long a journey to think of leaving matters so. Granted, it was a bit of a relief to find they could pass the time in easy silence, but it would be a waste of a colossal opportunity if he let it continue. He turned his gaze from the window with determination—and found her steadily regarding him. A warm light glowed in her eyes.

"What occupies your thoughts?" he asked guardedly.

She colored a bit and shrugged a shoulder. "Oh, I was just thinking of chestnut trees."

He blinked, but the corner of her mouth lifted and the back of his neck grew warm. He wanted to press her, but knew better. Yet he did not know how to turn her remark into a conversation, either.

But she smiled at him, all of her charms at full blaze, and he forgot to worry over it.

"You've been quiet as well. What is weighing on you, Stoneacre?"

He rallied his thoughts. "Two things," he admitted.

"Still wondering about my favorite color? It's pink. The soft pink of cherry blossoms—also my favorite flower."

"Thank you for sharing," he said seriously.

"But that's not what you were wondering about?"

He shook his head.

"Care to enlighten me?"

"Honestly, since you gave Bradford-on-Avon as our destination, I've been going around and around in my head, wondering what mischief Marstoke could be fermenting in such a small mill town."

"I should think you would know by now that Marstoke can stir up chaos anywhere. Chain him to a church pew in the country and he'll have the local parishioners in an all-out war within days."

"I won't argue that," he said wryly.

"But honestly, that village is not our destination. It is merely the closest spot that is large enough to disguise our presence."

"Where are we going, then?"

"A country house. Small. Out of the way. It sits outside of a hamlet called Farleigh Wick."

"Sounds like the perfect spot for a bit of illicit business—and nothing to tempt these London *Mesdames* to stay after they've made their payments."

"No," she said quietly. "Not any longer."

Silence fell again, but this time she was the one to break it after a few moments. "What was the second thing weighing on your mind?"

He said it straight out. "I was wondering if you were the one who absconded with that sack of Marstoke's papers. The one that went missing so long ago, on the very night that your friend, the Duchess of Aldmere, found his secret office."

The atmosphere inside the carriage shifted from languid to crackling in an instant.

She lifted her gaze to his. "Is that a question, Stoneacre?"

He lifted a shoulder, a deliberate effort to lessen the tension. "Yes, I suppose it is."

"And do you expect me to answer?"

"Well, I hope you will," he said honestly.

She settled back into her seat, watching him steadily. She took her time before she spoke again. "The answer is yes. And no."

He waited.

"I have the papers. But I did not take them." She sighed and fond remembrance softened her expression. "Francis brought them to me, thinking to trade them for a place at Half Moon House. Heavens, but she was so young, then. Having been under the care of that pimp, Hatch, she didn't understand shelter and safety could be had without a price."

"Why didn't you hand them over?" He didn't hide his faint disapproval.

"I did relinquish some of them. I had Aldmere mix them in with the ones your people confiscated from the office not long after I realized what they were. Most of that batch was related to bribes and blackmail."

He leaned forward. "What did you keep?"

Another hesitation.

"Lists. Names. Initials," she said at last. Thunder furrowed her brow and colored her words. "He kept a record of the women he mistreated, Stoneacre. Long, long lists. I had to recruit a friend to help me, as he kept some of it in code, but once it was broken . . ." She swallowed and looked away, out at the passing city outskirts. "It was all there. The trickery. The lies. Hints at the abuse. The ruin of so many. False marriages. Sham betrothals. A multitude of false identities. Women picked off the street and destroyed for his amusement. Others, of all classes, traded to pay debts owed to him."

She paused a moment and took a deep breath. "He toys with them. Torments them like a cat with a mouse, before he decides to finish or release them. An opera dancer here. A young woman of good family but not enough protection, there. It is a horrifying list that he continues to add to, to this day."

He made a noise of sympathy, but she hadn't finished. "Worse are the ones he warps. He takes a few and convinces them to play his Great Game. Like pieces on a board, he moves them at his whim and they help him, acting on his behalf to cheat, steal and ruin others. He uses them as weapons, where they will do him the most good or his enemies the worst."

"And what did you do with this information?" Because he was sure down to the soles of his boots that she had acted on it.

She didn't answer for a long moment. He was not perfectly sure she would. But then she heaved a sigh. "I tracked them down. Am tracking them down. One by one, I've searched out the women whose lives have been warped by Marstoke's touch."

"I can only imagine what you've found."

Swallowing, she nodded. "Yes. Some have been . . . hard. Some were gone already. Others beyond help. But there have been those that we found in time. Still within reach of a kind hand. There have been those, too, that moved beyond the experience, put it behind them and rebuilt their lives." One corner of her mouth twisted. "Some of those shut the door firmly in my face before I could utter more than a sentence or two. But others, some of those women have become our staunchest allies."

You are a wonder. He wanted to say it.

"Does he know?" he asked instead.

She shrugged. "If he does, he does not care. He's finished with them. What happens to them now, matters naught."

"Clearly, he did not feel that way about you," he countered.

"I'm the one he didn't break."

She said it so simply. Like it was not a monumental achievement. It was, he knew. He could well imagine it, though he had no wish to. This carriage was too small to contain the fury he felt when he thought of all that she must have been through.

He stuck to logistical issues instead. "I thought perhaps those pages contained information on his hideaways, since you knew where to find him in Somerset."

"No. Nothing like that." She met his gaze steadily. "That is not how I know how to find him."

Well. There seemed no way to respond—except to wait and see if she would expound upon it.

She did not.

Silence stretched out again. Not easy, this time, though. He allowed it to fill the carriage with awareness and expectation and whatever magic she spun that made him want to know every small thing about her, with the distance she always imposed upon them and his despair that he was never going to bridge it.

The Brentford tollgate came and went and at last he cleared his throat. "I had thought we were agreed," he began.

"On?"

"Have we not declared that we would be friends? This," he gestured, "does not feel friendly."

"No?"

"Friends talk. Share."

"I shared my favorite color," she said defensively.

"Friends converse. They laugh."

"I do have friends, Stoneacre," she said with a roll of her eyes.

"Then treat me as one," he challenged. "Or will it be too difficult?"

"No. Too dangerous," she countered with a direct look that beckoned him, like a shimmer of light from a long and shadowed corridor.

His heart suddenly tripped to a faster gait. "Less dangerous than the alternative."

"True enough." She leaned back. "But I have already shared a secret this morning. If you wish to further our friendship, then I believe it is your turn."

"Fine. But I do not wish any further discussion of Marstoke."

"I heartily concur." She raised a brow and he noticed it was blonde again, and briefly missed that earthy bit of red. "So, what shall it be?"

He opened his mouth, then shut it again. "I find myself perplexed."

She bit back a grin. "What was it you said to me? Tell me what you love? What you hate?"

"Very well. I love my sister."

"Not fair," she objected. "That can hardly count as a secret."

"It counts as a miracle."

She laughed. "Truly?"

"Without a doubt. She's just as stiff-necked and prideful as my parents and I hate the nickname she gave me as children with an unholy passion. Which is why she still uses it."

"Now, that sounds like a story to pass the time."

What on earth was wrong with him, bringing up such a subject? But he rather thought he'd tell her every embarrassing story he knew, to hear that laugh again.

"Very well." He settled back into the cushion. "We played at pirates, often, when we were small. We staged dashing sword fights and survived tempests and sea monsters and wicked French privateers out to capture us for reward."

"How intrepid."

"We were, rather. I received a splendid model of a two-masted schooner for a birthday present and I would take it across the lawns to the lake to sail it. Patrice was only allowed to the lake if her governess accompanied her, so whenever she grew tiresome and wanted to change the game to Pirate Princess or Pirate Bride, I would take my model and abandon her."

"Wretched boy," she said with feeling.

"I was, indeed. One day she evaded her governess and came after me. I had the boat in dry dock that morning, which meant I had it with me at the end of the dock while I tried to reattach a sail. She teased me, wanting to sail it on her own. I refused, naturally."

"Naturally."

"She fussed and fumed and tried to snatch it away. I pushed her back and she fell in the lake."

Hestia looked horrified.

"It should have been no great matter. My father was not fool enough to raise us near the lake without teaching us how to swim. But the shock of it—she opened her mouth and got a mouthful of lake water and in the ensuing coughing and sputtering, she became confused and frightened. She panicked. I couldn't get her to listen to me. I knew I had to go in after her, but in doing so, I tripped over my model ship and one of the masts stabbed deep into my thigh."

"Oh, dear. But you did save your sister."

"I did. And had to be stitched up, afterward. I walked with a limp for months, which sent my father into despair and allowed my sister to dub me Gimpy."

"No!"

"Yes."

"And one would think that she would be too grateful to torture you so."

"Alas, if only that were how sisters worked."

"I never had a sister. Not a blood sister, to share and compete with and all that comes with it."

"I know that Callie Russell certainly counts you as family, as does Lord Truitt."

"She is family, as far as I'm concerned. I have been gifted with sisters of the heart and they are all a true blessing."

They spoke for a while then, of the friends who had become her family. Callie and Tru. Brynne and her husband, the Duke of Aldmere. And of her son, Rhys, who had just married her protégé, the urchin they'd all first known as Flightly.

And all the while, Stoneacre rocked between wonder and despair. Here it was, everything he'd hoped for with Hestia. Conversation and a bit of teasing and a growing sense of intimacy. Heat and the sparkle of tension flared between them, increasing a little each time their knees brushed or their gazes met. But it was fleeting and the knowledge hurt. He wanted to shout in denial as the carriage began to slow.

He looked out. "Hounslow," he said. "We'll change horses here. We might as well disembark and freshen up and find a bite to eat."

He handed her down when they pulled into the courtyard at the Bear. And when the touch of her hand and the brush of her skirts against his leg caused his breath to catch—he told himself it was his own fault.

Every nursery maid, nanny and tutor that he'd ever had—and there had been a long line of them—had warned him to be careful what he wished for.

Now he knew exactly what they meant.

CHAPTER 7

Sometime in his reign of terror, Lord M—came up with the idea of marking his false brides. I myself wear the scar carved into my finger where my wedding ring would have been. When I tire of fighting his cruelty, I look at it and remember the sisters who wear the same mark.
—from the Journal of the Infamous Miss Hestia Wright

The Brown Bear was spacious, inviting and very busy. The late afternoon hour appeared to have brought a selection of locals out to enjoy the comforts of the taproom, which lay to the right of where Hestia stood in the entryway of the inn. Stoneacre spoke with the innkeeper, while she wondered why it appeared to be taking such a long time to settle an account for a change of horses.

Wandering toward the taproom, she peered inside. It held a loud and congenial crowd. They appeared to be embroiled in a rollicking debate over which sort of pig feed produced the best bacon.

Why had she hesitated to tell him about Marstoke's lists? Sighing, she admitted that she knew why. It was personal, her crusade to find those women. All of the work she did was valuable. She truly believed it. But finding those women felt special to her. Every time she could offer help or a shoulder to cry on, or even just a listening ear—it bound them. And it helped to heal her own soul, just a little.

Crusade was the right word, too. She followed that list with nearly religious fervor, determined to find them all.

But sharing something so meaningful—it left her feeling exposed. Letting him see that was lifting the mask a bit, allowing a glimpse of the private creature inside. And she hadn't allowed herself to feel vulnerable around a man in a very long time.

She supposed that was the least she owed him, for his help. But it felt . . . significant.

"It would seem there is a problem with their private parlor," Stoneacre said, approaching. "It is unavailable, but we can take a quick bite in the taproom, or request a box to take with us. There will be a small bit of a delay with the horses, however, as they only have one groom tonight." He paused. "I assumed we would travel on, at least to Reading. I know it grows late—"

"Yes, we should push on, but if we have to wait in any case, I don't mind the taproom." She took a step closer to the open door and looked over the crowd once more. "No one here *looks* to be a London brothel keeper en route to or from a meeting with Marstoke, but we should be careful. Inconspicuous."

She gave herself credit for not scoffing at the idea even as she proposed it. She had dressed in a plain traveling gown and pelisse, but Stoneacre, with his height and breadth, his striking looks and exquisite tailoring, looked every inch the lofty lord.

She kept her face turned down as they moved to a small table in a corner. A few men glanced at them, but the villagers in Hounslow were used to travelers. Their argument raged on as Hestia and Stoneacre settled in.

"Not one of them have the right of it," He leaned over her shoulder to speak as he pushed her chair in. "A hot mash of mixed grain is always best for bacon."

She glanced up in surprise. "Another hidden talent, my lord?"

"I do have an estate of my own to manage," he reminded her. "My tenants are quite as opinionated as these fellows on the matter. And a properly fattened pig can mean the difference between comfort and want thru the long winter."

She thought about that as the innkeeper's wife brought out slices of game pie and pints of her own home brew. "I assume you've undergone extensive training to take over your father's marquessate, as well?"

"Of course."

It was a casual answer. He was more interested in the excellent meal than in impressing her with his inheritance. Her heart swelled a little more with affection for him. Truly, he appeared to be Marstoke's opposite in every way. A man of power who viewed it as a responsibility instead of a right. One who did his duty and then labored in his spare time to improve the world, instead of grasping for more of it and casually destroying the rest.

Duty. The thought struck a chord as she took a long drink. "You mentioned your father was distraught over your accident with the model ship. Was it so bad? Did they fear for your life?"

"It was damned painful and slow to heal, but my father feared for my gait, for the most part," he said with a sigh. "He could not bear the thought of his son and heir walking with a limp for the rest of his days."

Her brow lowered. The question must have shown in her face.

"My father," he paused and appeared to be considering his next words. "My father is an . . . idealist. He has an opinion and a preference on all things and likes everything just so."

"I'm familiar with the type." Her heart fell a little and she told it sternly to stop. The Marquess of Woodbury's inclinations would never be anything to her. She also suppressed the sudden and terrifying urge to ask about his mother. That could certainly lead to no good. "That cannot have been easy to grow up with. I speak from experience, as he sounds as if he would get on exceedingly well with my father—who also wished for every small thing to perfectly align. But I imagine it was worse for you, being the heir."

"I was far from perfect," he said wryly.

"No one is perfect." She raised her pint. "But in all honesty, Stoneacre, you approach closer than most."

He laughed and raised his glass as well. "May the sentiment travel from your lips to my family's ears. Although they would think your standards are lamentably low."

No. Could they see the pair of them now, his family would think her an enterprising female of the worst degree, and would likely start planning on how to pry him from her clutches.

"They don't approve of your work for the Privy Council? I should think they would be proud." She paused. "Oh, but I know of several tricky situations you've landed in—and I'm sure there are countless more. They fear for your safety."

"Their concern would be more palatable if it had to do more with me and less with the transfer of the title."

"Ah. They are after you to *marry*." A ribbon of sorrow leaked from her icy core, easing from the crack that he'd opened with his kiss.

"Worse. My mother has progressed to the point of throwing available young chits at my head."

In the blink of an eye, sorrow to turned to indignation and a wholly unreasonable anger. Her fist tightened around her glass, but her mask—thank the heavens for her mask—saved her from betraying herself further.

Enough. She pulled hard on the reins of her wayward emotions. It was ridiculous to resent a concerned mother and some innocent, nameless girl.

Saints, but she did *not* want know that girl's name.

"You are no longer a young buck, sir. As I am no longer a girl. I suppose your mother is to be commended for waiting this long," she said lightly, though it cost her.

He snorted, but his mouth was full, so he did not reply further. She turned her attention to the crowd again. A few more locals entered, and another traveler. After a moment, though, she realized that they had indeed attracted some unwelcome attention.

A man stood next to the door. Tall, with a broad brow and thick black hair and strong, slashing eyebrows, he sipped his ale and glanced their way more than could be explained with natural curiosity. When he wasn't surreptitiously watching them, he was exchanging glances with a man at the bar. That one was shorter. He looked painfully thin and wore a sour expression on his long face. Leaning on the bar with his elbows, he ran a long, speculative gaze over Stoneacre.

The tall man appeared to be watching her closely. She gave no sign that she'd noticed their interest. She and Stoneacre finished eating quickly, though, and the innkeeper's wife returned to clear the table. "Your lady can use a private room to freshen up, sir," she said, glancing between them. "No need for her to go out to the common necessary."

"You are so very kind." Hestia stood. "I'll go now, if you don't mind, as the horses are surely nearly ready." With a nod, she followed the woman out, and noticed the thin man followed, crossing the room and taking up a position with the other man near the door.

In the entry hall, she touched the woman's arm. "Thank you again for your kindness," she said, her voice low. "I am thankful to be able to stay inside. There are so many strangers about, when one travels."

"Aye. And there is still occasional trouble about here, and no mistake." The woman kept her tone quiet, as well. "I got a feeling in my bones these last weeks. And there have been men about I don't know and cannot vouch for." She patted Hestia's hand reassuringly. "You'll be safe enough inside, though."

"Thank you. I know you must be busy in your kitchens tonight, with such a crowd. I can find my way if you'd like to just give me directions."

The innkeeper's wife nodded in gratitude. "I do have a mess of dough all risen and ready to be worked. Thank ye, ma'am. If you'll just head to the passage behind the stairs, you can use the first room to the left."

The woman bustled off and Hestia waited to be sure there was no one to see before she stepped behind the open taproom door. She just made it in time, too, as the thin man who had been watching stepped out. He crossed to the front door and looked out, then returned to his companion right inside the taproom. Hestia moved closer, squeezing into the narrowing space and listening.

"She'll be harder to grab if she don't go outside alone," he complained.

"Don't know as she's the one that they are looking for, in any case," the tall man countered.

"I do wonder," the thin man agreed. "This one looks younger than I would ha' thought. And not the least bit dangerous. Did you see her? She don't look tough. And he don't appear to be the bloke they said she'd be travelin' with."

In the dark behind the door, Hestia blanched. Had they been warned about her? And who were they expecting to be with her? Isaac, perhaps?

"Hmm . . . she is a looker, though, and they did say they'd pay well for any pretty ones we could bring in."

Hestia's eyes narrowed. So, Marstoke's London associates knew to watch for her—and they had taken the opportunity to watch out for themselves, as well. But Half Moon House had taken out miscreants like these before—vultures more than men, recruited to linger in streets, at stage stops and coaching inns, looking for women to abduct or trick away and sell into prostitution. Hestia and her people did their best to frighten them off, but hard cases were served their own brand of injustice and turned over to the press gangs. She'd make sure these two were given the same choice.

"What about the nob? Think she's his wife?"

"Nah. He's dressed finer than she. And did you see him fuss over her seat? She's got to be his fancy piece."

"Too pretty to be his wife, I s'pose."

"Worth the trouble, though? That's the question."

"Definitely worth it, if she's the one they asked about, but they'll take her anyway. I'd surely pay to diddle her, were I—"

A noise sounded on the other side of the door, in the entry hall. The men stopped talking. Footsteps approached and Hestia sucked in her breath, barely breathing behind the door. Through the crack she saw the innkeeper pause and eye the men with disfavor. "Here now, the pair o' ye. Stop lingering in the doorway, ye'll make the taproom look more crowded than it is, should someone come in. Go on in or get out. Can't have you chasing off business."

They grumbled back and eventually abandoned their ales and left the inn. Hestia waited for the entry hall to empty, then went to use the room offered by the innkeeper's wife. When she carefully emerged, watching the shadows, she returned to the taproom to find Stoneacre gone.

"Your carriage is all ready for the road, ma'am," the innkeeper said, leaving the taproom. "Your husband is just outside."

She thanked him and hurried out.

"Drake feels certain we can make it to Reading tonight," the earl said as she approached.

"Stoneacre, I've something to tell you—"

He opened the door. "Can you tell me once we're underway? There is still a way to go and a fog is rising on the heath."

"Yes, of course."

They pulled away and the coachman set a quick pace.

"Stoneacre, back in the taproom, two men—"

"I saw them. Both Drake and I asked around and there are rumors of thieves lately, abroad on the heath. We need to keep watch."

"It's worse than that." She told him all that she'd overheard.

"So the London brothel keepers knew to watch for you as they travelled?" he asked, perplexed.

"And must have known when they left, even before we visited Mrs. Ledger's. It doesn't make sense. Worse, we've lost any element of surprise we might have had, going in after them."

"Damn Marstoke," he cursed. "Well, at least for now, you've nothing to fear. Our driver is an old family servant. He's been with me through thick and thin. If trouble comes today, he'll know what to do."

"*When* trouble comes, I'm afraid."

He shot her a grin. "Still, I'd put my money on the pair of us over any number of highwaymen."

The silence this time was full of a different kind of tension. They watched and waited while the miles passed and the evening shadows stretched out over the growing fog. They'd reached a wild, empty stretch of long grasses and scrubby shrubs when they heard the first shout.

The carriage picked up speed.

Another shout. "Stand!" was all she could make out.

Stoneacre pressed a decorative scroll in the wood of the far wall. The panel beneath it slid down. Reaching into the cavity, he pulled out a richly decorated dueling pistol and extended it toward her. "Go carefully. It's loaded. You know how to use it, I assume?"

"Yes, but I've one of my own."

"Good. Save them both for when your shot will matter." He tucked the second of the pair into his waistband. "Now, would you be so kind as to move over to this bench?"

She complied and he bent down and pressed the bottom trim on the bench on which she'd been sitting. It tilted outward, all along the length of the bench, and this time he reached in and extracted a rifle. "A Baker," he said fondly. With unhurried movements, he started to load it. "With a Newland lock and a split stock." He pointed with his chin. "Back you go, please."

She moved back and he lowered the window in the door, then thumped on the ceiling. The coach, which had been slowing, gradually pulled to a stop.

"Everyone out of the coach!" The order came from outside. "Coachman, get your hands back on the reins where they can be seen!"

Stoneacre pointed the rifle out the window. "Now, Drake!" he said clearly.

Sudden light shone, illuminating the area outside of the coach and a bit of the inside as well. Raising her brows, Hestia slid away, into the shadows.

"Adjustable lantern of my own design," Stoneacre told her quietly. "And a mount that swings out to widen the illumination."

"One on each side?" she asked.

He nodded.

"Impressive."

"We've been in this situation before."

The mist outside swirled and a figure on horseback emerged. His hat rode low and he wore a kerchief pulled high. He held a flintlock pistol pointed in their direction.

"Another on the right flank, my lord." The coachman spoke loud enough to be heard by all. "Got him covered."

"If he approaches, shoot him between the eyes," Stoneacre called easily.

"Now, don't be hasty. It's you who will suffer, you fool, if you don't follow orders." The highwayman on their side of the coach motioned with his gun. "All we want is your fancy piece. Send her out and we'll let you go on your way, unharmed."

Stoneacre cocked the rifle.

The other bandit spoke, but Hestia could not make out the words.

"No," the thief on the door side answered. "We said we meant to have her and so we shall." He motioned again with his pistol. "Put away your gun and send her out—or we'll take a bit out of her before we pass her on, in payment."

No one moved or spoke.

Hestia jumped when the shot sounded and a bullet dug into the door at the window frame, sending splinters flying. The rifle roared as Stoneacre fired back.

"Damn. I missed."

She peered out as he reloaded. "You knocked him cockeyed, sent his hat flying and parted his hair for him." The bandit was cursing and wiping blood from his eyes and trying to control his frightened mount. "I see a familiar set of shaggy eyebrows," she relayed.

Stoneacre reached for the door handle. "Stay here."

"Be careful."

He was gone, out the door and crouching low. Hestia sat back a moment and considered, thinking fast. A low spate of cursing sounded and she moved to the corner of the window. Stoneacre was circling closer to the thief. The man's spent pistol lay on the ground. He kept trying to aim another at Stoneacre, but the blood was flowing freely into his eyes and his mount kept dancing away from the earl.

Two bandits. Both covered. Too easy.

Any number of highwaymen, he'd said.

She dug her own small pistol from the pocket hidden in her skirts. It was delicate, but deadly accurate, and she'd had plenty of practice with it. Waiting, she took her moment when she was sure both Stoneacre and the thief were occupied with each other. Sliding out the door, she crouched near the step up onto the driver's box. Straining, she tried to see or hear anything lurking beyond the circle of light.

Nothing.

Awkward, with two weapons in hand, she climbed up onto the step, startling the coachman.

"Get back inside, ma'am!" he gasped. She was pleased to see he kept his gun and his focus trained on the second bandit.

Ignoring him, she peered over the box and stretched her senses out again, scanning what she could see of the other side. But when she turned her attention to the road ahead . . .

There. In the roiling mist she caught the gleam of a metal barrel. Using her own pistol, she fired straight at it.

The flash of a return shot flared bright for a moment, but she couldn't tell where it hit. She kept her attention fixed ahead and suddenly a rider-less horse danced out of the mist and into the light.

Behind her two more reports sounded in rapid succession. The horse before her snorted and ran, disappearing into the fog. Rapid hoof beats faded into the distance.

"Stoneacre?" The lighted space behind her was empty now. No sign of either the earl or the bandit. Anxiety bloomed in her gut, but she turned and pointed the pistol Stoneacre had given her toward the second bandit. He still sat motionless, glaring at her and the coachman. They all waited.

"Stoneacre?" Only long practice kept her tone even and free of the first tendrils of panic stirring inside of her.

"Here! I'm fine, but this one is dead," he called.

Relief melted the icy fear. The waiting bandit sneered at her, then turned and faded away into the mist-shrouded night.

She grinned at the coachman, and turned as Stoneacre strode into the circle of light and came to lift her down.

"How did you know there was another one?" he demanded.

She shrugged. "I would have had someone held back, were I holding us up."

He laughed. "You terrify me. Now, let's take care of this and get back on the road."

CHAPTER 8

Lord M— has used other ruses in his faked marriages. He has hired actors to perform the services, and in more than one case bribed true clergymen to erase all evidence of some ceremonies. All told, we have discovered seventeen false marriages—seventeen ruined lives—and believe there are more to be found.
--from the Journal of the Infamous Miss Hestia Wright

Stoneacre strode about, tidying up. He found a blood trail in the road ahead, followed it a ways into the bracken, and came back declaring it not worth further chase.

"You must have hit him in a vital spot," he told Hestia. He was wrapping the dead bandit up in the man's own cape. "He's got a substantial enough leak that he won't be bothering us any time soon. As for this one?" He stood. "We'll leave him here. Either his cohorts will come to see to him . . ."

"Or they won't," she finished for him. Standing over the dead man, she found herself unable to spare him any pity. The self-serving violence of his life had bought this death. She was focused on the living—and specifically, at the moment, on Stoneacre.

What a revelation he was. Once again, they'd worked well together in a complicated situation. He was calm and competent, and shockingly, he'd held the obvious conviction that she was, too. She'd been in worse situations than the one they'd just conquered, and she knew how easily things could go horribly wrong. But they hadn't. The two of them were well matched in this and he wasn't put off by it.

She hadn't expected it to be so heady. She'd forgotten the relief of sharing her burdens. They were truly partners, in deed as well as name, now—and for this moment, despite all the trouble lurking ahead, she felt light and hopeful.

He came to see her into the carriage and stood close in the open door, his shoulders blocking out the world. "I think I will take the horse for this leg." Mist gathered like little pearls in those raven locks as he indicated the dead bandit's mount and the smell of bay rum and horse hung about him. "At least I will be able to listen better, in this dratted fog."

She nodded, feeling both disappointed and slightly relieved. "Thank you," she said. "For . . ." she gestured.

He waved off her thanks. "We did well." Bending over her hand, he kissed it.

Emotion spiked. Their gazes met. Faint music swelled within her. Heat rose from that chaste spot like water over a floodgate. And it mixed with those feelings she'd started to associate with Stoneacre. Peace. Warmth. Acceptance. Gratitude for his powerful and honorable presence in her world.

He started to straighten—and she reached out, curled her fingers around his neck and pressed her mouth to his.

STONEACRE STIFFENED IN SURPRISE, but the fight had already heightened his senses and the shock quickly unraveled into something far more heated and primal.

The taste of desire, the abrupt racing of his heart, the quick, tightening swell in his groin—after-battle-lust was something many men were familiar with.

This wasn't a role. It wasn't pretend. It wasn't something he would feel for any woman. This was *Hestia*—and so it meant so much more. A storm of long-denied craving had him grasping her hard. His tongue swept hers, and he kissed her with all the dreams and longing he'd carried, without hope. He twisted his hand into the fabric of her pelisse and wrapped the other one around the slender column of her neck. He kissed her forcefully. Relentlessly. And he waited for her to come to her senses and push him away.

She didn't. She leaned out and eased down out of the carriage, never breaking contact. Her body softened and went pliant against him. She kissed him back, measure for measure.

Her hands fisted around the collars of his coat. His heart thundered. She was here. *Stay,* he wanted to order her, for he craved more and more. He slid his hand down, settled it into the small of her back and tugged her closer. Lord, but she was made for him. *There she is.*

He could feel her nipple peaking against his other hand. Letting go of her pelisse, he covered her breast. Her heart drummed fierce against him.

She reached up, touched his face. And the kiss gentled. Below the towering desire lay more. All the things he craved. Pleasure. Comfort. *Home.*

He didn't want it to end, though he knew it must.

Sighing, she did it, breaking contact and pulling away. She pressed her forehead against his chest for a moment, then turned to climb back up into the coach. Squeezing his hand, she gave him a twisted smile. "I'll see you in Reading."

He nodded. Strode away from her, his mind awhirl, and mounted up.

COVERING her eyes with one hand, Hestia sunk down in the seat. Why now? How long had it been since she'd been stirred up this way? Veritable parades of men passed through her life. Diplomats, bankers, politicians, dukes, merchants, even a prince or two or three. She hadn't been the slightest bit tempted by one of them, not in years.

Yet, *now* she found one who raised her senses like a conductor calling music from his orchestra? *Now?* At the perfectly wrong time and in the most complicated circumstances?

She'd achieved a rapport with Stoneacre. It felt lovely and tenuous and she might have ruined it by acting worse than the youngest, most inexperienced tease of a girl, unsure of herself and playing with a man's desires.

It was wicked behavior. Utterly unfair to Stoneacre—and when he'd been more than decent to her.

She wasn't acting like herself.

And as the long hours alone with her thoughts dragged on, it became clear how wise he'd been to distract her with talk of friendship and sharing.

Alone, she fell prey to not only guilt, but to nerves and dark imaginings of what might come about when they confronted Marstoke. This trip was doing things to her. The thought of entering that house . . .

She bent over, feeling nauseated. She should be elated at the thought of finally finishing off her old enemy. She was. But right now she felt like the flailing needle of a compass—and steady, stable Stoneacre drew her like due north.

The moon climbed high as they changed horses again and went on. The hour was late when they reached Reading. Stoneacre's shoulders drooped with weariness. He registered them as brother and sister and scarcely spoke as they separated for the night.

She lay in the strange bed knowing he might despise her—and that she could not blame him. In the morning she would rise early and seize the chance to apologize—and to reestablish her equilibrium. Rolling over, she ignored the memory of his hands on her and sought out blessed sleep.

◞

THE NEXT MORNING, Stoneacre bounded up the stairs, note in hand, fighting to school his expression. Fortunately, he'd had the long ride to Reading last night to indulge himself—and he had, riding behind the carriage largely to hide the broad, recurring and no-doubt-ridiculous grin on his face.

Hestia Wright was not indifferent to him. He felt like singing the words out in song. She was not indifferent—no matter how much she would like to be.

That kiss had proved it. No mere after-battle affirmation, that had been a kiss of epic implications, gloriously heated and sweetly tender and utterly natural. They had both been present, aware and perhaps, a little awed.

But it had given him hope.

It had given her a headache, if her expression when they'd arrived last night had been any indication, so this morning, he went cautiously to seek her out.

The hour was early, but he found her leaving her room, fully dressed and seemingly ready for the day. He paused at the top of the stairs to gaze upon her.

There it was. The little catch of his breath. That moment of weightless, boundless anticipation that hit him every time he saw her anew. It could be filled with so much more, he understood suddenly.

She was backing out of her room, speaking to a maid inside about the removal of her valise. Early morning light streamed in the window just beyond her at the end of the passage. Her sturdy, dark navy traveling costume absorbed the rays, but the sunshine bathed her above the high neckline, creating a halo of her golden hair, hiding some of her features in the bright haze, and highlighting her delicate profile in soft, shell pink. She turned and blinked, her sight adjusting —and then she saw him.

He witnessed it. The slight loosening of her tense shoulders, the ease of a certain tightness around her eyes. The light that grew behind her eyes and the smile that began to curl the side of her mouth.

And he knew.

It lived there, between them. The potential for everything he longed for, all that he felt was missing from his life. And she felt it there, hovering, too.

There was no other woman like her. She was wily. Resourceful. Her eyes saw things others didn't. Different paths. Real truths. Her mind traveled in different directions.

And there was no other woman for him.

Only her.

She adjusted her expression as she moved toward him. Drew the shutters down once again. He understood why. Mountains of obstacles still loomed before them, all the uncertainty and the surety of Marstoke's wickedness, the harsh realities of the job before them and even the world they would return to.

But he didn't care. He knew now. Knew that he would not push her. That because of all that lay in her past and might loom in their future—that she would have to come to him. But he resolved with absolute certainty that he would shove against every impediment, fight and claw and do everything in his power to clear a path, to give her the freedom to choose.

To choose him.

The difficult enormity of the job made catching Marstoke look like child's play. But he would do it.

"Stoneacre?" she asked uncertainly as she approached and he did nothing but stare.

He shook his head and buried any sign of his decision—even as he took up the banner of this new crusade.

"Your gloves," he said awkwardly. "I like the color."

She looked down at the pair she carried. "Thank you."

"The perfect light blue, just the color of a robin's egg. I remember the first time I saw a nest of them. They dazzled me." And he was blathering like an idiot. He shook his head and recalled why he'd been coming up for her.

"I am glad you are already up and about." He lowered his tone. "I've received a note from one of my men."

That startled her. "Delivered here?"

"Yes. Crawford is one of my most trusted men. He has been in Oxford, searching out an old, disgruntled partner in one of Marstoke's schemes. When you gave me our destination the other day, I sent a fast courier with orders for Crawford to intercept the Bath Road, follow along it and seek out information on Marstoke or the associates traveling to meet with him. I mentioned we would stop here, at least to check for messages." He allowed his excitement to show. "It's good news. Crawford found several of the brothel owners stayed here in Reading, and they departed, heading west, only yesterday morning. He heard a mention of Farleigh Wik, as well. You were right! We are on the right track and if we set out quickly, we can reach the place this evening—and surely catch Marstoke still there."

"It's possible," she agreed slowly. Stoneacre was surprised she wasn't more excited. "But he won't linger, once he's taken everyone's payment and given new orders. Moving quickly and often has helped him avoid capture for so long, and he won't stay where so many people have known him to be."

"It's worth the shot, though, I think you'll agree."

"Definitely." She nodded. "Is the carriage ready?"

"I've just sent for it. If you don't mind a quick breakfast downstairs, I'll leave Crawford a note in case he makes his way back here."

Stepping aside in the narrow passage, he waved her ahead. They were shown to a private parlor and once they were seated, Stoneacre pulled his notebook from his coat pocket while Hestia was served a plate of shirred eggs and toast.

"Sir?" Jenny, the serving girl, stared at him with wide eyes. "I know you enjoyed the mistress's special tea this morn. I could tell. Shall I fetch you another cup?"

"Yes, that would be just the thing." Looking to Hestia, he told her, "The lady of the house makes her own blend and adds in cinnamon and spices. It's lovely. You should try it."

"It sounds divine." Hestia was watching Jenny.

The girl didn't notice. She stood rooted to the spot. Her gaze darted to his notebook, then back to his face.

"Thank you, Jenny," the earl said gently. "Forgive our haste. We are in a bit of a hurry this morning."

"Oh!" Flushing, she dipped a curtsy and hurried away.

He opened the book and glanced up to find Hestia watching him, a smile dancing around her eyes.

"What?" he demanded. She pressed her lips together to hide her amusement, but he could see it anyway. "What is it?"

"What is what?" She was all innocence.

"That look."

"What look?" she teased, but then she laughed outright and relented. "Nothing at all. I just enjoy watching a master at work."

"Master?" He wondered if he should be seriously affronted. "Of what?"

"Charm? Is that not what you called it when you spoke to the girls at Half Moon House?"

He made a noncommittal noise.

She leaned in. "A handsome gentlemen, polite, full of smiles and attention. You remembered her name! Heady stuff for a girl like that, it would seem." Her tone lowered to a rasp that made the hairs on his neck stand up. "Seduction, others might call it. You've won a devotee. That girl would be quite willing to show you to an empty room for a few, fevered minutes of passion."

"I, however, would not be willing," he said icily.

Smiling, she sat back. "And that's just one of the many reasons why I like you, Stoneacre."

He speared her with a mock glare. "You've no room, Pot, to call the Kettle black, in any case. Your soft words and quiet smiles have left jaws dropping on every ostler, groom and innkeeper we've encountered."

She started in on her eggs. "We do use what we've been given, do we not? And if it eases the way . . ." She lifted her shoulder.

"Well, you've eased the way and left a trail of daydreaming men all the way back to London, but I didn't point it out," he grumped at her.

"That's because you are a gentleman and I am no lady. You would do well to remember it, Stoneacre."

He sat back, triumphant, and grinned. "And that is just one of the many reasons why I like you, Hestia."

With a raised brow, she conceded him the win and took up a slice of toast. She wouldn't be so complacent if she knew how true his words were. He tried and failed to imagine Miss Chisholm or another of his mother's young candidates serving him with a bout of verbal sparring with breakfast. And then he imagined waking every morning to Hestia, to her wit, banter, and her lovely, expressive face—and he had to look down to his notebook again to hide the stab of *want* that surely must show in his face.

Slowly, he ripped away a piece of paper and ruthlessly suppressed the emotion. She was not ready for such truths yet.

"The innkeeper will surely find you some paper, if you do not wish to deplete your own supply," she said, eyeing his battered journal.

"No need. Crawford is used to my scribbles."

"And knows only to trust a page torn from that book—with a gilded edge and an old ink stain dribbled in the corner?" she asked pointedly.

With a rueful grin, he snatched a slice of toast from the rack. "You are quick this morning. Am I so obvious?"

"No. I've heard of such careful measures." Abandoning her eggs, she sat back. "Marstoke has a mark he uses in special correspondence. Did you know?"

"No." He frowned. "I can't recall ever seeing one."

"I don't believe he uses it for business or records. I've only found a few instances of it, and usually in messages we've intercepted. Direct orders to his highest lieutenants, as he calls them. From what I've seen, I think it denotes urgency, but it also authenticates the order." She nodded toward his journal. "As your unique paper does."

"Well, damn him for being intelligent and careful as well as ruthless." He sighed. "I suppose it's what makes him so dangerous."

"His black heart is what makes him dangerous," she corrected him.

"True enough." He stood. "I'm going to deliver this to the innkeeper. Can you be ready to leave directly?"

She stood. "I'll meet you outside."

They were on their way shortly, the horses eager in the cool, morning air.

"I hope you will not mind if I ride inside today," he said as he handed her in.

"Not at all." She gave him a solemn look as he settled across from her. "It gives me the chance to apologize." She ducked her head for a fraction of a moment, but then lifted her chin and met his gaze straight on. "I do apologize. I should not have . . . jumped at you like that."

Stoneacre laughed. "I thought you might demand that *I* apologize. For once again, I quite enjoyed it."

Her lips pressed together and he grew serious. "There is no need for remorse here, Hestia. Tensions are high on this mission of ours. The stakes are higher. Our very lives are at risk—as yesterday proved. Unpredictable reactions are to be expected."

"Thank you. It's true." She swallowed. "My emotions are unexpectedly wayward."

"Well, do not fear. I'm not likely to cry foul and demand compensation for my damaged virtue."

That dragged forth a wisp of a smile.

"There, now." Switching tones, he went business-like and brisk. "You'll have to tell me if you object, but I'd planned for us to masquerade as a married couple when we arrive in Bradford-on-Avon. I think we'd do well to switch identities and modes of travel as we go."

She nodded agreement. "It will make us more difficult to track." She worried a loose thread hanging from her pelisse, winding it around her finger in one direction, then another. "A wool merchant would be a good guise, and one that would ring true."

"Exactly what I was thinking. A merchant with an eye to a profitable deal, and a continuing trip to Bath with his wife to celebrate."

"It sounds just the thing."

Her gaze wandered to the window and he took a moment to appreciate the beauty of her, even with tension creeping back into her spine and tightening the angles of her face.

"Hestia? What's worrying you?"

She gave a short, bitter laugh. "Everything."

"Are you thinking of what we'll find tonight? How do you think Marstoke is handling these people?"

"He wants something besides money or he wouldn't have summoned them out here," she mused.

"Will he welcome them as guests, do you imagine? Or will it be direct to business?"

"I don't know," she said, suddenly sharp as the knife in his boot. "We could find anything at Farleigh Wick. Anything at all. He could be throwing a lavish party or marching them in like the meanest supplicants. It depends on his mood, and what he might need from them and whether he believes he'll be more likely to get it using charm or his fist." She drew a deep breath and shook her head. "I gave up trying to predict his ways long ago. I also refuse to give him any more of my time than absolutely necessary." Drawing a deep breath, she gave a half smile. "Surely we can find a more enjoyable way to spend our day of travel."

CHAPTER 9

Opera dancers and actresses—I send you fair warning. Lord M—appears
to have a singular antipathy for those women who take to the stage.
Many of your numbers have come forward with tales of his cruelty.
--from the Journal of the Infamous Miss Hestia Wright

S he'd phrased that badly. She could see it in his cutaway glance
and feel it in the heavy pause that weighted the air between
them.

"You were right, yesterday, when you said that we were friends
and should share. It truly passed the time." Shifting in her seat, she
eyed him, contemplating. "Never let it be said that I don't play fair. It
is my turn, is it not? You shared something you hated."

She narrowed her gaze, thinking, while some of the tension faded
from his frame.

Inspiration struck. "Ah, I know! Have you by chance noted the
very fine astrolabe hanging in my private parlor?"

"Yes. It is a lovely piece. I have wondered about it."

"I loathe it," she said simply.

He blinked. "Loathe it?"

"I do."

"Was it a gift?"

"No. I purchased it myself. It is exactly like the one my father kept in his study."

She could see him pondering. "Did he sail?" he asked.

"No. He used it to survey field placement, or when he added new land to an estate. He would use it to consult the stars on exactly the right day to plant seed or harvest crops. I was fascinated with the thing. Dazzled by the shine, all the markings. I would stand before it, marveling at its intricacies and longing to know its mysteries."

"Did he teach you the use of it?"

"No. He refused. He would not burden a girl's mind with such heavy matters. He taught my cousin, however. A boy of twelve. The heir presumptive for my father's title and wealth."

"Ah." Wisely, Stoneacre said no more.

"It was one of the first things I bought, once I had a decent amount of money of my own. I hired a student to teach me the workings of it."

"And do you use it?" He was patently curious.

"I occasionally use it to calculate the exact time of sunrise or sunset, if a particular raid or enterprise counts on such things. But no. For me, its most important function is to be there when I am told that I cannot or should not do something. When someone reminds me that something important is out of my sphere. When I am told I am too young, or too old, too weak, or something is beyond my reach because I am a woman. Then I go and I stand before it and I think of all the things I have done and accomplished in the face of such opposition."

The look he gave her was full of warmth and approval. She wanted to lean forward and bathe in the heat of it, but she stayed where she was.

"Then it is a valuable piece, indeed." He folded his arms. "And now that you tell me, I believe that I love it."

She laughed. "Ever contrary."

"Oh, yes. I fear so. I'm surprised you hadn't sussed that out yet."

"I should have known, when you said you were resisting your mother's attempts to marry you off," she teased, just to remind them both not to enjoy this *too* much.

"Oh, I started my career in stubbornness much earlier. When I was barely breeched, my family likes to remind me, I heard someone say that a man was known by the strength of his swing and the cut of his blade. They were talking of earlier times, I realize now, but back then I went straight to the library, climbed a table and took down a rusty sword from the wall. Somehow I managed to knot the thing to my belt and I wore it everywhere. I went outside every day to practice my swing. I refused to be parted from it for weeks."

She snorted. "My father would have loved that, if he'd had a son. As it was, I spent a large portion of my childhood attempting to do every small thing a daughter was not supposed to be able to. He enjoyed it for a time, but as soon as I sprouted breasts, I became . . . expendable. An asset to be bartered, perhaps, for something more useful. "

"He sounds like a damned fool," Stoneacre said baldly. "Perhaps fatherhood does something to men. Certainly, my father has had his moments of foolishness."

She brightened. "We could entertain ourselves for hours if we compare the ridiculous things our families have said."

"Too easy." He raised a brow. "Tell me instead, something they said that turned out to be true."

She stared at him. After a moment, she shook her head. "You do like to challenge me, Stoneacre."

He laughed. "I do. I truly do enjoy it, I confess."

Her eyes narrowed. Her voice lowered and she startled even herself when she heard how much she sounded like her father. "You'll go out and meet many people in your lifetime. They will seem fine, upstanding, even pleasant, but the vast percentage of them won't care two farthings for you or what happens to you."

His eyes widened.

"A harsh truth," she said evenly. "Harsher still to discover that he was part of the vast percentage." She'd suffered many instances of being forced to concede her father had been right—and had despised him anew each time.

She was, after all, the infamous Hestia Wright. Hundreds, perhaps thousands of people knew her name. Thought they knew her story. She'd met a great many of them, too. They greeted her with a variety of reactions. Avid curiosity. Palpable desire. Disdain. Fascination. Mortification. They all wanted to meet her. Damned few wished to know her. Fewer still cared those two farthings worth.

Stoneacre, however, appeared supremely unaffected by this basic, terrible truth. "Eh." He lifted a shoulder. "One only needs a few real friends in life. It doesn't matter if the circle is small as long as the caring is real."

She was impressed. It had taken her a long time to understand this was true, as well—and it had saved her. It didn't help her now, though, as she was starting to care for him.

Another harsh truth. Beyond his broad shoulders and fine, strong cheekbones, and the utter masculinity that kept tickling her senses and reminding her how sweet it was to react with prickling skin and tingling nerves and a thumping heart, she liked better his wit and quick smile and ready courage.

Her mouth opened. Closed. But then she said it—the further bit that made her feel even more miserably like her father. "Yes. A few are enough, as long as they are the right ones."

He wasn't the right one. Not for her. She had to keep reminding herself. Reminding him. They were spending this time together with a purpose. Once they'd dealt with Marstoke, she would go back to Half Moon House and he would go haring off wherever Prinny sent him— and he would eventually go to the altar with one of those sweet, inno- cent girls his mother pushed at him.

Damn the truth, anyway.

"My father told me that people will admire your virtues but remember your mistakes," he told her.

She grimaced. "He was right about that."

"Also, to always give substantial vails to the servants at coaching inns and house parties. It is the largest part of their livelihood and your best path away from scorched meat, lost buttons and scuffed boots."

She laughed. He was clearly trying to lighten the atmosphere. She followed him into an exchange of amusing-but-true advice until he left her laughing with a last gem from his father.

"In case I was worried about growing older," he said. "My father reassured me that an elderly man might find it takes longer to cock the gun, but his aim is just as true."

She laughed, imagining his reaction to hearing the innuendo. "And I always heard your father is straight laced!"

"He is."

"Oh, well, it must have been something that was worrying you greatly, then, for him to loosen up, so."

"I wasn't worried about it all, until he brought it up!"

They both laughed then and Stoneacre shifted on his bench and she abruptly realized that one of the reasons she'd been feeling so warm and comfortable was because one of his long legs had been pressed to hers, in the narrow space between them. And she hadn't even noticed. Or allowed herself to notice.

She straightened, moving away, and then they both looked up as the carriage noticeably slowed.

Stoneacre lowered the window and peered ahead. "We're in Lambourn already," he said, surprised, as he drew back in. "We'll be able to stretch our legs while the horses are changed."

It felt good to walk about a bit. Hestia spoke with the wife of the inn's owner for a few pleasant moments, but there was no news of any trouble or of any obvious London bawds. Mindful of Stoneacre's life lesson, she gave the woman a coin and turned away with a smile as the earl came hurrying from the stables.

"Good news," he said as he approached. "The grooms tell me of a new bridge open on a road we'll meet just before Liddington. It will allow us to take that route and head more directly south and west toward our destination. It means leaving the Bath Road for smaller lanes, but the roads are dry and it should cut several hours off our journey. What do you say, Hestia? Shall we take the gamble?"

She stilled. The music faded, that faint, gentle song that he'd spun and let loose inside of her. Their intimate interlude was over. Reality intruded. Marstoke awaited—and what could be the most dangerous confrontation of her life.

"Hestia?"

"Yes." She took a moment to mentally fill in the crack he'd made in her icy core. "Yes, let's take it. Let's get there quickly and see what we find."

CHAPTER 10

Should you find Lord M—or one of his minions in the Green Room,
ladies associated with the theatre, please beware. The last one associated
with him was found floating in the Thames.
--from the Journal of the Infamous Miss Hestia Wright

Hestia grew quieter and more withdrawn as the hours passed and they drew nearer their destination. Stoneacre spent the time cleaning his pistols and the rifle from the bench and left her alone. Everyone prepared for battle in their own way.

They stopped in Sandridge to change horses for the last time and Hestia asked him to delay a moment before they started out again.

"Would you pass down that small case at the top?" she asked Drake, gesturing to the luggage tied at the back of the carriage.

The coachman eyed the horses being settled into harness at the front, then cast a questioning glance his way. Stoneacre raised a shoulder and gave a nod, curious to see what she was up to.

She took the case, balanced it on the footman's step on the back and cracked it open. His brow rose when she pulled out a long, thin, firmly braided rope and ran it through her fingers.

"Is that silk?" He held out a hand.

She nodded and handed it over.

"It's so light."

"And strong." She started to reach for a folded leather bundle, but then she stopped and looked to him. "Do you have your lock picks?"

He patted his coat. "At the ready."

"No need to duplicate, then." Instead she took up a small, stitched bag that could have been a lady's reticule. "Extra powder and bullets." They were tucked away into a fold of her skirt. Taking back the coil of rope, she reached to raise her skirts, but then thought better of their location. "Come along to the other side of the coach, gentlemen, and provide me with a screen."

Obedient, he and Drake turned away, but stood to block her from view while she attached the rope. He turned to find her swaying and checking the fall of the heavy fabric and laughed. "I never knew a woman with such a penchant for storing implements beneath her skirts."

She snorted. "You disappoint me, Stoneacre. Surely you are experienced enough to know that all women keep their finest tools beneath their skirts."

Drake turned a laugh into a cough and she looked between the coachman and him. "I've been thinking that we shouldn't delay. When we reach Bradford-on-Avon, or perhaps before, we should stop at a livery and hire a couple of horses. Stoneacre and I can set out for Farleigh Wick." She nodded at Drake. "You can go on and see to getting us rooms."

The coachman looked startled. "But, what shall I say to the proprietor, when I arrive with coach and luggage and no passengers?"

She shrugged, unconcerned. "Tell them we are newly married and stopped at a pretty spot outside the town."

Stoneacre grinned as Drake colored.

"It will look odder still for us to arrive and immediately set out on horseback," she told him.

"She's right." Stoneacre waggled his brows at her. "Of course, that means that I'll have to play the besotted groom when we arrive."

"Have at it," she said with a wave of her hand. Looking ahead, she motioned. "The horses are all rigged up. Let's go."

They found a livery on the outskirts of Bradford-on-Avon and followed her plan. Hestia hung back while he hired the horses, but she swung into the saddle easily enough, and spread the dark wool carriage blanket across her lower limbs, where her traveling gown lacked the extra fabric a riding habit would have included. Drake and the carriage continued on into the town and toward the sign of the Three Feathers while he and Hestia circled north and west.

They'd only ridden a mile or so when she pulled up in a copse of trees. "The light is fading." Buttoning up her jacket, she completely covered the white shirtwaist beneath it, and nodded toward his ivory waistcoat. "Is that lined in black? You should turn it around or leave it behind. We'll want to blend in with the shadows."

Dismounting, he handed her his reins. "Even better." He pulled of his coat, unbuttoned his waistcoat and firmly told his nether regions to stand down, despite the seclusion and the undressing. "Reversible," he said, holding up the garment and donning it black side out. "And I commandeered this from Drake." He wrapped a dark scarf around his neck, hiding his white linen.

She nodded approval as she tucked her blue gloves away and donned black ones. "Make sure it is anchored tightly. You won't want it coming undone if we have to move quickly."

She had a scarf as well, and removed her dainty bonnet and tied the scarf over her hair, hiding her bright locks. She knotted it in the back and he tried not to stare at the long, slender column of her neck. They mounted again and moved out. The track here was wide enough for them to ride side by side, so he nudged his mount up next to hers. "What do you know of this place? Anything useful?"

After a long pause, she answered. "It's ancient. An old priory for a small sect of monks. It has a Great Hall, where Marstoke is likely entertaining his guests, if they are still there. A low, stone wall surrounds the house, gardens, stables and outbuildings, but it is easy to get over. We'll leave the horses at the back corner of it. It is far enough away that we won't be seen and there are trees to provide cover."

Stoneacre merely nodded, but his busy mind was conjuring reasons for her to be so familiar with the place—and hating every one of them. He knew the bare bones of her story, probably more of the truth of her history with the wicked marquess than most. He knew she'd somehow rejected Marstoke when she was young and untried. Knew that, furious, the marquess had conspired with the man she did have feelings for. He'd heard the rumors of the elopement and the faked wedding and the fact that she'd ended up in Marstoke's clutches —and had been kept there for an undetermined length of time. He'd also heard that their first meeting had occurred in Bath. They were close to that city now. Could this have been where some of that drama had played out?

The thought sickened him. Under normal circumstances he would never ask her to return, but nothing about this mission was normal— and he knew she wanted Marstoke to answer for his sins more than anyone. Still, his respect and admiration for her strength soared yet again, and he rode silently from then on, allowing her to gather whatever defenses she might.

SHE JUST KEPT RIDING, focusing her mind on logistics, on one plan, then another to back it up, lulling her brain while they drew closer to the place where she'd sworn she would never return.

Each new landmark brought fresh pain. She'd made it to that rickety bridge the first time she'd tried to escape. The second time she'd only made it to this crossroads. Closing her mind's eye to the past, she rode on.

And then they were there, at the back border, tying off the horses. She draped the blanket over her saddle and went to scramble over the low wall. She landed on her feet before Stoneacre had a chance to object, and stood, staring toward the house.

It was still hidden behind trees, but she could feel it, lurking. Waiting.

Stoneacre dropped down beside her. "We need to make a circuit around the place, see what we can, get an idea of what we are up against."

"We'll have to be careful around the stables. They are close to the house and after our escapade in Kendal a few weeks ago, they are sure to post guards there."

He nodded and they set off. Stoneacre did blend well into the shadows, bless him, especially with that raven-wing hair. Memory invaded—how soft it felt beneath her fingers—but she pushed it away. Adjusting her scarf, she pushed on.

"It's quiet," he whispered as they paused behind the dairy shed, long empty. He stared at the house in frustration. "Do you suppose we've missed them completely?"

"Not completely. Look to the window above the main door and to the right. I saw movement."

Tense and on edge, they waited. Stoneacre's long form loomed slightly behind her. The slightest hint of bay drifted over her. She'd been so angry and upset at the thought of returning here and furious with mortification at the thought of him witnessing it. Yet, kneeling here before the dark, wicked old pile, fighting back the memories that skittered like mice across her mind and up and down her spine, she felt grateful for the comforting bulk of his presence.

"Yes," he said suddenly into her ear. "There. I saw it too. Someone is in there, watching out the front."

"There's a hedge at the back border of the kitchen garden. Let's follow it to the other side. We should be able to get a glimpse of the stables without being seen from there."

They kept their heads down and crouched at the far end of the hedgerow. "No guards. I don't see anyone at all." Stoneacre cocked his head down at her. "Shall we go in for a look?"

She frowned. "Wait. Listen."

She held her breath. Only the breeze stirred.

In her ear, Stoneacre huffed in frustration. "I'm going in."

She clutched his arm before he could stand. "Go around the back. It's built into a small hill. I think there is a door opening into the hayloft back there."

He nodded.

"And be careful. If they are there, they are armed."

He looked back toward the house, judged his moment, and sprinted away.

She cursed as he went. She hated being left behind. Waiting. She watched him run, to distract herself. Her eyebrows rose. Saints, but he could move quickly. Those long legs, no doubt, and the lean muscled—

He peeked around the barn door and held up his hands.

She frowned.

He held up one finger.

"One?" she mouthed.

He nodded and mimicked four running legs with his hand.

"One horse?"

He nodded again.

Possibilities crashed like billiard balls in her head. A trick? A trap? Were they too late? Or had she been wrong all along?

But no, Stoneacre's man had heard mention of this place. And she knew Marstoke. Knew in her gut that she had not been wrong.

Emotions struck off each other in her chest, too. Damn Marstoke. Damn his endless game playing. She was sick to death of it all.

She stood suddenly. Glared at the back of the house. Spinning on her heel, she turned and walked into the open barn door.

"*One* horse?" she demanded of Stoneacre. "And no one else?"

"No one." He watched her, alight with curiosity.

"Could it be your man's mount?"

He frowned, considering. "No. Even if it were he inside, waiting, he would never stable his horse here, for fear of someone returning. Or arriving. He'll have hidden his mount somewhere near, as we did."

"Very well, then." She gestured toward the placid mare, watching them. "Bring her along, then."

She marched out and around the barn, climbed the short hill and waited for Stoneacre to catch up, leading the mare. When they all stood in the lane that led to the loft door, she took hold of the horse's halter, brought her forward a few spaces, then slapped her rump, urging her away.

"What are you doing?"

"Inconveniencing someone, I hope."

She waited until the mare wandered around the curve of the wooded lane, then turned and stalked back the way they'd come.

"*Now* what are you doing?"

She kept marching. "At first, I'd thought we'd sneak in the back," she told him as he followed her. "They never did discover how I managed to keep escaping. The way is surely still usable. I thought the place would be crowded and we would slip in and mingle a bit, gathering information before we made our move—or were found out."

She didn't attempt to hide this time, just strode along the path toward the house. When she came to the front she stopped and glared at it with all of the loathing in her heart.

"This place. It all began here. The lies, the manipulation, the pain. Here is where I began to understand Marstoke's great game—and vowed to beat him at it. So many years since I left here, I've spent watching and maneuvering. Anticipate and strike. React and counteract."

The sight of this place, though. All of the dark memories rising. The recollections of helplessness, despair and sheer, stubborn determination . . .

None of it made her feel the way she'd thought it would.

"I'm beyond tired of it all," she said suddenly. She started for the front door. "It's time Marstoke began to dance to *my* tune."

Something dark was rising inside of her—and Hestia was going to go along with it.

CHAPTER 11

To any gentleman perhaps tempted to associate with Lord M—, we ask you to reconsider. He is easily offended and always looking for betrayal. Should he find it, or think he has, it may be the women in your life who pay the price.
--from the Journal of the Infamous Miss Hestia Wright

Stoneacre followed Hestia into the house, his every sense on alert. She'd stopped just a few steps past the arched double door. She stood, her color high and her spine ramrod straight.

He gazed about. A great hall lay to the left, littered with all the signs of a grand party. A grand, *debauched* party, he mentally revised, taking it all in.

Furniture had been moved about and left in odd groups. Wine glasses and decanters sat on every surface. Several bottles lay about on the floor, amongst discarded gloves, slippers and at least one leather boot. A woman's garter hung from one light sconce and a shawl from another. An arched window was cracked open and a gentleman's cravat hung over the sill, fluttering in the breeze.

"Smell that?" Hestia asked quietly. She had her chin lifted as she tested the air.

It was no hard feat. Despite the cracked window, the sweet and heavy scent of blown fruit and burning hung in the air.

She turned her gaze to the rickety stair ahead of her. It hugged two of the stone walls and ended on a dark passage high above. He looked at her, nodded, and they set out, climbing slowly and trying to keep as quiet as possible.

The first landing held a dark opening in the stone.

"The monk's cells are down that corridor," she said in a whisper.

Turning, they continued upward. They were nearly halfway up to the passage when a figure emerged onto the final landing above.

They both froze. A bit of light showed behind him, casting the man's features in shadow. Stoneacre saw Hestia's hand dip into the folds of her skirt.

"You are earlier than I expected, sir."

Stoneacre put a hand on her arm to stall her. "It's Crawford," he said in relief. "He's mine."

Her muscles relaxed under his hand.

"Come on up," Crawford said. "We can talk and keep watch."

They stepped through a thick stone passage and emerged into a sun-filled room that stretched across the width of the hall below. Window seats were situated facing both the front and the back of the building. Carved, paneled wood covered the walls in Jacobean splendor. A massive fireplace with a marble surround centered on one wall.

"You must have traveled quickly." Crawford moved to look out at the front of the house. "I didn't expect you to make it from London until late tonight, at the earliest."

His man stepped toward them again, making a bow to Hestia before moving into Stoneacre's quick embrace. "How long have you been here?" Stoneacre asked, clapping his friend on his back.

"I followed a group of them from Reading. They set out before dawn and arrived yesterday afternoon. Other groups were already here." He shook his head. "You missed quite the party."

"So we gathered from the aftermath. You were here for it?"

"Yes. I watched the arrivals from outside. Everything was quiet in the afternoon. Whatever business they had to conduct, they must have done so then. The evening turned into something else altogether."

"You invited yourself in?"

"I did. After a certain point, no one would have realized I didn't belong. They were entirely caught up in their . . . pleasures."

"Of several varieties, I noticed."

"Yes. Notably—Marstoke partook in none of them. He waited until it started to get rowdy and then he left late in the evening, with several of his lackeys."

"Did you learn anything about the business they conducted? Or were they too far gone?"

"Their pleasures were the business," Hestia answered for him. "You smelled it. Opium."

Crawford eyed her with admiration. "You are quick in more ways than one, ma'am. But there is something you should see."

Hestia raised a brow.

Crawford glanced outside again, then crossed to a doorway in the corner of the room. He swung open a door and indicated that they proceed him.

Stoneacre sensed Hestia's hesitation.

"That was the abbot's office, in antiquity," she told him. "Later Marstoke used it for his chambers. There is nothing in there I am going to want to see."

Yet she pressed her lips together and followed the sweep of Crawford's arm.

She stopped just past the threshold. Stoneacre, on her heels, stalled as well.

The place had been transformed. It looked like a pasha's tent—something one would find in a desert oasis. Patterned silks draped the ceiling and covered the walls. Cushions were strewn across the floor. A low chair, lower table and a set of pierced lanterns defined a space in the center.

"Theater," Hestia said with a sigh. "He always had a weakness for theater—with himself in the center role." She stepped in, her head moving to take it all in. "Can't you see it? He has them escorted here and they are struck by the opulence, the decadence—"

"And the Eastern supplier he kept by his side," Crawford added.

"He received his tithes and notified them all they were to begin dealing in opium as well as flesh?" she asked.

"That's what I heard. Some were enthusiastic about the idea. Others were annoyed at losing rooms for their usual business and at the thought of the cost of setting up a space like this."

"He wouldn't have given them a choice."

"No."

"But he did give them a taste of the wares," Stoneacre reflected. "The party must have gone on all night."

"It did—but that didn't stop his men from booting them all awake early this morning and moving them all out. Back to London, to get to work."

"New revenue streams," Hestia said, meeting Stoneacre's gaze. "You've been shutting them off, now he's looking for new ways to make money." She nodded absently. "Suddenly it makes sense, why he chose this spot."

"Why?"

"Way back in the beginning, Marstoke started his illicit business with smuggling. That's when he began to recruit malcontented sons of the aristocracy. The ones who weren't to inherit the family money —and might be willing to commit a bit of treasonous smuggling to make their own. This place has vast cellars and used to be a regular stop along their routes."

Stoneacre stood still, absorbing it all. This mission was growing bigger all of the time.

"There's more." Crawford shifted, uneasy.

"What is it?"

His man pointed with his chin. "On the table."

He exchanged glances with Hestia and together, they approached.

A sealed letter lay on the table, Hestia's name scrawled across it.

"Did you read it?" Stoneacre asked sharply.

"No!" Crawford raised his hands. "There seemed no need. Everyone was gone and I knew you two would be arriving eventually."

Her face ashen, Hestia picked it up and began to read.

SHE REFUSED to let her hands shake as she held up the missive.

HESTIA, *my dear,*

Thank you for coming. The world changes, but I find comfort in the idea that you are always where I expect you to be—chasing after me, always a step or two behind.

I am grieved that I cannot wait for you, be there with you, right where it all began. Ah, the memories. How young we were. How lovely you were, and how innocent. Have you visited your cell? I have. There are still manacles attached to the wall in there. I have walked all over this house, remembering. The bloodstains still color the cracks in the marble in the solar hearth, did you notice?

Our games have been magnificent. I have always felt a strong sense of pride in you, even when you enraged me. I feel it now, even as the curtains to our drama draw to a close. I admit that my victory will have a hollow quality, without you to witness it.

But alas, I must bid you . . .

Adieu,

M

AN ICY CHILL ran down her spine as Hestia looked up. "There is someone here."

"No." Stoneacre's man sounded decisive. "I've searched the place."

"Not all of it," she returned flatly. She looked to the earl. "One horse." She waved the letter. "And this—"

"The whore is correct."

They all turned. He stood on the threshold—a small man, short but sturdy looking—and with no expression to be found on his countenance at all. With one hand he tugged down his lavishly embroidered waistcoat while his other held a steady grip on a shining pistol.

"Move away." He pointed with the firearm. "Step back from the woman. It is only you who must die, Hestia Wright."

She sighed, even as the chill faded and embers of fury began to glow in her belly. Slowly she reached up and began to unwind the scarf from around her head. "He found the secret passageway, did he?"

The man's brows raised in surprise. "No. The hidden panel next to the great hearth." He nodded. "But he'll be interested to hear about a secret passage. Thank you, for that."

"A bit of icing to go atop my death?" She could hear the hard edge to her own voice as she let the scarf drop.

The man shrugged, still flat of manner. "I've been given the job. You know him. You'll know I must complete it."

"Oh, no." Stoneacre words emerged softly, but carried deadly intent. "You must not."

She looked over to see him pointing one of his dueling pistols at the newcomer.

It didn't unsettle the man in the slightest. He merely raised his other hand and widened his stance, standing with his arms angled and covering both of them with a weapon.

Angry flames licked higher inside her. They tightened her chest and climbed into her throat and threatened to block her words. She forced them out. "Know him?" She spit the question as if it were a bullet that would take him down. "Oh, yes. I do. I'll wager I know you, too." And she let all of the revulsion and loathing she felt show in her face. "Someone, somewhere, possesses something that you feel should be yours. Curse the whims of fate, someone else has inherited the estates or won the girl or covered himself in glory that should be yours. Likely a mixture of all three." Gesturing, she sneered. "Look at you. Well fed. Well shod and clothed. Manners. Education, presumably. And those lovely pistols earned some gunsmith a month's good living. All blessings in your life, without doubt. But you cannot see or appreciate them over the bitter taint of envy that has permeated your soul."

The first sign of emotion showed in him when his mouth dropped open a little.

"I can see I have the right of it."

"That's enough." He frowned. "You don't know. The army? Because it's family tradition?" he scoffed. "Why? What should I do there? War's over. Laurels have all been handed out. No chance to have my reputation made in battle dispatches. No opportunity to capture enemy supplies or pay and share in the booty. Shall I rot in some wilderness or babysit a failed, fat emperor on a wasted island?"

"You might protect your country, perhaps? See to her interests at home and abroad? Or find some other occupation that would satisfy your family and let you follow your own interests? But no, so much better to join with a traitor and kill women at his bidding. Is he still promising to overthrow the monarchy? To do away with primogeniture? Because you are so much more likely to inherit based on . . . what? Merit? Your honor?" She laughed.

"Stop talking," he said, raising the weapon pointed at her a little higher.

"Or what?" Damn him. Damn them all. She scarcely recognized herself. That damned insulting letter had jolted her mask loose and the appearance of this poppycock of a would-be assassin had knocked it clear away. If she were meant to die, she would do it with a curse for Marstoke and his morally weak minions on her lips.

Stoneacre made some slight move and the stranger glared his way. Smoothly, Hestia pulled the tiny Queen Anne pistol from her pocket, her hand just as steady and her resolve as set as the man who meant to murder her. Her finger caressed the trigger. She braced herself—

And the stranger jerked and dropped as another gun barked. A red hole bloomed at his temple as he fell. Hestia spun and glared. Stoneacre still stood at the ready, but Crawford was lowering his smoking weapon.

"I was ready to—"

"I know you were," he said respectfully. "But I didn't like to think of you carrying that death around with you for the rest of your days."

Hestia opened her mouth to answer him, then shut it again. He'd meant it as a kindness. It *was* a kindness. Why, then did it feel like another blow? Another man believing she couldn't do what needed to be done?

"*A sense of pride*," she muttered, her gorge rising. She stared at the dead man. Fury choked her. Anger, grief and despair threatened to crush her with their combined weight. Gasping for breath, she stumbled out of the room.

Yes. Light and air. Space. She leaned a hand against the wooden mantle on the fireplace and fought to breathe. *Hollow victory be damned*, she cursed silently.

Her gaze fell on the marble surround. Oh, saints in heaven, he was right. *Bloodstains still color the cracks* . . . Revulsion speared her from brain to gut. She flung herself away, shuddering.

Damn him. Damn her. Damn them all.

"Hestia?"

Stoneacre and his man stood in the doorway. Their eyes widened as she raised her pistol and aimed for those loathsome stains.

The crack of the shot was followed by a ping as the bullet ricocheted off of the hardened stone.

"Hestia!" Both men ducked.

She stared at the small indentation in the stone and then blindly at the pair of men, then back. It was all too much. Being here was bad enough . . . Rage rose to heights she hadn't imagined she could reach. She struggled to contain it. She had to . . . She had to . . .

She ran.

Out through the passage and down the stairs. Past the remnants of Marstoke's revels. Out into the clear air. She walked until she hit green lawn and then she breathed deeply, reaching for control.

From the corner of her eye she saw the two men emerge from the main door. They conferred, murmuring, and then Crawford slipped away, moving down the front of the house and heading toward the wood on the east side. Stoneacre started toward her and she turned away. Still, he came. He was still several feet away when she spun about.

"Three times!" she spat, throwing a hand out toward the house. "Three times I escaped this wretched place and three times they dragged me back. I never truly despaired, though. Because they never discovered how I got out. And because I knew I would not break, no matter what Marstoke did to me. I *would* make it out."

She paused, breathing her way through horrid memories, glaring at the house. "But the fourth time, it was different then. I prepared thoroughly. I stole a pair of stained breeches from a courier's saddlebag and took an old tunic a groom left drying in the bushes. I stashed away provisions. I did it because I knew this time had to be different. I couldn't come back again, because Marstoke had finally done it. He'd finally found a way past my defenses and I feared I truly would break if it continued."

She glanced back. Stoneacre stood, tense and still. He'd closed his eyes. "Don't you want to know how he did it?"

"No!" he rasped. "I don't."

"He brought another girl into the house," she continued relentlessly. "Not educated or refined in any way, but very sweet. Bewildered. He brought her along to my room. It was one of the monk's cells, where I was kept confined, most days. He proceeded as usual, but this time, when I defied him—he punished *her*."

Now her eyes closed. "How long?" she whispered. "How long do you think I could stand by while he struck her? And worse?"

Stoneacre didn't answer. He only shook his head.

"She came creeping back later," Hestia said hollowly. "To thank me. And she kept coming back. She wasn't confined nearly as much as I was. I imagined she was too ashamed of her bruises to venture out. Too cowed. Or perhaps she had nowhere to go." She sucked in a breath. "She brought me extra food from the kitchens. And she talked endlessly about her village and the people there. She said it was far away, and she wasn't sure which direction."

Hestia sighed. "I was furious—and I was worried. I was set to escape, but I knew I couldn't leave her behind. I had to take her with me—and it was going to make everything so much harder. But I made preparations, and I waited for the right time."

Her heart began to pound again as the memories rose up. "Except. . . one day I noticed a bruise—a split on her cheekbone that I had not seen Marstoke make—and I began to wonder what else was happening to her. So, the next time I was released and set to helping the maid with the laundry, I took a stack of linens upstairs—and began to creep about, searching for Beth."

Stoneacre started. "Beth? Not that frightened girl . . ?"

"Yes. The very one. Her manner makes her appear so much younger. But back then, I worried that one of the servants was mistreating her. Bad enough what Marstoke was putting us through. I couldn't imagine being frightened even when he was not around. None of them had tried anything with me. But they might think they could get away with it, with a timid girl like her."

She sighed. "I knew her room was in the upper floors. I went searching, but the bedrooms were all empty." Her tone hardened. "The solar was occupied, though. Beth was there—on Marstoke's lap—and not because she'd been forced there. She was grinning and unbuttoning his waistcoat while he complained that it was taking too long for me to trust her."

"No!" Stoneacre looked aghast. "She wasn't . . ."

"She was. It was all an act. She assured him it wouldn't take much longer, as I'd accepted her offerings from the kitchen and listened to her stories. She told him I'd soon be talking back—and they would find how I was escaping—and could move on to other . . . plans for me."

Stoneacre gave a grunt of distress. Hestia kept going. It was too late to stop now. She had to tell it all.

"I crouched there in the shadows like a fool, but I couldn't take my eyes off of them. Couldn't stop staring. It was like a dream. Marstoke grasped Beth's chin, rough as usual, but she pushed his hand away. 'Careful,' she admonished him. 'I caught her looking at my cheek—and thinking. Always thinking, that one is.' She began to untie the laces to her peasant shirt. 'Pick a spot that won't show,' she whispered to him. 'And make it good.'"

Hestia cleared her throat and wished she could clear her head of these memories. "I was sick. Almost physically ill at the thought of being played for such a fool—at the thought that she would do such a thing to me, a girl no older than I and yet so—"

"Evil," Stoneacre whispered.

She swallowed and pushed on. "I didn't make a sound. Didn't move. But Marstoke bade her fetch his strap and when she climbed off of him, she spotted me. I whirled to run, but she was quick and caught me by the hair and dragged me into the solar. I was beyond livid. And she was mocking. I struck out at her. She hit back and soon we were struggling, while Marstoke watched, all amusement. Finally, I broke free and pushed her away. I headed for the stairs, but Marstoke caught me. It was several minutes before we realized that Beth had gone quiet. She still slumped on the floor. She'd struck her head on the marble when I shoved her. The smear of blood down the surround showed her path down. She lay there still, unconscious."

"No more than she deserved," Stoneacre snorted.

"For four days, she slept, and when she awoke, her wits were gone. She was scarcely the same girl. Marstoke tried to use her to torment me further, blaming me for her illness and for her new condition." She shrugged. "I was past caring. She'd earned what she got, as far as I was concerned and nothing he could do could touch me now. I was blank. Empty. Not even defiant any longer, just uncaring." She gave an ugly laugh. "He tired of that soon enough. If only I had known! I gave him nothing. Neither the terrified surrender he enjoyed with other girls nor the fight he usually got from me—and suddenly he wasn't interested. He set me free, dumping me alone and penniless, in rags, miles away."

She breathed deep, remembering the joy of that moment.

"Hestia," Stoneacre reached out.

She drew back, shaking. "No! Please, do not. I'm fine."

"You are not fine," he said gently.

"I am! I got past it. I forgave her, eventually. I'll *never* forgive him—but I will defeat him. I just need . . ."

She was coming undone with the effort of holding on to so many emotions. Her mask. It felt long gone and out of reach. If she could just find it again . . .

"Please," she begged. "A moment alone. It's just, coming back here, and that letter, and that boy . . . it's dredging up so much . . . Just let me be. I need a moment to push it all back down."

"Why?" he asked.

"Why?" She stared, dumbfounded. "Why, what?"

"Why push it all down, banish your feelings?"

"How can you ask that?" She nearly shouted it, lashing out in sudden anger. "Do you think I want Marstoke to define me? Control me? You don't know—you cannot!"

"No, I cannot. I cannot imagine the incandescent anger you must feel." He shook his head, gazing at her in what looked like admiration.

Admiration? No. That couldn't be right.

"I'm in awe of you, Hestia Wright," he said softly. "You must have carried all of that with you for so long, rigidly controlling it. Allowing it to fuel you, I suspect."

She wanted to cringe. She shouldn't have told him. He was stripping her naked. Seeing right down into her soul.

"But you paid for that fury with blood, sweat and spite. And now it is out—and you deserve the chance to feel it. Let it out. Let it go. Some of it, at least."

She frowned. Shook her head.

"He only wins, Hestia, if you act against your feelings. Or let them harm you."

Harm her? By all the saints, her hate and anger were part of her. But was that allowing Marstoke to define her? Only if she couldn't control it. She'd always believed that. But this, how she felt now, here, it was beyond anything that she'd had to bury before.

She turned toward the house—and her breath began to come faster at the idea of it. Could she? But she knew—now that idea was in her, now that the thought of release hung before her—she must.

She took a step toward the place. Stopped. A noise came out of her that she could not contain, could not recognize or categorize. The flames inside her were leaping again, growing—and she knew.

Suddenly, she was running again. Toward the house, this time. She lifted her skirts and her feet flew and she was inside, and heading for the bright light of the library. Yes. The liquor cabinet still stood there, in this place where ancient monks must have labored over their manuscripts. She picked up a chair and smashed the glass front of the cabinet and plucked several bottles of brandy from the shelves.

Dragging the broken chair and the bottles, she went back to the massive hearth at the Great Hall. Wood had been stacked here, and kindling. She started a fire, threw the chair onto it, too—except for one leg. She fetched the cravat from the window, wound it around one end of the chair leg, sprinkled it with brandy, and held it in the fire until it started to burn.

The odd sense of urgency had left her. Calm descended, settling like a mantle over her shoulders as she climbed the stairs and took the dark passage off the first landing. Even the light of her makeshift torch couldn't chase the bad memories of being dragged down this corridor. She took a swig of the brandy as she stood on the threshold of the cell where she'd been imprisoned, and then she began to sprinkle it about. She poured it over the manacles on the wall and left a thick trail leading away. Near the door again, she tossed the bottle back onto the bed, held the torch to the brandy and let it light the puddle at her feet. Small, dancing flames flared up, crept across the floor and began to climb the wall. When the bed linens caught, she turned away.

Up. Up to the solar, now. Moving almost woodenly, she pushed into the pasha's tent. Stepping over the body still on the floor, she crushed one of the pierced lanterns and allowed the oil inside to drip and leak over all the surrounding cushions. Pursing her lips, she tossed the torch into the wreckage.

With a whoosh, this fire roared to life, hot and fierce. Her grin echoed it as she left. She moved more quickly now, her step lighter, the weight on her shoulders lifting with each crackle of growing flame.

Smiling, she walked through the thickening smoke and out the main door. The wood was old. The whole place would burn quickly. No one would be imprisoned here, hurt here, again.

And this was only the first blow she meant to deal Marstoke.

Stoneacre stood silently where she'd left him. Bless him for giving her the idea—and for allowing her privacy to carry it out.

"Where's Crawford?" she called as she approached him, suddenly struck with the notion that the man might have gone back inside . . .

"I sent him after the bawds." Stoneacre was staring above her, where smoke had begun to leak around the solar window. "Oh," he said, his eyes widening. "But what of the—"

"The house will be his funeral pyre," Hestia answered roughly. "And it's more a marker than he deserves."

The earl did not get the chance to object. She'd reached him by then, and she didn't pause, just stepped close, grasped his shoulders and pulled him down. And when he bent to her, she kissed him, long and hard and without mercy, but with all of the relief and leaping passion in her unexpectedly lightened heart.

CHAPTER 12

Friends and business partners who fall from Lord M—'s favor have
suffered beatings, destruction of property and other unexpected mishaps
—but the marquess has also demanded payment for debt or default
through the services of wives, daughters and wards.
--from the Journal of the Infamous Miss Hestia Wright

S he tasted of brandy and smoke. He savored it, drinking it in. Her
fingers had drifted to his hair and he shivered at her touch, pleasure coursing down his spine. Her tongue swept his, challenging him
and he gave a low growl as he answered. She moved against him. He
could feel her everywhere, supple and hot and utterly enticing.

Oh, damn, yes. His body knew just how to respond—but the rest
of him felt like the kaleidoscope his sister bought for her nursery—so
many emotions tumbling about inside of him and he didn't know
which to feel.

Pulling back, he gazed down at her, then at the burning house.
"Not that I'm objecting to the current situation, but I am wondering
just what your thoughts are?" He gestured. "On all of this?"

"I'm not thinking," she answered. "I'm feeling—just as you suggested."

"I congratulate myself on the excellent suggestion, then."

"As do I. And eradicating that house from the world is making me feel very happy indeed." She stepped toward him again, but they both started when a tinkling crash echoed from the house.

"That's all very well, but do it from further away." He tugged her hand, pulling her further out onto the lawn and wishing he could protect her from more than fiery sparks and bursting glass.

She followed, searching his face. "I'm feeling grateful, too, Stoneacre."

"So am I—grateful you are alive." And happy that she had exorcised some of the dark emotion that had held her. But also violent, furious and gutted at her story. And filled with murderous intent toward Marstoke. Oh, and yes, still scorched with desire for this brave and beautiful creature.

"I am grateful for you."

"Me?"

"Yes." She cocked her head. "Marstoke is not the only man to despise me, but truthfully? Most men like me."

"That's easy to believe."

"Some like the way I look—"

"No," he interrupted. "We *all* like the way you look, Hestia."

Her mouth quirked at the corner. "Some approve of the work we do. Others like my sardonic humor. Some just like that I have a scandalous name." Her brows rose. "But there's not one man in a hundred who could watch me fall to pieces the way I did today, then tell me that they admire me for it."

Oh, he was so damned far past admiration. How could he not be? He had no idea what had been in Marstoke's letter. He suspected it had been all taunting and insults, and still it had been the least of all the evils she had faced this afternoon. Not one woman in a thousand could have borne it. He was surprised she hadn't collapsed under the weight of so much—and inordinately proud that she had faced it all with righteous anger, defiance—and, yes, flame.

But he couldn't say a word of all of that. So he raised a brow instead. "Yes, well, I'm not like most men."

"No," she agreed decisively. She looked back at the house for a moment and he followed her gaze. Evening was coming on and the rising smoke drifting out from the corners and eaves blended easily with the shadows.

"I've worn a mask for a very long time," she said carefully. "It's comfortable and useful. And it works in two directions. From the outside it helps me appear poised and strong. Unflappable. But it turns inward, too, and helps me remain calm and in control."

Turning back, she met his gaze directly. "I don't know how you see past it. No one ever has. It's . . . disconcerting. But right now, it feels very freeing, too. No one else could have convinced me to cast it aside today. But you did—and now it is off—and I find that I'm in no hurry to don it again."

Her eyes widened and his attention was torn away as a great boom sounded and the roof over the solar collapsed inward. She drew a deep breath, a look of satisfaction moving across her beautiful face.

Her arms flew out. "This could have been a disastrous evening. And somehow, because of you, it is not. Tonight—it feels like we are floating. Free. We are disconnected from the real world and our usual lives."

"True enough," he said ironically. The flames showed against the darkening sky now. They should move on before the fire started to draw attention.

She grabbed the edges of his coat in two fists. "It's almost as if we don't exist right now. No one knows where we are." She snorted. "Marstoke likely believes us both dead." She flattened her hands against his chest as she gazed up at him with an odd expression. Like she wanted to implore him, but wouldn't allow herself to do it. "I want to leave the mask off. And the rules that go with it. I want you, Stoneacre, for this time that doesn't exist."

The kaleidoscope whirled again. His first instinct was to refuse. He wanted her for all of her days, not just this one. But despite her emotional victories today, he knew she was still fragile. He could not bear the thought of harming her. Nor did he wish to jeopardize their mission by making her uncomfortable or introducing discord now. But looming larger than all of that was one thought.

This was his chance to show her how they could be together. How much easier to convince her to leave that mask off than to persuade her once it was back on? And if she couldn't be convinced at all? Then this might be his only chance with her—with the real Hestia—the one he'd been longing to know.

She searched his face, looking for the reason for his hesitation. "Come, Stoneacre," she cajoled. "Let's go find the rooms that Drake rented us. I believe you meant to play the besotted bridegroom this evening, did you not?"

And the decision was made. "I did." He kissed her hands, first one, then the other. "I do. Indeed."

THEY MADE their way back to the horses. The animals were nervous, spooked by the noise and the smoke in the air. Her mount was fidgety and required a firm hand and a good deal of attention, in her eagerness to leave the place behind, but Hestia didn't mind. She didn't want to think. She didn't want past memories or future worries intruding on what was happening now.

Stoneacre. That's what was happening now. He rode beside her, focused and cautious in the dark and the unfamiliar countryside. She didn't want to think about how or why he saw her so clearly or understood her feelings so completely.

She just wanted him.

She strolled away from the livery while he dealt with the return of the hired horses. The town lay quiet. Most households were abed. The moon hung heavy and bright above the trees and lent sparkle to the River Avon. Strolling out onto the bridge, she leaned on the stone railing, enjoying the beauty and peace of the scene.

His footsteps sounded behind her. She turned and he kept coming. Even in the moonlight, she could see determination in his face and she felt it in his touch when he took hold of her shoulders, backed her up against the stone and kissed her.

Oh, my. Yes. So gloriously good. Why was kissing Stoneacre so much *more* than with anyone else? He was serious about it, too, that much was clear. His kissed her deeply. Demandingly. His tongue moved insistently against hers and he widened his stance, pressed closer and angled his head to deepen the kiss even further.

She shivered with the delight of it. Joy and anticipation jumped, jostling beneath her skin. *Joy?* Wonders never ceased.

And then he stopped. He cupped her face in his hands. "I should be utterly convincing as a randy newlywed." He took her hand and pulled. "Let's go."

Biting back a smile, she followed.

A light still burned in the entry of the Three Feathers. Hestia stepped closer to Stoneacre when someone stumbled toward them out of the taproom, but relaxed when it proved to be Drake, the coachman. He must have been keeping watch—and having a pint or two while he waited.

"Sir!" He stood straight, but blinked at them, rapidly. "The rooms are ready, as requested. I'll show you upstairs."

He led them to a room with a wide bed and a view over the kitchen gardens. Hestia stood at the window as Stoneacre stopped in the doorway and prevented Drake from entering.

"I've taken the servant's room next door, sir, as you said. You can sleep there and I'll head out—"

"No need," Stoneacre interrupted. "You take it. We'll be fine for the night. We'll get an early start in the morning." He shut the door on the man's startled, still blinking, expression.

Hestia laughed. "We've shocked him, the poor man."

Stoneacre looked unconcerned. "He'll be happy enough not to have to make a bed in the stables." He secured the latch and turned, already shrugging out of his coat. "Now."

"Yes. Now." She leaned against the bedpost and opened her arms. She'd often wondered if she'd be able to do this again. But she didn't feel any of the things she'd worried about. No old memories or bad feelings. Stoneacre banished them all with his smile and his big, wide shoulders that were strong enough to block out the world—and her past.

He stepped into her arms—and the kissing felt wonderful again. He was so large. Strong. And his hands were busy this time, too. Surely there was magic in that slow, deliberate touch. Everywhere it roamed, she twitched and jumped. Everywhere else strained, pressing closer because nothing else helped the aching need that he built inside of her.

"I'm not swiving you up against the bedpost, damn it." Stoneacre's hands were on her waist and then she was in the air and being tossed onto the bed. She laughed and threw her head back as he crawled up, straddling her and caging her with those long limbs.

"You are not swiving me at all," she informed him. "You are going to make glorious love to me."

"You are right about that," he breathed. Reaching up, he pulled a pin from her coiffure. And another. And suddenly, they were all out and her hair cascaded around her shoulders and across her chest. He pressed his face to it and breathed in—and retreated, coughing. "Smoke," he choked out.

She laughed again. "I'll rinse it with rose water sometime and you can try again."

He wiped his eyes. "You normally smell like spring, but if you are taking requests, then can it be lilacs?" he asked with a watery grin. "I like lilacs. They smell like home."

Her smile faded. There was the future, trying to push in. She banished it with the brush of her finger along the rough stubble of his jaw. "Yes. I will. If you will rid yourself of all of this." Her hand moved down, taking its time going over the scarf he still wore, past his shirt and waistcoat to his trousers.

He sat up and removed it all, piece by piece. Not hurrying. At the end he stood by the bed again to peel away his small clothes and remove his boots. She rolled over and reached out a hand to brush it against his broad shoulders, along his long torso, ending at a curved scar on his side. He was perfect. Strong. A warrior with a wry grin on his lips and laughter in his eyes.

"All the saints in heaven, preserve us," she whispered. Then she clapped a hand over her mouth. That saying was pure Pearl, her old friend, long gone. The past trying to push in, too. But it was fitting, in this instance, she decided. Pearl had been her savior. And today, Stoneacre had been one, too.

The last boot dropped and he turned and stretched out beside her. "Now your turn," he said easily. He put a hand to the dark jacket of her traveling outfit and grinned down at her. "So many buttons. How did you know I like buttons?"

"You like buttons?" Her mouth twisted. "And I'd thought I'd heard about every fetish known to man."

He made a face at her. "I like anticipation. Why hurry? All the best presents come wrapped up, bright and tight." His fingers moved nimbly down the row of carved buttons, undoing them one by one. "There's fun to be had in the unwrapping."

"That's all very well," she said he helped her out of the sleeves. "But have you considered the present's feelings?" She raised a brow as he pulled her skirt away.

"Don't you think the present enjoys the tension as it builds?" He breathed the question in her ear and sent shivers down her spine and raised goose bumps on all her limbs.

"Perhaps the present is in a hurry to be free." She shimmied out of her petticoat.

"There is no reason to fear, or to hurry." He grinned and let his fingers trail up and along her leg, pausing to tease her thigh where her garter was tied. "After all, the present is receiving a present as well."

"Is it?" She propped up onto her elbows, watching him.

He nodded, concentrating on his task. All of her focus narrowed, too, onto that light, teasing touch. Desire pooled, thick and hot, in her womb. "*What* is it?" she rasped.

"Me," he said with a satisfied smirk, before he bent down to nuzzle the spot his fingers had been caressing.

With a little laugh, she fell back. When had she laughed in bed?

When had she felt light and happy and utterly involved in the growing intimacy? Never. Never before. And if that boy of Marstoke's had succeeded today, then she never would have known. Would never have experienced the bliss of a smart, funny man igniting her senses with wit and care and just the tiniest of nips and touches.

He raised up then, and moved upward, smiling as he came. He breathed in her ear and she shivered again. His mouth moved into the curve of her neck and her nipples hardened as she gave a soft, happy moan.

"Ooh," he said, looking down at her. "That's my new favorite sound."

"What was your old favorite?" she asked, watching him work the laces of her corset.

"Your laughter." He kept unlacing. "I've only just heard it recently and thought it the most beautiful sound. Until now." The last lace was undone and he pulled. She arched her back to help and then she was free. Only her shift was left and by the quickness of his breath, even Stoneacre had had his fill of anticipation.

Grasping the hem of her shift, he lifted it up and over her head and she was nearly naked—only her stockings left—and he was looking at her with a very serious expression.

"Stoneacre?" she whispered. She was no young debutante, but . . .

He looked up, directly into her eyes. "You are the best present I've ever got," he said simply.

She melted. Eased back like a puddle of heat and want and longing. And they were kissing again and moving against each other, skin to skin.

Distant noises sounded. Laughter. Doors closing. The clink of metal pints. Tavern life. But it lived far away. Everything important right now narrowed to this cocoon of warmth they inhabited and the excitement coiling in her veins.

He bent his head to her breast, found her nipple and claimed it. Her back arched as he suckled and his hand moved to the other and brushed it with his thumb.

Yes.

Bless him, he still didn't hurry. He took his time and she reveled as he sucked and teased her with lips and teeth. There was no escape, no retreat as he licked, pinched and rolled her nipples and sent heat jolting to the depths of her belly.

She didn't want him to ever stop, but his hand moved down, right to her molten center. When he touched her, slick and ready, he groaned.

"You are right." She grinned up at him. "That is a good sound."

"Yes." He moved back down the bed. "Open your legs, Hestia. I want to hear you make it again."

She hesitated only for a second, then spread her legs wide. He moved between them and she wriggled at the rush of air over her exposed, swollen cleft.

And he was there, at her core. His fingers slid over the wet folds of her sex and her legs dropped wider. And then his tongue was on her and she jumped. He gripped her hips and held her still while he explored, uncovering all of her secrets, delving into all of her feminine places, paying special, sweet attention to the sensitive bud that swelled like a moon over her slick curves.

Oh, and she made the sounds he wished to hear. She didn't recognize them, even as they came out of her. She didn't recognize herself. She'd never felt such desire, never known that heat could move under her skin, melting every barrier she normally kept in place—even during moments of intimacy.

The room—the world—faded. She was lost in a golden haze. He had taken her somewhere where she could let go, let loose the tightly bound grip, the control that took so much energy and attention.

He raised his head. His eyes were hot. As he climbed over her, she reached for him, clutching, taking the strength he offered her with sweet laughter and tender worship and his powerful body.

She touched him, too. She needed to put her hands on him, to give as much as she received. Exploring his warm, hard chest, she grew bolder and watched his expression change when she reached down to grasp the rigid length of him.

He sucked in a breath.

She moved her hand and he growled.

She kept it up, enjoying his pleasure, until, with his knee, he nudged her legs apart. Her eyes closed as he moved into position, but then he stopped, poised at her waiting, writhing core.

"Hestia." His voice sounded rough and his erection pulsed urgently against her.

She looked up into his face and found concern.

"I need to know you are here with me."

She reached up and touched his face. "I am here. I don't know where. It's entirely new. But we arrived together. Perhaps we created it together." She moved her hands purposefully down to grab his hips. "Now let's finish it together."

He thrust, fiercely, and they both cried out.

Saints, but he was big and she was ready. Crossing her legs behind him, she surrendered to fullness and perfect, searing heat.

He pumped further, widening her, searching deeper with each stroke. And then he was fully seated—and she burned with the sweetness of it.

They held there. Pelvis to pelvis. Eye to eye. Balanced on the edge of something greater.

And then he began to move.

"Yes." It came out in a rush. "Yes. More."

He adjusted his position. Dug in and pumped harder. His eyes had gone dark, his expression intense, yet utterly open. He hid nothing of what he felt, showed every bit of desire and determination and enjoyment.

She couldn't give him any less. She could not. She braced her feet on the bed, lifted her pelvis and met him thrust for thrust. She was caught, helpless beneath him, but fully a participant and filled with ancient, feminine, carnal power.

It was fierce. It was tender. It was exquisite—but it could not last. He adjusted his stroke slightly—and *yes, there*—he had it just right. Pleasure built. It drew tightly from her scalp to her toes and from every point of her body.

"Hestia," he whispered her name. "Let's go together."

Her inner muscles tightened. His thrusts rocked her. Her hips rose and rose and his dark eyes were peering into her soul. Climax hit her, lifting and buffeting her higher, higher than seemed humanly possible. But it was all right. He was there, soaring beside her and when she reached the peak and began to fall back, he caught her. They drifted aloft, in sweaty, air-deprived bliss for many long minutes.

CHAPTER 13

*If you would not care to have your wife beaten or debauched or your
daughter deflowered, it would be wise to avoid entanglement.
--from the Journal of the Infamous Miss Hestia Wright*

When Stoneacre awoke, Hestia's side of the bed was empty. He
turned his head to see she'd dragged a chair to the window.
She sat in her shift, staring out at the early light, idly brushing her
hair.

He watched her, drinking in her beauty, knowing the change she'd
started in him was a permanent one. Last night had been incredible.
She'd been open and giving and free. All of that reserve and distance
had vanished. But she'd made it clear that it had been temporary. A
glorious victory—but he was wise enough to know it had only been a
battle. The war for her heart still stretched ahead—but he'd fight for
her every day until they'd both won.

She turned to set down her brush and take up a ribbon—and saw
that he was awake. She straightened. "The leaking information—the
culprit must be one of my people. Marstoke knew I was coming."

He sighed and scrubbed his face with a hand. "The real world calls us back so quickly, eh?"

She lifted a shoulder. "I feel the pull of it, I admit. I'm just . . . sick over it. I cannot see any of my people going over to him. Not willingly."

Stoneacre sat up. "Perhaps they didn't. I did report to Prinny before we left. I didn't give him specifics and I tried to do it as privately as possible." He shrugged. "But in that environment, one can never truly know."

"Ah." Some of the strain eased from her expression. "Yes. That is a real possibility. Someone might have heard, or the Prince Regent might have mentioned it unwisely." She thought it over for a moment, then swung around to face him fully. "So, where do you think Marstoke has gone to, now?"

He considered. "Well, smuggling is no easy feat. He has an entire network to set up and oversee. If he'd planned a storage spot at the priory, then he's likely bringing the opium up the Bristol Channel."

"He won't operate out of Bristol, though. There are established rings there and they'd give a newcomer no end of trouble." She frowned. "He'd find a lonely spot of the coast. Just far enough from a village to be private, but near enough to hire landsmen."

"There must be fifty such places along that coastline. He could be setting up anywhere. It could take weeks to track it down." Not that that sounded like a bad idea. They could stretch their mission out, exploring the coast, admiring the views, making love on cliff tops and sheltered in long sea grass . . .

The echo of her smile told him she knew where his thoughts had strayed. "He might have gone another direction entirely. He'll need to set up his lieutenants to oversee the transport, find storage along the way, a building or warehouse in the city, townsmen to make the deliveries and hundred other details."

"Again, a near impossible task, to find him," he sighed.

"There is one other possibility," she said, her brows raised. "Bath."

He frowned. "I did find a reference to Bath in his papers. An inn." He thought back. "The Red Fox."

"He does love Bath," she mused. "It's been a favorite haunt of his for years, although I believe he uses more than one name there, depending on the reasons for his visits. And it would make sense that he would seek out buyers for his opium closer to the coast. Less storage and transport would mean more profit for any he could sell here."

"You're right. He could be there. We really shouldn't leave until we investigate."

He moved to the edge of the bed. She stood and stepped closer. "It would be irresponsible," she agreed.

"And then there are the added benefits," he said, reaching out to tug her between his legs.

"Much easier to keep the real world at bay . . ." she finished.

"Just a little longer," he whispered.

She bent to him and he kissed her, languorous and long. And then they were in the bed, tangled together again, pressed flesh to flesh. She touched him with a charming mix of knowing and curiosity—and both were wildly arousing.

And damnation, but he couldn't move slowly this time. He lifted her shift away and ran urgent hands over her, teasing, wakening. She was ready as quickly as he was. He lay back then, and let her climb atop him. Sunlight gilded her lithe form, turned those blonde locks into a river of gold. He sucked in a breath while she straddled him and he used every ounce of discipline he had to hold himself still while she took him deep and set a sweet, then increasingly pulse-pounding pace.

Soon enough they were both alight with the building pleasure of it. She tossed her head back and cried out at her release—and he followed.

They lay for time afterwards, sated and happy. Talking a little and absorbing contentment as if they could stockpile it for later. But eventually she rolled out of bed and retrieved her shift again.

"I need a real bath, before we leave for Bath." Leaning in, she gave him a smacking kiss. "And for you, I shall ask if they have lilac soap."

He grinned. "Already, you spoil me."

"But would you or Drake do me the favor of summoning a dress-maker? A village of this size should have one." She shot him a mischievous smile. "No dark clothes and scarves today. This is going to be another sort of hunt altogether—and will require a very different role."

～

HESTIA LIFTED her fork and bit into her pastry with glee. She felt . . . light. Happy. She knew darkness and trouble waited just beyond the horizon, but she was determined to ignore it. For now. For right now, she had her favorite indulgence on a plate in front of her and a delicious man in the seat across from her.

He was looking at her as if he'd rather devour her than the bun in front of him. Easing a hand over her skirt, she silently thanked the resourceful dressmaker from Bradford-on-Avon. The woman had asked no questions about their need for such quick service. Once assured they were willing to pay for it, she'd just showed up with a perfect day gown of a rich sea foam color, decorated with a bit of scalloped lace to soften the square neckline. She'd taken a nip here, a tuck there and added another bit of lace as a flounce to account for Hestia's height. She'd sold them her own ivory pelisse to go over it. Stoneacre had required only a new bit of linen and they were outfitted before mid-morning, which meant they'd made it to Bath in time for an early tea, and here they sat, with Hestia looking like a proper matron and feeling surprisingly good about it.

Stoneacre's fixed attention had much to do with that satisfaction—because it was so much more than the usual scrutiny that men gave her. Stoneacre saw *her*. She knew he appreciated her looks, but he was the only one who had looked beyond them. Now he knew bits of her ugly past that she'd never shared with any man—and he still looked at her that way. The knowledge of it fizzed along like champagne bubbles under her skin.

"Go on," she urged him. "Eat it while it's hot and let the butter melt down into the cracks."

She spread a bit of jam onto a bite and closed her eyes in bliss. "These are my favorite," she sighed. "And you can only get them here."

"They are good," he acknowledged. "But is that the only reason we are here?"

So he had noticed her close perusal of the bakery's public rooms. "No." She lowered her voice. "If Marstoke is in town, there is one person who will know it—or can find out quickly."

He raised a questioning brow.

Hestia spread clotted cream and jam on one last bite. She savored it before she sat back and regarded him seriously. "You have searched through those files of yours, learned about the men Marstoke has bribed, cheated and corrupted. You've seen then, how he keeps an eye on them afterward, watchful lest they think of exposure or revenge."

He sighed. "Yes. It's made the job difficult."

"Those men remain cowed and fearful. Now, imagine how much worse the women he's abused feel."

He shook his head, his eyes sad.

"Most of them refuse to say his name. They are terrified at the thought of ever seeing him again. But him. There's a difference in the way he treats them." Her chin lifted slightly. "He has a pattern. He amuses himself hurting women—but when he's done with them, he often keeps them until he knows they are not with child. I was an exception. Circumstances have created a couple of others. He sends his lackeys to check on those few, but the vast majority—he ignores. He doesn't waste his resources and spies on women. He imagines he has broken them, has done with them, and they are thereafter incapable of anything save obscurity, ruin and slow decline. And in too many cases, he is right."

She took a sip of her tea. "I told you that I had found a few women who had moved past the horror of it, put Marstoke behind them and gone on to make something of their lives."

He nodded.

"Well, I only ever found one who outsmarted him."

He straightened in surprise.

"It's true. And it's quite a story."

"Well, come on then," he urged. "Tell me."

"It began about a year after he cast me out. Using a false name, he masqueraded as a businessman and courted a wealthy shipping merchant's daughter in Bristol. She was a bit older than his usual prey, but pretty and very intelligent. Her father was thrilled with the match. He believed he was getting an investor as well as a husband for his only daughter. The wedding plans were set. But Marstoke began to talk privately to her of an elopement. He told her they had no need to wait and painted a grand picture of the drama and romance of it all. But he had chosen poorly, or perhaps not extended enough of an effort to understand her."

She paused. "I've often wondered about that. The girls he tricks with fake betrothals or marriages with usually stand out in some way. Either they are connected to men he hates or resents, or like me, they might have snubbed him or rejected him in some way. But none of it seemed to be the case with this one. Perhaps he was growing cocky. Or it might have been the settlements. She came with an enormous dowry—and a part of her father's empire. I've often wondered if he meant to actually marry her, and so didn't bother with actually trying to win her affections."

"More likely he meant to run off with her and come back alone," Stoneacre said cynically. "She was likely meant to meet an unfortunate accident."

"You may be right. But as I said, he'd miscalculated with her. The girl had gone along with her father's plans, accepted his courtship, but she was marrying him for duty, not for love. She declined a trip to Gretna Green. And when he began to press her, she became suspicious."

"Did she tell her family?"

"Of course, but her father waved off her concerns. So, she set a couple of the family footmen to investigating her betrothed—and discovered he didn't exist. But when she took the evidence to her father, he was furious at *both* of them."

"He was angry at her?" Incredulity caused his voice to rise a bit.

Hestia nodded. "Marstoke was a cheat and liar and her father had him run off. But his daughter was willful and unfeminine for disobeying him and acting on her own."

"I've never heard such rubbish. He should have been ashamed to have failed her so," he grumbled.

She shrugged. "It's not the first such reaction I've seen. But she is the first and only woman I've encountered who beat Marstoke at his own game. She didn't discover who he truly was, not then, but she escaped his clutches." Hestia let her gaze circle around the room once more. "I've often wondered if there might be others like her, out there."

Shaking her head, she recalled herself to the conversation. "In any case, her father washed his hands of finding her a husband. So, she set about doing that job herself, as well. She found a lovely man, a minor baron who suited her well and who had an estate outside of Bishop Sutton and a house in Bath. They were happy for a few years, but he developed a gastric condition and passed on. After his death, she took up permanent residence in Bath and started up a somewhat unconventional cultural salon. When I found her, we struck up a friendship and she became my eyes and ears here."

He blinked as she finished her story. "I cannot wait to meet her."

"And so you shall. She often comes here for tea, but since she has not, then we will likely find her stirring up the afternoon crowd at the Pump Room."

He tossed back the last of his tea, then stood and extended his arm. "Well then, let us go and find her."

"The fashionable hour at the Pump Room will not begin for another hour or so," she said as they made their way outside. She stepped aside as a delivery boy approached, pushing an empty cart with the bakery's name on it.

"Perhaps we should find lodging then, in the meantime."

"Yes." She squeezed his arm where her hand rested in the crook of his elbow. "A comfortable room is definitely in order."

His gaze heated at her use of the singular and he shot her a wicked grin. But then he paused. "Hold that thought a moment." He turned back and called to the delivery boy. "Emptied your cart, have you?" he asked.

"Aye, sir." The boy tugged at his cap. "Lady Darby always serves our cakes at her dinner parties."

"And do you make morning deliveries, perhaps?"

"Aye!" The boy raised a proud head. "I've a special, portable oven cart and I deliver our buns warm to many a household hereabouts."

"And to customers at an inn? Will you deliver to them?"

"Of course, sir."

"Very well, then." Stoneacre cast her side-glance. "Will you deliver half a dozen to . . ." He paused. "Where did your brother recommend that we stay, my dear? The Red Lion? No, the Red Cub—The Red Fox!"

"Yes, I believe that was it, *dear*," she said with a twist of a grin.

But the boy tugged his cap off, his expression wary. "Beggin' yer pardon, sir, but the Red Fox is no place fit for the likes of your lady."

"Is that so?"

"Yessir. You should take rooms at the Queen's Crown. It's on Henry Street, not too far from here. It's just right for a real lady and they already have a standing order for our buns in the morning. You'll get them hot and fresh." He gazed admiringly at her and Hestia smiled at him.

"Thank you for the recommendation," she told him as Stoneacre nodded and handed him a coin.

He blushed and wheeled off in a hurry.

"Another conquest?" Stoneacre laughed.

"A useful one, perhaps. Shall we take his advice?"

"I believe we shall. Let's see the Queen's Crown, then we'll find your friend—and then, we shall see what is to be found at the Red Fox."

CHAPTER 14

The Great Game is Lord M—'s greatest passion. He plots to meddle in the affairs of crowns, royal families and nations. He longs to maneuver himself into a place of even more wealth, privilege, and especially, power.
--from the Journal of the Infamous Miss Hestia Wright

L aughter and conversation and music bubbled up toward the ceiling of the Pump Room. The room was light and airy and big, and it all conspired to make one think that the famous waters might taste like sparkling wine. It did not. Having tried it before, Stoneacre had no inclination to taste the warm, heavy, mineral-laden stuff again.

He led Hestia aside as they entered, out of the general flow toward the marble vase of waters and their flanking fireplaces. They strolled along one long wall while she searched the crowd.

"There she is." Hestia indicated the direction with a nod of her head. "Lady Cartweld. Dark hair and a forest green gown."

He studied her friend. The woman stood across the room, near the musician's dais. She had a small crowd gathered around her, but there was an open space between them and the rest of the chattering socialites. A bit of snobbery in action, that.

The woman was pretty, but in a different way. Her beauty had a sharp, precise nature to it. She looked all angles and points, from her fine nose to her thin shoulders, to the long, slender fingers wrapped around a glass of the waters. Just then, her entourage broke out into fits of laughter at something she said. True laughter, not the false, polite tittle so often encountered at the *ton's* social events.

He rather thought he might like Lady Cartweld.

"I'm surprised Marstoke hasn't tried to take some sort of revenge upon her," he told Hestia. "He's certainly followed a path of vengeance after you."

"She doesn't defy him the way I do. And her father never admitted her role in unmasking him." She tilted her head. "It's only a bit of justice then, that the baronness believes that Marstoke has tried to avenge himself on her father. His business suffered several unex-plained losses of cargo over the years. There were other, mysterious mishaps, and someone scuttled one of his coastal schooners. But when I tracked the lady down and shared Marstoke's true identity, she did pass the information on to her father."

"What happened?" He was fascinated with the whole of this tale.

"One of Marstoke's biggest warehouses in London burned down almost immediately afterward. I am not aware of how the message was passed as to its cause, but Lady Cartweld said the mysterious attacks on her father's business ceased thereafter."

He laughed. "A formidable family." He glanced toward the baroness again. "Does she have much contact with them now? Her family?"

"Not much. Her father still disapproves of her independent ways."

He made a sound of disgust.

She cast a curious look up at him. "Why do you ask?"

"I just . . ." His shoulder lifted. "I suppose it feels similar to my own experiences with family."

Curiosity shifted into surprise. Her brow furrowed and she started to ask—

"Hestia!"

The shocked call came from across the room. "My darling!" Lady Cartweld approached, cutting through the crowd like a clipper under full sail. She marched right up, embraced Hestia and kissed her on both cheeks. Both women were laughing with pleasure, even as the ladies and gentlemen around them cast sly glances and whispered behind gloved hands.

Stoneacre stiffened, but made himself relax when Hestia turned to him with a smile. "Lord Stoneacre, if I may present my friend? This is Lady Amelia Cartweld."

He bent over her hand. "A pleasure, my lady."

She curtsied and smiled up at him. "The pleasure is mine, meeting a fine gentleman brave enough to show up here with Hestia Wright on his arm." She turned to Hestia. "And today of all days." She leaned in. "I had every intention of writing to you today."

"Oh?" Hestia glanced between them.

"Indeed. For just today I've heard talk of our old, mutual friend, seen here in Bath."

"That is exactly why we've come to you, my dear." Hestia pressed her hand. "What is the news?"

"I've heard only a secondhand whisper. I'd expected to see the lady who told the original tale here this afternoon." She craned her neck. "Let me make the rounds and see if I can find her. I'll bring her over and we'll see what she has to say."

The baroness started to move away, but Hestia stopped her with a hand on her arm. She looked around meaningfully. "She may not care to make my acquaintance."

Lady Cartweld tossed her head. "There are more than a few nose-up, high sticklers in Bath. They might try to cut you, my dear, but Virginia Reeves is not one of them."

Hestia glanced about again. Some of the surrounding people watched them with avid curiosity. Others, mostly ladies, had pointedly turned their faces away.

It made Stoneacre's lip curl. Hestia was worth ten of any one of them.

"Nevertheless," Hestia said with determination. "I've no wish for the lady to feel reluctant or uncomfortable." She glanced up at him. "We'll take a stroll just outside and you can bring the lady to us there."

"Very well," Lady Cartweld sighed. "You are not in a hurry, are you?"

"No."

"Good. Give me a moment. I'll strive to bring no untoward attention to any of us."

Stoneacre took a good, long look around the room. He was thorough about it, taking particular notice of those who watched with sneers or disdain, and letting them know he saw it, too. Then he offered Hestia his arm and escorted her outside, away from all the superficial snobs.

Torches burned high, just outside the pedimented entrance. Hestia leaned against one of the columns, but Stoneacre walked on, pacing across the uneven flagstones in front of the building, his fists clenched. He could feel Hestia's gaze resting on him.

"It's nothing, Stoneacre," she said softly when he came stalking back.

"It's not nothing!" he snapped. "It's everything."

"Don't let it bother you so."

How could he not? Fury and frustration coiled around each other in his gut. He wanted to go back and blacken the eye of every hypocrite inside. He wanted to take Hestia in his arms and shield her from such boorish behavior forever.

He could do neither of those things.

He kept pacing, instead.

"I think you are reacting to more than just a few raised brows in there," she said, the next time he came close.

"There were more than raised brows and you know it, Hestia," he growled.

She waited.

"I know you likely face all that and more when you move in Society, but it infuriates me. And the censure with which they looked at your friend, as well." He wanted to hit something. "It's the hypocrisy of it all that makes me so damned frustrated." He flung out a hand. "One of those women who faced away from you—she has a son widely known to be the seed of a Royal Duke, instead of her husband. Another keeps a fleet of handsome footmen busy, year round. Half the men in there keep a mistress. The other half gambles or drinks indiscriminately. One removed the housekeeper from his ancestral home and set her up with her own house in London."

She shrugged. "Their sins are hidden in a cloak of respectability. Mine are out there, defiantly in the open."

"But still, the sins exist! And they presume to judge!"

"It's the way of the world."

"Yes, hypocrisy makes the world go 'round! As I well know!" It emerged, bitterly. A curse.

"Tell me," she said simply.

He walked away again. He'd never spoken of it, to anyone. He had to be careful . . . But she'd bared some of her darkest secrets. How could he do less? And if he ever had a hope of anything lasting coming of this . . .

He came back and stood before her, waiting until a departing couple passed by. "I thought it was just my family, for the longest time," he said at last.

She looked surprised, but said nothing.

"I grew up, often in despair, thinking I could never do it. I could never do enough, be enough, to meet my parent's expectations. I am the heir. I am to uphold the accomplishments of generations, bear the weight of their history, their names and reputations. Go away to school? No. I had to stay at home where my father, who did not want the work of educating me, nonetheless required frequent reports of my progress. Flawless French. Letter-perfect Latin. A thorough knowledge of the classics, of estate matters, of the workings of parliament and the government. I wished to learn science? On my own time, if I must. I wished to learn archery? Fencing? Very well, but I must practice until my aim is perfect and my every thrust hits home. I must excel. I must be the most accomplished of my acquaintance. I must remember that I am an earl and a future marquess. Always,

always, I must look, speak and act the part. And remember that my actions reflect on my father and family."

"It does sound exhausting," Hestia admitted. "But I can tell you that no expectations can be as damaging as too many."

"I do know that to be true. And in all honesty, part of me is grateful for the pressure, for the opportunity and for all that I learned." His mouth twitched. "I'd be far more grateful if I hadn't discovered it was all a sham."

She blinked.

"It started with my sister's betrothal. My father arranged it. He chose Sayer Cunningham, the heir to Viscount Sydham. I did not approve of him. He is . . . oily. Sly. The sort who always speaks decisively, and yet somehow you know he always means the opposite of what he says. I did not like the match and I told my father so."

"He didn't listen?"

"Why would he? To the world the man looked a perfect match. He had the title, a vast number of acres in Yorkshire, and pots of money. I knew he gambled actively and often, but so do many other men of means. Still, I just did not like it. But my parents did not care that the man beneath the surface might be lacking, when the outside was so very shiny."

"It sounds like a great many matches I've seen, but the lack can go both ways." She shrugged. "It's the way of the marriage mart. It's often made me glad I had no part in it."

"All true. And my sister was content to go along with it. My father seemed unduly excited. It wasn't until later that I learned why he was so eager for the match to go through."

He sighed. "Cunningham is a . . . schemer. An enthusiastic investor in mostly bad or doomed business plans. But he managed to not only hide his failings, but to persuade my father to go along with them. They first suffered large losses investing in a played-out Scottish coalfield. Then Cunningham sold my father on the idea of a gun manufactory. He knew that the British had pledged to help rebuild the Portuguese army and that the number of promised men, arms and money kept rising. He convinced my father that the gun manufacturer could not produce muskets, pistols and carbines fast enough. They could not lose money backing him."

Stoneacre stared up, into the flames of the torch mounted above them. "I tried to caution my father, urged him to look into the contracts and the men who made them, but he insisted all was well. At first he appeared to be right—until he accidentally discovered that the reason their profits were so high was because the manufactory was compromising the quality of the guns."

Hestia's eyes rounded. "But that's—"

"Yes," he said shortly. "Providing British and allied troops with substandard provisions can be construed as treason."

"Good heavens."

"My father was in complete distress. I'd never seen him so upset." He closed his eyes. "The worst part was that he was not horrified by the danger in which he'd placed good British soldiers and our allied brothers. He didn't think about the deaths he might have caused or the military losses that might have occurred. No. He was worried about people in society finding out. About the stain on his reputation. What his friends would think. How it would affect his name and how it would look to the rest of the *beau monde*."

"Oh," she breathed.

"I was disgusted. Sick. I railed at him. What use is his good name if corruption and rot lies beneath it?" He sighed. "But I knew my duty. I started investigating. I discovered what compromises were being made and by whom, and how they would affect the use of the products. I found who knew about them and who did not. I gathered papers, contracts, letters and testimonies of men involved in all aspects of the deals. I proved to myself that my father truly had not known of the cheating practices going on—and then I forced him to confront Cunningham and the others involved."

"I can guess how that went."

"I'm sure you can. They refused to change anything and tried to threaten my father into silence. And once he knew the real faces of the men he was in business with, I made him go to the Board of Ordnance."

"Cunningham knew, then?"

"Yes. But it was kept quiet. All of it. In some circles my father was lauded a hero for coming forward. But he knew. And there are some canny men in the government. They knew, too. And some of them knew what I had done to protect him. One of them is a member of the Privy Council. I was summoned before them and questioned. And then I was told that my father and brother-in-law would suffer no consequences if I were to consent to do the same kind of work for them—unofficially, of course."

"Ah," she sighed. "I had wondered how you wandered into that role."

"Honestly, I didn't mind. As I grew, I'd so looked forward to getting away from home. I thought Society would be different. Less focused on artifice."

She made a sound that was not quite a laugh.

"Yes." He shook his head. "Instead I just found more of the same. An entire community of people concerned with appearance over substance. I had been planning to go abroad, hoping to find something . . . meaningful. So, when I was more or less commanded to dig into the council's work, I decided to find meaning in the job."

"And you have," she said warmly.

"I have," he agreed. "I feel confident that I have contributed something to my fellow man. Not in the same way you have, Hestia. Hell and damnation, you put every well meaning Englishman to shame."

She snorted. "Tell that to the crowd inside."

"I wouldn't waste my time. And in case, they know it, deep down. It's too much, however, for them to face the truth." He dismissed them all with a roll of his eyes. "I'm content with what I've managed to accomplish. I still find value in the work." He stepped closer. "But for months, I've felt unsettled. As if I'm missing something yet." His heart began banging against his ribs. "Do you not ever feel that way?"

Her eyes looked huge in the firelight. He'd thought she might avoid the question, but she kept a steady gaze upon him. "Yes."

Just the admission was a step forward. A triumph. She was so damned lovely. Her heart was pounding too. He would wager anything on it. He held her gaze, allowing the trust and partnership they'd shared, the passion they'd acknowledged, to fill up the space between them. It wasn't a fair move. He didn't care. He'd use every weapon he had to bind her to him.

She looked away first. "But that aspect of my life is better now," she told him, almost defiantly. "I have my son, returned to me by that sprite of a girl who stole those papers, years ago. And now she is my daughter. And I have Brynne and Aldmere. Callie and Tru. Isaac and the girls at the House. We've created our own community. Our own family."

He was going to get himself included on that roll call.

"You deserve every bit of it—and more."

She tossed her head. "I don't need more."

A lie. She knew it as well as he did. He was going to prove it—and prove himself to her. He would bewitch her if he must, tempt her with pounding blood and sweet kisses and burning caresses—and with truth and trust and caring and *love.* Everything they were both missing and could find—gloriously—with each other.

"We are going to finish Marstoke," she reminded him. "And this will be over. My family will be free. I will be free."

Heat curled from him to her and back again. An invisible swirl of awareness—and so much potential. "You will be free," he agreed. "Free at last, to do exactly what you wish."

Her gaze narrowed. "Don't get any ideas, Stoneacre," she warned.

He laughed. "Oh, I have ideas. Ideas and plans and designs." He reached out to touch the curl that lay along her nape. "And propositions."

She didn't flinch. But there was no anger in her. Her blue eyes were filled with uncertainty and with more than a bit of longing.

He was going to count that as another victory.

"There you are." Lady Cartweld emerged from the doorway, another lady on her heels. As I said, Mrs. Reeves, here they are." The baroness made the introductions and the other woman looked intrigued at meeting Hestia—and flushed at making his acquaintance.

"Now, Mrs. Reeves, these two have an interest in Mr. Denton Coombs and I'd like you to tell them your story."

Denton Coombs? That name, it triggered something. He looked to Hestia, but she nodded for the woman to begin.

"Well, and I'd like to know what you want of the man, for I believe he's more than a bit of a rogue, myself," the lady said indignantly. "First there was all the ruckus over the Stokes girl—and such a nice, sweet young thing she was. We all thought him a good match for her, a stable, older businessman—until the pair of them up and disappeared."

Ah, now he understood. And her words sparked his memory. He'd found a mention of Denton Coombs in Marstoke's papers.

"It near to killed her mother," the lady continued. "The girl going off without a word. And then the mother and her other, older daughter just left town, too, with no more of a by-your-leave. Shady dealings, if you ask me. But this morning I caught sight of Mr. Coombs."

"Here in Bath?" Hestia asked. "Today?"

"This very morning." She sniffed. "I was driving by that rattletrap, the Red Fox, and there he stood, large as life and red as my cook's pickled beetroot. Shouting right there in the street."

"Who was he shouting at?" asked Stoneacre.

"I didn't know him. A clerk, perhaps? A young man, in any case, standing hang dog and taking it while Coombs rang a peal over him." She lifted both hands. "I stopped my carriage of course."

"Of course," Lady Cartweld said encouragingly.

"Well, I did wish to have word of the Stokes family. Lovely women, all of them. I called out to the man. Shouted his name, almost. He never turned or acknowledged me in any way."

"Could you tell why he was angry?"

"No. Not really. He was going on about someone. She was to be fetched. But then he stopped shouting, snapped at the porter strapping luggage to his coach, climbed inside and left."

"Left? Left town?"

"I do believe so, my lord."

Stoneacre glanced at Hestia and found matching frustration in her expression. "Did you happen to hear where that coach was heading, Mrs. Reeves?"

"No. They just wheeled off without another word."

"Thank you, ma'am." Hestia pressed her hand. "We do appreciate your help."

"I'm happy to give it, my dear. And if you find that rascal, please discover what you can of the Stokes family, will you? Lady Cartweld will pass along any news, I'm sure."

Hestia smiled. "I can put your mind at ease right now, ma'am, for I am well acquainted with all three of the Stokes ladies and they are quite well."

"Well, that's a relief!"

"And I can tell you that Miss Laura Stokes, the eldest girl, is the Duchess of Rothmore now. So they are all quite safe."

The woman's eyes grew as big as saucers. "A duchess? Laura Stokes?"

"Indeed."

Mrs. Reeves put a hand to her chest. "And the youngest girl? Married?"

Hestia grew serious. "No. But I think you will agree that that is for the best. She is well protected and happy now, and if anyone asks, that's all I hope you will say."

"Of course! My word. A duchess! Well, please pass my felicitations to them all, if you will."

"I will be happy to do so. Thank you again for your help."

Mrs. Reeves nodded, bobbed a curtsy and wandered back inside, still looking stunned at such news.

"Thank you," Hestia said to her friend.

"We should still check out the Red Fox," Stoneacre said. "We might discover where he was headed." He raised a brow. "Or what he was doing there."

"A good notion, but there is no 'we' to be had in the idea," Lady Cartweld said smartly. "Ladies do not frequent that particular inn." She chuckled. "Vixens, perhaps, but not ladies."

"I'm no lady and you know it," Hestia told her.

"Well, you are dressed like one, and if you accompany Lord Stoneacre, you will attract attention and prevent him from discovering anything at all. Let him go and you come home with me. If you'll recall, the last time we spoke, I said I would try to find a list of business contacts—ones that my erstwhile fiancé claimed? I've found some leads. Some were fictitious, but others live and breathe in Bristol."

"Business contacts in Bristol? Marstoke's?" Stoneacre couldn't deny that could be invaluable. He looked to Hestia.

She nodded. "Very well."

He turned to the baroness. "My lady, if you will, please see Hestia safely delivered to the Queen's Crown after your visit."

"Of course."

"Thank you. It was a very great pleasure to make your acquaintance." He bowed and then turned to Hestia. "I shall meet you at the Queen's Crown in an hour or two." He didn't bother to hide the promise in his tone.

"I will see you then."

He strode off, wishing his errand finished already.

CHAPTER 15

Though women are the most numerous and harshly used of Lord M—'s victims, the Great Game leads some of Society's finest young gentlemen into his dangerous reach.
--from the Journal of the Infamous Miss Hestia Wright

Hestia scanned the names on the baroness's list. She didn't know any of them, but she knew they might prove to be invaluable in their investigations. She looked up as a servant entered with a tea tray. "I'm a little surprised your father shared this information."

"Oh, he refused when I asked." Her friend poured tea and handed her a dish. "So I went to the family solicitor myself. He refused too, on the grounds of client privilege and privacy."

"How did you get it, then?"

"I hired the man myself, at twice the price. And I told him, as the main party nearly ruined by the marriage settlements he arranged with an imposter, that I wanted to know about the business practices and recommendations that had tricked him into it."

"Ah, guilt is often an excellent motivator," Hestia said with a tip of her teacup. She picked up the list again, suddenly struck. "You haven't spoken to any of them, have you?"

"Heavens, no. I've no wish to spook them. And I've nothing specific to ask them, in any case. I meant to leave all of that to you."

"As you should. You've risked enough. But I thank you."

"You are quite welcome." The baroness leaned forward in her chair. "And I will take payment in gossip. Tell me about you and Stoneacre."

Belatedly, Hestia reached for her mask. She'd forgotten it. Grown comfortable without it—and that thought alone set her nerves to jangling. She couldn't allow Amelia to see what came to mind—and to heart, gut and various other interesting bits—when she thought of Stoneacre.

"Hestia!" The baroness's eyes widened. "Are you *blushing?*"

"Of course not," she answered crossly. "As for Stoneacre, you can blame Prinny for that." She distracted her friend with the tale of her meeting with the Prince Regent.

"So, we've come to the endgame," Amelia mused when she'd finished.

"Yes. One way or another, it will all be over soon."

"Marstoke will be over," Amelia said decisively. "And then you can figure out how to fill your free time."

"There will still be plenty of work to do."

"Yes, and you can start by working on Stoneacre." She raised a hand. "Don't bother to deny it. I saw the pair of you. Just because it's been a while since I had the chance to act on such . . . stirrings . . . doesn't mean I don't recognize them when I see them." She sat back and set her fingers in a steeple. "I did consider Stoneacre as a potential husband once, you know."

Shock rattled her and Hestia set down her cup and saucer. "Did you?"

"Yes. I saw him at a country assembly in Wiltshire once. There is no denying his looks," she said with a sigh.

She held herself rigid and silent.

"It was the family that decided me against him as a candidate, in the end."

"Stoneacre's family?"

"Yes. They are . . . stiff. The lot of them. I thought I'd have the same sort of fight with them that I already had with my own family. Do you know what I mean?"

She nodded. She knew a good bit more about Stoneacre's family than anyone might suspect.

"The father seems a tough enough nut to crack, but the mother, I think the mother is the real dragon there. And Stoneacre seemed solicitous of her." She raised a brow. "Not that you could not best her. I'd never bet against you, dear. But I thought you might like to know what you would be up against."

"I'm not up against anyone," she said curtly. Even though it wasn't strictly true. Her friend's words were kindly meant, but it was a warning, nonetheless. One she would never need, she sternly reminded herself. She already knew how dangerous Stoneacre's mother could be.

They spoke of other things, then, but Hestia could not focus. As soon as she could, she took her leave.

"I wish you luck against Marstoke," Amelia told her, gripping her hands. "And if I can contribute in any way, just ask. I'll do anything you need."

"Thank you," Hestia said, truly grateful. Impulsively, she squeezed the baroness tight for a moment. "You are a good friend. And heaven knows I need one."

Amelia grinned. "I'm a good enough friend to tell you I think you should take your chance with Stoneacre." She squeezed her back. "Live a little, my friend. What else is all of this for?"

Hestia refused the offer of a carriage. She needed to walk. Ignoring the footman Amelia sent to see her safely back, she strode out ahead of him, her mood plummeting with each step.

Why could not this one thing be simple? She'd wanted this . . . detached . . . time with Stoneacre. She'd made it clear that it was strictly temporary.

It had to be temporary. Nothing else would work, not once they'd returned to London and their duties and the people in their lives. She shivered in the cooling air. It had been so wonderful, though. She'd felt like she was coming alive once again, under his hands. Music wafted, sang and soared in her blood again, after years of silence and dust. How could she blame him for wanting more when she craved it too?

He did want more. She'd seen it in his eyes, felt it in the graze of his fingertips. He'd even said as much, talking of ideas and plans and designs.

He should know better than to ask. No good came of yearning for what you couldn't have. She'd learned that at her father's knee. And he'd learned to ask for better at his father's. His family would demand the best for him, and in their eyes that meant a girl with family, fortune and a good name.

The footman left her when she reached the inn. She stalked in with thunder echoing in her empty heart and darkening her expression. The clerk at the desk nodded to her as she passed.

"Oh. Ma'am! Excuse me?" Lost in her thoughts, she did not realize he was addressing her until she'd taken the first step and he reached out to touch her arm. It was a reflex to jerk away and turn, snarling.

"Oh! I beg your pardon. I did not think you heard me." He held up a letter. "It's just . . . this was delivered for your husband."

She ignored the wrench at his words. "Thank you." Woodenly, she took it and turned to continue on.

"And ma'am?" he called to her again. "I just wanted you to know that the letter—that is the condition in which I received it."

Pausing, she looked over her shoulder and he nodded at the paper in her hand. There was a lantern mounted on the wall in the first landing. She climbed up to stand next to it and held the letter up. She frowned. There was an extra, thin lip of wax on the seal. It might have come from someone lifting the seal with a hot knife.

She nodded at the clerk and he returned to his post. Sighing, she held the paper up to the light to look again—and saw something else.

Time stopped.

Shock and sudden horrid awareness raised gooseflesh all over her.

There it was. Even through the folded paper she could make the image out.

She sank down onto the step. Hands shaking, she turned the paper all around. No name. It wasn't addressed to anyone. Steeling herself, she took a deep breath and cracked the seal.

One sentence.

Bring her to Clevedon.

The words didn't steal her breath away. It was the image. A chess piece. A tall, elaborately crowned king piece, standing tall amid a collection of much smaller, toppled pieces.

Marstoke's mark.

The image he sent only to his top lieutenants. The mark that conferred the highest urgency to his commands.

No.

She sucked in a deep, shuddering breath. *No. No. No.*

Not Stoneacre.

She refused to believe it.

"Ma'am? Is something wrong? Are you ill?"

She looked up. The clerk was back. He puzzled up at her from the bottom of the stairs. "There is no name on this letter." Her voice didn't sound right. "How did you know to deliver it to my husband?"

"A messenger boy brought it. He described you both to an inch." He frowned, suddenly apologetic. "I am sorry. Have I erred in passing it to you?"

"No. It's fine. When did the messenger come?"

"This afternoon, ma'am. Very soon after you departed." He took a step up. "Are you well? Shall I help you to your room?"

"No. I'm fine. No." She climbed to her feet, feeling unsteady. "Thank you. Good evening."

She made her way to the rented room. Sank down on the bed.

Eyes unfocused, she stretched a hand out across the coverlet. It was not possible. She *liked* Stoneacre. She was an excellent judge of character. He could not have fooled her so thoroughly.

You will never see it coming. The final blow approaches.

This wasn't what that cryptic note had meant, back in London. She could not believe it.

She'd spoken of this mark. Told Stoneacre about it herself. He hadn't known about it. She hadn't described it. He had not asked. He hadn't seemed especially surprised, either.

It meant nothing.

He was close to the Prince Regent. He would have known about the request from Miss Smythe, perhaps even before the Prince saw it himself. He could have leaked her true identity. He would have known how dangerous she could be to the Regent and the monarchy.

Her mind kept ticking off facts, even though she didn't want to think about them. Face the possibility.

He hadn't known their destination the night that they invaded Mrs. Ledger's brothel, and the staff there had been unprepared, hadn't had an inkling they were coming.

He *had* known they aimed for Bradford-on-Avon, and anyone working with Marstoke would have guessed they were heading for the priory. And Marstoke had expected her, prepared for her arrival.

Stoneacre had known about the Red Fox Inn and Marstoke had been there as recently as this morning.

Almost against her will, her mind ranged back, months ago, back to the time when they'd actually caught Marstoke. He'd been locked up in Newgate while the crown dithered, scurrying to discover the extent of his crimes and trying to decide what to do with him. Stoneacre had been a frequent visitor, as he tried to decipher the marquess's coded records and convince him to cooperate with the crown's investigations. No one knew how the Wicked Marquess had escaped. She recalled how cold and broken she'd felt when she heard. She recalled how furious Stoneacre had been.

She recalled that he had been Marstoke's last registered visitor.

A great, forlorn shiver went through her.

She stood. Seizing the grief and crushing disappointment that welled higher with every second, she crushed it, used it, and coalesced it into anger and purpose.

Sticking her head out of the door, she hailed a maid down the passageway, carrying an armful of linen from a room. "Send to a livery and have a horse saddled for a lady and waiting in the court-yard. Fifteen minutes. No more."

Moving swiftly, refusing to think of anything except speed and escape, she stripped off her finery and donned her serviceable, dark traveling clothes.

She couldn't go back to Amelia's. That was the first place he would look.

But, where?

It didn't matter. She had to *go*.

It took only twenty minutes before she mounted up and headed out of Bath.

STONEACRE LURKED in a narrow stairwell at the back of the Red Fox Inn. Below, in the basement, two men worked, shifting crates and barrels.

"Damn that man, straight to hell," one of them rasped. "Who in bleedin' hell does he think he is? The only smuggler in Bath lookin' for storage?"

"Why bother wit' him, then?" the other asked. Derision filled his tone. "He's naught but a toff."

"Naught but a toff?" the first repeated, incredulous. "And here's ye, askin' every week why I don't hand the place over to ye? And then you up and just bleat out somethin' so damned ignorant?"

"Ignorant? Why?"

"If ye think *he's* just a toff and not the most vicious whoreson you ever met, then ye don't deserve to empty dustbins, let alone run my business." The first man spat audibly. "Now move those casks closer to the stairs. I'll put the crates over here and we'll leave the whole wall open for him.

The other man grumbled again. Stoneacre didn't make out the words.

"Aye. Aye. Just stay on his good side, 'tis all we gotta do. Hell's bells, at least we ain't transformin' the whole place, like old Geordy Tieck. Damned fool should know better than to go all in with a man like that."

The sound of rolling casks drowned out the rest, but Stoneacre had heard enough. Damned if Hestia hadn't predicted exactly this development. It must be Marstoke they spoke of, and now he had storage for his opium and perhaps even a functioning den on the way, if he'd interpreted that last exchange correctly.

He moved silently to the top of the stairs and peered out. No one moved in the corridor, thank heavens. He'd had to nurse a pint in the taproom for too long. Listening to the ebb and flow of the patrons, he'd gleaned nothing. But his luck had changed when the man behind the bar suddenly berated his son for being slow to arrive and dragged him off below stairs for urgent 'rearrangement.'

He slipped out and kept his head down as he maneuvered out of the inn and into the streets. Moving quickly, he made his way back to the Queen's Crown. He was eager to share his findings and see if the list the baroness had collected contained any intersections with his own files.

He was eager for other reasons, too. He'd pushed Hestia too hard, earlier. He'd seen it in her eyes. She felt the connection between them, he knew. She just wasn't ready to acknowledge where it was going to lead them.

He passed a florist's shop and something caught his eye. A gorgeous vase full of pink and white flowers, framed by stems full of cherry blossoms. He stopped and bought them at once. Tonight, he would reassure her. Distract her. Let that connection lead them to a place where only the bliss they gave each other mattered.

His blood was already up when he entered the inn. Nodding to the man behind the desk, he took kept careful hold of his bouquet and took the stairs two at a time. Pushed open the door—

And frowned.

Had she not returned from Lady Cartweld's? No. Her fine clothes were draped across a chair. Was there a shared bathing room? Setting the vase down, he went out, called out to a maid passing on the stairs and asked.

"No, sir," she assured him. "Should you care for a bath, we'll set it up in your room."

"Perhaps later." He went back—and caught sight of a piece of paper on the bed.

Clevedon? What did it mean?

He took it downstairs. "Do you know who delivered this message to my wife?" he asked the clerk.

The man looked nervous. "I gave it to her, sir. I didn't know it would upset her. But it was delivered earlier today—and meant for you."

"Upset her? Explain."

The man told him what had occurred. "I knew it must be urgent. I thought perhaps she had found you, the way you hurried upstairs."

"Found me? What do you mean?" He slapped a hand on the high desk. "Where is she?"

The man's eyes had gone wide. "I don't know. She left right after she read it."

"Left?" Stoneacre's mind was racing. "How? With whom? How long ago?"

"Alone. On horseback. Not quite an hour ago."

"Damn it all!"

The man cringed.

Stoneacre stared at the note again. "Where the hell is Clevedon?" he demanded.

"On the coast?" The clerk seemed uncertain. "Somewhere near Bristol."

Bristol. What had happened? He stared at the note again. At the image stamped there. And the memory stirred in his head.

Marstoke has a mark he uses in special correspondence. Did you know?

She'd told him, back in Reading. He hadn't known. And she had not described it. But looking at the image now, it seemed exactly the sort of thing Marstoke would commission. Yes, he enjoyed thinking of himself as above all men, the grand master of his Great Game.

And a message bearing that mark had been delivered to him? It made no sense—

He stopped. No. She wouldn't. She couldn't.

Had Hestia truly believed that he, Stoneacre, could be one of Marstoke's chosen players?

Fury and disbelief erupted. "Damn it! Get me a horse. Now!"

CHAPTER 16

Lord M—targets younger sons and men who lay far from the succession
of their family's titles and wealth. He stirs up feelings of discontent,
jealousy and ill use and recruits them into his Game with ideas of
change, of revolution, of plots to reinvent the systems of inheritance and
promises of favor and influence in the new regimes.
--from the Journal of the Infamous Miss Hestia Wright

The moon had not yet risen above the horizon when Hestia left the lights of Bath behind. She pushed the mare on while the darkness closed in on her, pressing in on her chest and shoulders, making it difficult to breathe.

No, that was grief, and the weight of her burdens settling back into their accustomed places. She should have known better than to cast them aside, even for a short time.

They were so very difficult to pick up again.

Because, for the first time, she'd had someone to help carry the load.

Not that she would ever disparage the hard work and support that came from her family—from Brynne and Callie, from Rhys and Francis, from Isaac and the others at Half Moon House. But even they hadn't made her feel seen and safe and cherished the way Stoneacre had. And it had started months and months ago, at the very beginning.

Had he been playing so deeply, for so long? Hestia reined in her mount as they passed over a fast moving stream, her thoughts racing just as quickly. Had she missed something? A sign? Her head could pick out all the logic, all the points where it made sense that the earl could be the one working with Marstoke. But her heart—her heart did not want to believe.

She began to mentally review their association. Back from the start of it. Slowly, she let each interaction sift through her head. One by one. Each thought and feeling recalled and scrutinized. And the further she went, the more certain she became.

She was a fool.

A suspicious, reactionary fool.

This. This is how Marstoke would win. If she let his wickedness color her own view. If she looked for deceit and betrayal from the people around her. This was a battle she'd long fought—to remember to look for human decency. Friendship. Love.

And that's what it came down to. She was more than a fool. She was a coward.

Her feelings for Stoneacre had surprised her. Scared her. Gone beyond the desire for a short, physical escapade. She wanted more—and she could not have it.

It was going to hurt to let him go. She would have to do it. She knew it—and Amelia's warning had driven the knowledge home.

How much easier to allow Marstoke to convince her to doubt him? It had been her chance to get out with anger instead of pain.

She hung her head, ashamed.

But she'd never been a coward. And she would not start now. She would not believe such a thing of Stoneacre. Not when he had continually shown himself to be a strong, kind and generous man. A man who had given her respect, patience, friendship and passion.

Of all the evil Marstoke had done to her, this might well be the worst.

She would not hurt Stoneacre this way. Neither would she allow Marstoke to steal his friendship from her, or the last, precious moments they had alone out here.

Her heart pounding, she pulled the mare up, spun her about and sent her racing back to Bath.

STONEACRE WAS TAKING the reins of his hired horse from the ostler when Hestia came riding into the courtyard.

There she is. Something frantic inside of him eased.

"Hestia! Thank God." A great relief swept over him and he held onto the saddle for support. But then he stiffened his spine. "What's happened? Where have you been?"

She slid out of her saddle and moved right for him. He turned the reins over to the boy right before she launched herself into his arms. "I'm sorry," she whispered. "So sorry."

He couldn't stop himself from holding her tight, even as anger and disappointment tried to choke him. "You believed it? You thought that I—"

He couldn't finish.

She reached up and framed his face with her hands, forced him to meet her gaze. Her eyes shone with tears in the torchlight.

"I allowed myself to believe it. For a short while."

His eyes closed against the stab of hurt.

"Because I was a coward," she whispered.

That startled him. "A coward?"

Her hands drifted down to grip his shoulders. "I'm so ashamed. But I was already fearful and then along came that note, and the idea, and . . ." She swallowed and her fingers tightened. "It was so much easier to latch on to hurt and betrayal than to admit how afraid I was."

Sudden understanding and wild hope melted some of his pain. "Why were you afraid?" he asked gently.

"I have feelings for you, Stoneacre. I didn't want to, but there you are."

She sounded almost cranky about it. He could not laugh, though, even though he wanted to—nearly as much as he wanted to shout his triumph out loud.

"They are real and strong and dreadfully inconvenient, but I cannot deny them," she continued. "No one has ever seen me like you do—the real me, flawed and uncertain but still determined. The defiant, contrary me."

"I do see her," he whispered. "And I find her fascinating."

"There's no accounting for taste," she said with a sigh. "No one has ever challenged me like you do. No one has ever lightened my burdens just by standing at my side."

Suddenly, she ducked her head and pressed close. "Part of me doesn't want this to end. It's going to hurt like the very devil to let you go when this is over."

Something twisted inside of him at her words. He couldn't think of parting with her. "Perhaps—"

"No." She stopped him with a finger to his lips and gave a mighty frown. "Saints and baby cherubs, Stoneacre. How did this happen?"

He did laugh, then, and shrugged. "Oh, the usual. Brothels and highwaymen. Assassins and arson."

Her chuckle sounded painful, but then she sighed. "Kind words to my wild houseful of girls. Friendship. Secrets."

He nuzzled her hair. "Don't forget the buttons."

She closed her eyes. "It has to end. And it won't be pleasant. But I will treasure the memories we've made, Stoneacre. And tonight—tonight is still ours."

"I want more than tonight, Hestia. And I won't stay quiet about it any longer."

"I know you do. You do want more. Right now. Things will look different when we go back, but surely we can hold the world at bay just a little longer."

In answer, he picked her up in his arms and carried her inside.

Behind him, the ostler called out. "What about your mount, yer lordship?"

The porter standing over a pile of luggage in the corner snorted. "Send it back, lad. The gent and his lady have other plans tonight."

HESTIA BURIED her face in the crook of Stoneacre's neck, breathing in bay rum and reveling in the electric charge of anticipation between them.

She would not be forlorn. She would not worry that this might be their last time together. She would relish the sweet and leave the bitter for later.

They were in the rented room almost before she finished the thought. Stoneacre set her down. He drew her in and wrapped his arms around her.

There was no teasing this time. No laughter. His expression shone intense and solemn—just the way she felt.

"I want it to last," she whispered. "I want to fill your senses. I want you to remember this night years ahead, when you close your eyes. I don't want you to forget me."

"Never," he vowed.

She stepped back a little, peeled off her pelisse and turned to drape it over a chair. He stepped in close behind her. His hands ran down her arms and her breath caught when his tongue traced the outline of her ear.

Heart pounding, she sank back against his tall, warm body. His tongue journeyed lower and shivers wracked her, from scalp to toes. His mouth was warm and wet as he kissed his way along her nape, then gave a quick, hard nip at the curve of her neck.

Her nipples stood at attention. His hands moved along the curve of her waist, climbed higher over her ribs. He cupped both breasts and brushed his thumbs over the extended peaks.

"Oh, yes," he whispered in her ear. "Your nipples are hard for me already." One hand moved steadily lower. She arched her back and made a sound of protest, but he only chuckled—and ran his hand over the length of her thigh. Tucking his fingers behind her knee, he urged her leg up and placed her foot on the chair. "I want to see if all of you is ready."

Soft fingertips teased her ankle, circled it, stroked up her calf. He grasped the hem of her gown and began reeling it in, inch by delicious inch.

Cool air brushed over her heated skin. Pleasure spiraled through her, centering in heavy coils in her womb. He teased the inside of her thigh and she sucked in a breath.

She knew what his seeking fingers would find. Wet heat and proof of a woman's passion. But it didn't compare to the oceans of joy and gratitude and delight in her heart.

He kissed her nape again as his fingers explored amongst her curls, then he slid a finger into her folds and a jolt of excitement arced between the two spots.

His fingers moved on her and they both moaned.

"So wet," he whispered.

He found her swollen bud and she jerked against him as he teased her, circling in a delicious, slow motion.

She cried out and reached behind her, grasping behind his neck. His other hand pinched her nipple through her bodice and she bucked, aching for more. She was lost in the pleasure, at his mercy. She thrust forward, asking—and he answered, letting a finger slide into her, then back out and up to rub hard against her nub.

She cried out, inarticulate with want, entranced with the sensations that danced along all the nerves in her body. He repeated the motion and reason melted. She was only a shower of light, of need, all focused on the delicious movement of his hand.

And then the light exploded outward and collapsed, rushing in again to gather at her pulsing womb, sending ecstasy tearing through her.

She moaned a little when it was through with her. She hung in his arms and he cradled her against him while he murmured in her ear.

Only for a moment, though. Mind and energy and determination returned—a determination to give as good as she got.

She stood straight and turned in his arms and kissed him deeply. "Your turn," she rasped.

He smiled, but she pulled him to her, kissing him soundly and without mercy. Pulling back, she nudged him to move until he leaned back against the tall bedpost. Pausing a moment, she searched his face and was satisfied with the anticipation she found there.

She took her time, kissing him thoroughly, loosening his cravat so that she could return the favor and rain soft, nuzzling kisses over his neck. She ran eager hands over his broad chest and along the narrowing slope to his waist.

Then she dipped lower and cupped the rigid length of his erection. He made a choked sound and thrust into her hand. "Are you ready, too, then?"

He growled his agreement and she dropped to her knees before him.

"Hestia—"

"Shh. I want to drive you wild, as you do to me." Efficiently, she began to loosen the fall of his trousers.

In seconds, he sprang free and she had him full and hard in her hands. She eyed his dusky, red length with approval. When she gave him a long stroke, he shuddered all over.

"Yes," he breathed. "Touch me."

She did. Eyeing him with a raised brow, she rested the tips of her fingers on him. Carefully, she began to explore his entire velvety-smooth expanse. He was firm and alive beneath her touch. And then she bent forward and put her mouth on him.

He moaned out loud.

Slowly, gently, she treated him to the same exquisite torture he had shown her. With soft touches and a gentle tongue and the lightest of caresses, she found all of his sensitive spots and veined ridges and teased his high, tight sac.

His gasps and low exclamations told her how much he enjoyed it.

And then she gripped him firmly and pumped. His chest heaved and his rod lengthened and hardened even further.

Abruptly, he reached down to lift her to her feet. With a quick, smack of a kiss he urged her toward the bed. "I need you, now."

She was ready. She wanted him hard and deep. She wanted him to brand her with every inch, to take her hard and long so that she would always remember.

Turning, she bent over the bed. Spreading her legs just a bit, she hiked her skirts, looked over her shoulder and smiled at him.

"Hell and damnation, Hestia. You're going to kill me." He moved to cover her, to run his hands over her and kiss her neck. "I don't know what I did to deserve you."

He was there then, at the entrance to her core. He pushed her legs a bit wider apart and eased the broad head of his cock just inside her.

"Damn, but you are so tight," he groaned. He rocked his hips, advancing further. She threw back her head, feeling her body change, feeling stretched and unbearably empty all at once.

Slowly, he worked her. And her body gave way, welcoming him home. *Saints, yes.* She put her head down and focused on the incredible sensations, until, suddenly, he was fully seated.

He moaned his triumph and began to move—and she moved with him. It was wild and lovely and oddly intimate. They strained together, rocked together, read every nuance of position and tone. As one, they climbed.

She tilted her hips and he slid in deeper, touched her at just the right spot. All of her muscles responded and clenched tight.

With a gasp, he began to thrust, hard and fast. And then he reached around and stroked her center.

And she was no longer in control. She jerked and rose and fell as his fingers and body dictated—and he carried her higher than she'd ever gone before. He was inside and outside and all around and he touched her with loving and tender care—and she was gone. Lost to herself. Totally abandoned to the storm of pleasure he brewed.

Convulsions gripped her and him and she let them shatter her. She was safe. With him. She flew apart, knowing he would be there to help her pull herself back together.

They crawled into the bed minutes later, once they had come back to themselves, and lolled there, recovering.

"Don't go to sleep," Stoneacre warned. "There's still a long night ahead of us, and I intend to make full use of it."

And so they did, loving each other until the hour grew late and falling into an exhausted sleep, entangled together.

In contrast, the hour was early, although the room was still dark, when Hestia came suddenly awake. What was it? A sound? Inside the room?

Not Stoneacre. He slumbered deeply at her side, one hand flung possessively across her hip.

She caught a scent. Sickly sweet. Her eyes flew open, but a cloth quickly covered her mouth and nose. She struggled, frantically trying to pull away, to hold her breath. It was no use. She breathed it in . . . and the dark beckoned.

Still protesting, she fell into it.

CHAPTER 17

*Lord M— makes these young men of good birth his 'lieutenants'. They are
tasked with doing the deeds he doesn't wish to sully his hands with.
Everything from extortion to bullying, smuggling and yes, killing.
--from the Journal of the Infamous Miss Hestia Wright*

The incessant rocking was making her head ache abdominally.
Hestia frowned, her eyes still closed. What devil was thumping
his pitchfork on the inside of her forehead? And why was he rocking
the bed?

With a gasp, she sat up—and moaned out loud. She clutched her
head with one hand and steadied herself with the other. The bed
wasn't rocking. She was in a carriage. Naked. She glanced down at the
blankets she'd been covered in, now pooled about her lap.

Her ear caught the sound of the driver's panel sliding open, but she
couldn't move her head quick enough to see anyone peering through.
The carriage began to slow.

She struggled to *think*. Peering outside, she winced at the light.

Saints above, the sun hung nearly directly above. Where was she? Who had taken her? Where was Stoneacre?

The door opened. She braced, desperate enough to fling herself out—until she saw who stood there.

"Isaac?"

He tossed in her traveling clothes. "Get dressed. Quickly."

Her mind raced, but her movements were slow and careful as she struggled into her shift and gown. It hung on her without her corset, but there was nothing to be done about it.

She'd just finished and was trying to swallow back her nausea when the door opened again. Isaac climbed in and sat across from her. The carriage started up again.

She stared, aghast. But she was too smart to make the same mistake twice. "He has Rachel?" she asked, finally.

Tears sprang to his eyes.

She shivered. In all of the years they'd worked together, with all the ugly and terrible things they'd seen, she'd never seen him cry.

"Both girls, too." He hung his head.

She stared. "He got past the guards posted around your home?"

He nodded. "We were so careful. We've always been so careful. How did he find them?"

She sighed and sat back, resting her head against the seat. "We are nearly at the end. He's throwing everything at us at once. I'm so sorry."

After a moment, she opened slatted eyes. "Where's Stoneacre?"

"I left him where he was. I dosed him heavier. He's likely not awake yet."

She sat up and cradled her aching head. "Did you have to dose either of us? Couldn't you have just asked?"

He shot her a candid look. "I'm to bring you. Just you. Do you really think Stoneacre would have allowed you to go without him?"

She didn't answer. She knew he was right.

"I'm sorry, Hestia."

"Don't be. We all agreed to the pact. All of us. If he has one of ours, we give him what he wants—and we fight from there." She looked up suddenly and groaned again at the backlash from within her skull. "Did you send that note?"

He nodded. "It seemed the easiest way to separate you."

"It almost did." She looked away, watched the scenery pass without noting it. There was no need to let Isaac see what she was feeling.

"You have feelings for him."

She swallowed. She should have known he'd see it anyway.

"I knew it when you turned around and rode hell for leather, back to him. I was following along, giving you a bit of time." He glanced away. "I would have given you more time, if I could have."

Together, he meant. Together with Stoneacre.

A long breath slid out of her. She would *not* cry. She had to look ahead. Prepare herself. "Marstoke told you he'd let them go, if you turned me over?"

"Yes."

"Take them and get them away safely, as soon as he gives them over. Don't look back."

"You'll need help," he began.

"No. That's why we made the pact. So our innocent loved ones wouldn't pay the price for our war. You take your women and you get them far away."

"Hestia, there's no one else. I sent Aldmere a note, but neither he nor Tru will be able to get here in time. You'll be on your own."

"I don't care," she said fiercely. "I've faced him before on my own. I got away. I'll do it again." She reached across and took his big hands in her own. "And if I do not, I need to know that you are going to carry on. Keep the girls safe. Keep the house open." Squeezing, she glared at him. "Promise me, Isaac."

He merely looked at her.

"*Promise* me."

At last, he relented. He gave a slow nod.

"Send me a signal when you've got them safely away." She frowned and laid her head back again. "And then I will begin to play his game in earnest."

~

THE HOUSE HUNKERED SQUARELY in a field of sea grass, set back a ways from a cliff. The road curved close to the edge on the way toward it and she looked down to the rocky beach below. The whole place looked sprawling and utilitarian rather than elegant or homelike.

"How the mighty have fallen," she said as the coach pulled away.

She recognized the two men leaning against the low stone wall before the house. They had once been bully boys for the pimp, Hatch. They didn't move as Isaac escorted her past. They merely looked at her and exchanged a long, telling glance.

The door opened as she approached. She did not know the man there, though he was clearly not a servant. He appeared to be expecting her, though. Silent, he held the door wide to admit them.

A large entry hall lay just inside, all done up in dark carved paneling and old wooden floors. Crates were stacked against two walls. Men hovered about, some of them digging in open crates, packed with straw. They all grew silent and still with her entrance.

One man set aside a clipboard and beckoned them. He opened a door. "This way."

They followed him down a long passage. The sweet scent of licorice hung in the air. In one room she caught a glimpse of a scantily clad man tending a bubbling cauldron. In another, men bent over clerk's desks, busy with paper work. Their escort led them to a set of ornate doors and pushed them open with a flourish.

Hestia strode into what might have once been a small ballroom. It was a great, open space that now looked like a . . . den. The makeshift home of a disturbed mind.

A wall of windows took up one side of the room. They were open and a slight sea breeze drifted in, but the wooden frames looked warped and they and the floor all showed signs of damp. The musty smell of decay hung in the air.

A tall stack of rugs stood piled along one wall. Thick and richly colored, they were being counted by a man with a pencil and paper. Nearby stood an easel and an artist painting upon it, his palette in hand. She craned her neck to look—it was a portrait of Marstoke dressed in flowing Eastern robes.

She bit back a dark laugh. In a corner a group of dirty children played a dice game. One of them heard her and glanced up, then elbowed the others. They all stared. Beyond them, a weather-roughened man sat at a stool. He had a large, forged iron hook in one hand and was attaching it to fishing net. A number of finished specimens bunched around his feet.

She halted next to a dining table set up in the middle of the room. It was still covered with dishes and the remnants of a meal. Ahead, she faced a raised dais. Created for musicians, it sat a couple of steps above the main floor and held a single, elaborately carved chair.

Trust Marstoke to set himself up with a throne.

It sat empty. Hestia turned completely around, searching, but her nemesis was nowhere to be seen.

"Wait here." Their escort snapped his fingers at one of the boys in the corner and bent to give quiet orders when the boy answered the summons.

Perhaps he was sending for Marstoke, but there was no need. Her spine tingled in dread and anticipation as a door opened and her old enemy walked through. Another young man followed on his heels, listening to him talk and apparently taking dictation.

" . . . at least twelve feet by twenty-four," Marstoke was saying. "And to be outfitted in the opulent style of the East." He waved a hand. "Rather like the Royal Pavilion, but with actual taste."

He stopped dead in his tracks when he caught sight of Hestia and Isaac.

"Well done, my boy," he whispered to Isaac. "Very well done."

He frowned at Hestia. "You burned down my house." he said, suddenly loud and distinctly unhappy.

Everyone in the room stopped what they were doing.

Hestia drew herself up. "You sent an assassin to kill me!"

He pursed his lips, whatever else he'd been going to say dying away. "Yes, well . . ."

She looked him over. It had been some time since they'd faced each other directly. "You are not aging well, Marstoke. You look like hell warmed over. Not as bad as Captain Wilson has aged, but . . ." She shook her head and roved a disparaging eye over him.

"I lay the blame directly at your door," he snapped back. "Yours and your fat prince's, as well." He smoothed a hand over his receding hairline. "As for Wilson, I should hope I look better. He's dead. Your last encounter was too much for him."

She fought not to touch the scar on her ring finger. "Good."

He waved away the man hovering near him. Slowly, he climbed the dais and took his seat.

Without a word, the children gathered up their game and filed out. The painter collected his tubes and brushes and scurried out while the rug counter held the door. After another moment, the door opened again and other men and women streamed in.

Silently, they gathered, a motley mix of the people she'd seen on the way in, and others, including several young men of quality and more than a few thin, hard faces—men and women she'd think to find in London's back streets. Without a word they all took up watchful positions along the back wall. Two of them, the size of behemoths, moved forward to take up positions at either end of the dais.

Marstoke just sat there, looking at her. "It would have been cleaner, had you died." He scowled. "Ever the thorn in my side."

She gave a little curtsy.

He merely sat and watched her for a long moment further. "No," he declared suddenly. "This is better. I am glad you are here now. This will be a more fitting end to our game."

"Not yet. First, you must finish your business with Isaac."

The marquess's eyebrows rose.

"You have his family here, I assume. Bring them out. Set them free." She stretched her hands out. "He did as you asked. Here I am. Now it's your turn to keep your word." She glanced at her friend and then at the group standing silently behind them. "It's just good business, Marstoke. I imagine that you've made quite a few promises to these people, too."

He glared at her, then rolled his eyes. "Bring them!" he called.

They waited. Marstoke called for one of the men in the back and held a whispered conference before sending him out.

Still, they waited. Marstoke brooded. Twice more he called up a minion and sent them scurrying off. Hestia could not help but think that none of this activity boded well for her.

Finally, two men returned, hauling Isaac's wife Rachel and their two young daughters between them. Hestia felt Isaac stiffen beside her, but he gave no outward reaction.

"You need to follow your own rules, Marstoke," Hestia reminded him. "They leave now. Free, clear and unmolested."

"Yes, yes." He sounded impatient.

"Go," she said under her breath to Isaac.

He lurched forward suddenly, and picked up a girl in each arm. His wife looked at him with love and relief and implicit trust.

Hestia turned away. She could not show even a hint of weakness before Marstoke. She watched the marquess as the family hurried out, but he showed not a whit of concern about their release.

Silence descended again. A watchful, alert silence that somehow seemed to become a presence in the room.

"I understand that you've been searching out old acquaintances of mine," Marstoke launched the words into the quiet, shattering it with tense disapproval and anticipation.

"Searching out your victims, I think you mean? Offering assistance? Cataloging your sins? If that is what you refer to, then the answer is yes." She sneered up at him. "I've been kept disgracefully busy."

"Well, tit for tat, my dear. I believe it is time we listened to some complaints against *you*." He lifted his chin. "Get her a chair."

One of the men brought one from the dining table and leered at her as she sat. Another man offered her a glass of wine, but for several good reasons, she refused.

Marstoke raised a finger then, and the man set down the wine, and came back with a rope. The leering man held her in place while he began to tie her wrists to the chair arms.

Her heart dropping, she struggled. Though she knew it was futile, she fought. His minions were merciless, however, and the truth settled heavily onto her soul. He was going to win. She was likely going to die here.

She craned her head and looked over her shoulder at the gathered crowd. There were the dissatisfied younger men of good families he'd recruited with his whispers of rebellion. The few women he'd convinced to play his game. The criminals he'd recruited into his service.

They all watched her with hungry anticipation. She was far outnumbered. There were no allies here.

"Settle in, my dear, and listen," Marstoke said with an air of satisfaction that made her nervous.

But then, through the open window, echoed the sound of four distant gunshots.

Marstoke sat up. "See what it is," he ordered. "Make sure we are not disturbed."

But Hestia knew. It was Isaac's signal. They were safely away. She grinned up at Marstoke.

Fine. He would win, in the end. But she still had plenty of play left in her.

Now the game would truly begin.

CHAPTER 18

Several of these young blue blooded 'lieutenants' were recently tried and transported for the sins committed at Lord M—'s direction. Only their family names saved them from the gallows.
--from the Journal of the Infamous Miss Hestia Wright

Stoneacre rolled over—and nearly cast up his accounts. What in damnation was wrong with his head? "Hestia?"

Lord, his mouth felt like he'd slept with a woolen scarf stuffed in it. "Hestia?"

He groped across the empty bed. It was still dark. Had he heard the door close? Was she feeling ill, too? Gathering his strength, he lifted himself up enough to peer over onto the floor.

Empty.

Perhaps she'd gone to the privy? Or to the kitchens for something to help a pounding head? He lay back, gathering strength for another push, to make it out of bed.

When he opened his eyes, he was unsure how much time had passed. "Hestia?"

She still had not returned, but he felt marginally better. It was light out, though. Alarm pierced him nearly as painfully as his headache. He swung his feet out of bed and hung his head in his hands. After a few seconds, he stood up—and nearly fell forward onto his face.

He fought through the dizziness, now beginning to really worry. Had Hestia been struck with the same illness? Was she lying somewhere, unable to make it back? Oh, Lord. Or had Marstoke had something to do with this?

He pulled a blanket from the bed and staggered to the doorway. He stood there, panting, holding his aching head and waiting.

Eventually the boot boy came scurrying up the stairs. "Here, lad. Come here." He beckoned and the boy cautiously approached. "Have you seen my lady? I fear we've caught something. Do you know where she is?"

The boy did not. "Didn't you lose her once already?" he asked.

"Coffee, lad," he ground out. "Fetch me coffee." His stomach objected to the notion, but he needed to clear his head. "And send up the innkeeper. We need to find my lady."

He managed to get dressed, forcing coffee down as he did so—and his headache did settle to a dull ache. His alarm had only risen, though. No one had seen Hestia. Her travel clothes were gone again.

He did not believe she had left him. Not voluntarily. Not after last night. He didn't know what had been done to him, but he was sure now, that it had been Marstoke.

Had they done the same to Hestia? Taken her while she was incapacitated? He had to find her. And he had only one clue. Clevedon.

But where was Clevedon? On the coast near Bristol was all he knew. And even if he went straight there, he couldn't scour the whole town. He went in search of someone to ask and found the clerk from yesterday downstairs, talking to a groom.

"Excuse me, I need to know more about Clevedon. Where is it in relation to Bristol? And how big a place is it?" he asked, striding up to them.

The clerk looked startled. "It's a small coastal town, I believe. But my lord, you need to hear this groom's story."

Stoneacre turned to the man. "Have you an idea where my lady has gone?"

"Might be so, yer lordship. I was up early, changing a poultice on one of our coach horses. Saw a man bring something from the inn and load it into a carriage. It might have been a woman, bundled up in blankets."

Stoneacre's heart sank. "Did you get a look at the man?" He knew he was grasping at straws. "Did you know him?"

"No, not him, my lord, though he was a big 'un. But the driver. I do think I knew him. He's one of the stablemen at the Red Fox."

Determination chased the rest of his lethargy and nausea away. "Thank you, sir." He passed the groom a gold coin. "Get me a mount right away, will you?"

Ten minutes later, he rode into the courtyard at the Red Fox. The yard stood empty. No one came to take his horse.

He hitched the animal to a post and strode inside. "Fetch me the owner of the place," he demanded of a porter coming down the stairs with a lady's valise. Its owner trailed after him, and she ducked her head at Stoneacre's request.

"He's not here," the young man replied, nervous.

"Where is he?"

The boy flushed bright red. "I couldn't say, sir."

The woman behind him tugged her hood further forward. He stopped to look at her. She was too short to be Hestia. But he caught a glimpse of her as she turned away—and he stalked across to take her roughly by the arm.

"What are you doing here? Where is she? Where's Hestia?"

The woman tried to pull away. "You're too late."

"Why are you here?"

"I've been summoned," she answered. "We've all been summoned."

MARSTOKE CROOKED a finger and the opulent doors behind her opened again. She looked over her shoulder to see a small man pass through. His face was stained with soot and sweaty rivulets ran down his face and neck, leaving streaks. She smelled sour ale and sweat as he passed and he paused to cast a menacing look over her. She frowned as she realized he was the man who had been stirring something in the cauldron. Did she know him, perhaps? She strained to remember.

He came to stand before Marstoke, looking up at the marquess expectantly.

"You know the lady, Gordie?"

The man nodded and shot her another dark look—and with a sudden flash, she realized that she did know him.

"I understand she's done you a wrong turn?" Marstoke prompted.

"The worst, yer honor, sir."

Marstoke gestured impatiently. "Well, then, come on, man. Tell us about it."

"Well, and I had a little house, sir, where I lived and kept my whores and made decent enough money. Until she bought the lease out from under me and turned me out."

Hestia scoffed. "You never held the lease. You were just squatting in that house."

"Yes, and well enough, until you put me and all me girls out onto the street."

"Half of your girls came to *my* house, you cretin. I saw the bruises you put all over them."

"So? You've got to hit whores," he said reasonably. "Naught else makes 'em behave."

She shook her head. "The girls who came with me are safe now, working decent positions where they are paid good wages and they don't have to fear such abuse. Do you think they are complaining about that?"

"I'm complainin' about it!" Gordie retorted. "Without a house, the rest of me girls got took by other pimps—and some o' 'em are wors'n me!" he declared triumphantly. "And I had ter get new work," he grumbled. "Look at me now." He wiped his face with his dirty shirt. "And 'tis all thanks to yer interferin'."

Hestia merely raised a brow and looked pointedly past him at Marstoke.

Gordie frowned and looked back—and alarm blossomed over his face. "Not that I ain't that grateful, sir, ter be working fer yer honor, sir."

"Yes, yes." Marstoke had heard enough from Gordie. He waved a hand. "Bring in the next!"

A tall, gaunt man shuffled in now. He looked them all over with disdain and didn't appear to be happy to be there.

"State your business," Marstoke commanded.

"I'm a kidsman."

Hestia had already known it—she'd recognized him instantly. But she hadn't known he was still working his disgusting trade. She'd shut down the last flash house he'd run, and taken over a hundred half-starved children out of it.

"State your grievance against this woman," Marstoke repeated with an impatient sigh.

"I had a good thing going in London. Trained up a good-sized crew o' street rats and the livin' had started to come easy." He frowned at her. "But she brought in the constable and magistrate and they took ever' one o' them away. Had to skip out o' Town and start over from scratch—and just no one don't appreciate how long it takes to train up a kid the right way. Too many of 'em get caught at first, and they're no good to me one-handed or transported off. I'm still barely makin' enough to eat."

Hestia glared at him, knowing those children probably were not eating at all, and made herself a promise to find his new enterprise and give him more of the same.

If she made it out of here alive.

The next 'witness' accused her of snatching away his sister. She had to speak up when he accused her of spreading the rumor that she had the French pox.

"She does it have, Eustace, you idiot," she raged. "She must have picked it up as a child, too, so far has the disease progressed."

"You don't know nothin' about it," he sniffed.

"I know it's eating her mind away," she retorted. "She thinks she's five years old and you were 'punishing' her by whoring her out—and you were spreading the pox across London."

"She brought in good money—and she didn't remember it hours later anyways." He lifted his booted foot. "Since you took her, my circumstances is severely reduced—I had to get these off of the resurrection men!"

Marstoke's lip curled and he dismissed the man. She wanted to scream at him. Disgusted by a dead man's boots, but unmoved by a man who would treat his own sister so?

But the testimonies went on. Marstoke called up pimps and madams, abusive husbands and old women who ran roughshod over young flower girls and street sweepers. It went on and on. Even the audience tired of it. The malevolent silence turned to shifting and sighing. Only Marstoke seemed to be enjoying himself and he conducted the enquiries with a dignified delight, urging each witness to damn her for her life's work.

It only strengthened her pride, to have thwarted all of these selfish, despicable specimens, to have given aid to those with no voice and no hope, to those abused by this soulless horde.

At last, though, the parade of accusers ended and Marstoke stood.

"All of these stories have been most affecting. You have much to answer for, Hestia Wright, but none of these victims have complaints to match my own, I think."

She bit back a laugh. Ah. Here was what all of this theater had been leading up to—a public airing of Marstoke's grievances.

"So long, you've been irritating me, I should have grown a callus." He climbed out of his seat and walked the diameter of the dais, his hands clasped behind his back. "The personal affronts have been insult enough," he began.

She choked. "Personal affronts? To you? Have you lost your wits? You haven't been dabbling with Eustace's sister, have you?"

That brought the silence swooping back in. She rather thought all of them were holding their breaths. One of the bulky guards ahead of her looked horrified, but she was incensed. "I was barely more than a girl when you engineered, then hijacked my elopement! You invalidated the marriage by disguising yourself and acting as the vicar—then you took the place of the groom on the wedding night! You held me prisoner for weeks! You beat and raped and abused me and you have the sheer, unmitigated gall to talk to me of personal affronts?"

Someone hissed from the back of the room, but Marstoke's glare cut it instantly off.

"You are an evil-tongued witch," he said to her, low and fierce. "You have maligned me from the highest reaches of Society to the lowest. You made me the subject of the caricaturists and the broad sheets! And what of your larger sins?" He raised a hand toward the crowd. "You have thwarted our efforts at change at every turn."

"Your plans for harming the monarchy and threatening the stability of our country?" she asked tartly.

Marstoke raised a haughty brow. "The king is mad. His fat, philandering son is an imbecile. They do not deserve to rule."

"I do not believe in your grand vision for a new order, Marstoke—and I do not believe that you do, either."

"You may believe what you wish."

She snorted. "I know you. Better than any of these minions of yours."

He glanced over the audience behind her and then descended to stand before her. Her fists clenched helplessly in her bonds.

"I rather think you are right about that," he mused. He spoke in a quiet tone that wouldn't carry. "No one else defies me the way you do. It is stimulating, I do admit it. It's possible I might actually miss it."

She ignored the direction he was moving the conversation. "Your grievance with Prinny is personal. I know it, because I know you." She lifted her chin. "You punished me because I rejected you. You destroyed Wilson because we were young and foolish and cared for each other. Those girls you took as payment due—it was because someone in their family defied you. You are always harshest with those who make you feel slighted in some way." She leaned back. "It's a shame that your character failing has been so dangerous to the rest of us."

He only looked amused, the bastard. "It's true. You are more intelligent than any of this lot," he said with regret. "Certainly you exceed the Prince Regent's mental capacity." He sighed and walked all the way around her. She ignored it, refusing to look anywhere but straight ahead.

His lips pursed, he stopped when he came back around to stand before her once more. "He wasn't always so fat, but Prinny's always been a fool. Not that it mattered," he said bitterly.

"Outshone you, did he?" she asked sardonically.

"As if he could," he scoffed. "Those days were different, you must know. More . . . savage. We ran wild, the young men of Society. We made today's rakes look like country vicars. We got up to every wicked thing imaginable—gambling and racing—and putting the fix in on both. Drinking, even smuggling—and the women." He sighed. "We could do anything to them. And I led them all. I took those boys to places they'd never dared to go themselves. And today they sit in judgment on me, as if they'd never examined the dark side of their souls."

He stood silent a moment, lost in memory. "Yes, I was their captain, until the young Prince of Wales showed up on the scene. Then they flocked to him. At the balls, the theatre, even at the fights and the races and when we went carousing amongst the low-born street rats, they all lost their minds bowing and scraping and your highness-ing."

"He stole your thunder," she said, nodding. "But I'll wager it was more than just the attention." She stared directly up at him. "What was her name?"

He looked at her with active dislike—but then he surprised her by answering. "Margaret Bronhold. She was nobody. A theater seamstress. But she was quick and intelligent and stunningly talented. A beauty—and damn, but that woman could flay you with her tongue. She was fearless. I was wild for her. We all wanted her. I did everything to win her—and she preferred that royal fool. The prince only dallied with her because his married mistress was pregnant and off on her lying-in. But she liked him. Not only because of who he was, which was even more infuriating. They shared interests. History, literature, painting and the like. She chose him and he took her, then cast her off quicker than any of his other flings."

He shook his head and gave a sudden laugh. "You would have liked her. She would have liked you. I suppose you are alike, in many ways." He paused and stared down at her. "Do you know, I sometimes think about it—how things might have been different. If only she had chosen me. If only you had given in to me. If you had agreed to partner me in the Great Game." He sighed. "What might we have accomplished, together?"

"Where is she?" Hestia asked quietly. "Where is Margaret Bronhold?"

He scowled. "Dead. Long dead." He gave a dark laugh. "Did you doubt it?" He backed away and raised his voice again. "Dead, as you soon will be. Because you had to fight me. Over and over and at every turn, you fight me."

"You know, you might have taken your fight directly to the Prince."

"On the social level? He's a prince. And you saw how well that worked out for Brummel, did you not?"

"You might have fought him in Parliament."

He waved a hand.

"Too much like legitimate work? Was it so much better to scheme and plot and lure weak-minded and dissatisfied young men into your machinations? To use innocent young girls as pawns?"

He leaned in and gifted her a slow, simmering smile. "Not only better, but more fun. *The Game*, Hestia. The Game is everything." He turned and waved a hand at the watching crowd, raising his voice as he did. "And do be careful, my dear. Those men you call weak-minded are among those sitting judgment on you today."

He frowned suddenly. "And innocent and young is not what I would call you or your coven of harlots. You stole my fiancée, did you not? A grand move of revenge, that was."

"I didn't steal her. She ran from you. She didn't even know we had a history when she came looking for help."

"A likely story. Such a ragtag group you've gathered. Whores and street rats and royal bastards." His face darkened. "And the lot of you sent me to Newgate! Me. In that rotting, stinking pit," he spat. He paused to collect himself and draw a deep breath. "Your fate was sealed that day, Hestia Wright, and at last your day of reckoning has come."

She stiffened her spine.

Behind them, the double doors opened again. Marstoke's eyes widened and then he smiled broadly.

She turned to look back with trepidation, sure that nothing that brought him such pleasure was going to go well for her.

It was so much worse than she feared.

CHAPTER 19

You might join me, dear reader, in asking how Lord M— became so wicked? Was he born with this evil in his soul? Or did he grow to enjoy and pursue the pain and subjugation of others? I fear we may never come to understand it.
--from the Journal of the Infamous Miss Hestia Wright

S toneacre stood framed in the doorway. Her heart jumped—and then plummeted.

His eyes locked on hers, and there it was again—that feeling of every nerve under her skin jumping to life, yearning toward him. He looked as rumpled and tired as she felt. The day old grain of his beard showed stark on his jaw—and all she wanted to do was to run her fingers over it.

How had he found her? Surely no one else could have done it. It seemed impossible. She blinked back tears. But he'd already shown her he could do the impossible. He'd seen past her mask and convinced her to set it aside. He'd set a match to her soul and held it there until it sparked back to life.

Relief showed in his gaze—but she knew it was ill founded. Marstoke would not be kind to either of them.

"Lord Stoneacre," the marquess purred. "You have arrived ahead of your slotted time." Marstoke shrugged. "No matter. We will find you accommodations while you await your turn." He turned to cast a truly malicious gaze at Hestia. "And I have lately learned that you might have a vested interest in today's proceedings."

The guards on either side of him prodded Stoneacre into the room.

"Sit him at the table," Marstoke ordered. "And do not take your eyes off of him."

Hestia's mind whirled. She began to work against her bonds in earnest. Bad enough that she might lose everything to Marstoke in this ridiculous farce of a trial, but she'd be damned before she let him harm Stoneacre. She cast her gaze about, looking for a sympathetic face, something she could use as a weapon, anything.

A stirring in the crowd behind her caught her attention and she craned a look over her shoulder again. A woman entered the room in Stoneacre's wake. She was covered in a hooded cloak—and Marstoke looked delighted to see her.

He descended from on high once more, and went to meet the woman. Murmuring a greeting, he led her forward and brought her up onto the dais to stand next to his grand chair.

Hestia's skin prickled. Who was it? Not Amelia. The woman up there was too short and slight of build. None of her girls would stand there so docilely. Who, then?

"Lend me your attention, my faithful and most devoted followers. I wish to present someone truly special to you all. You know my complaints against Hestia Wright. We've heard all of yours today, as well. But this woman might just be the one with the most egregious grievance to lodge against her." He shot a look of triumph at Hestia, then bent down solicitously toward the newcomer. "May I take your cloak, my dear?"

Hestia held her breath. Her mind raced, trying to predict who could hate her so much as to help Marstoke in this—but the woman threw back her hood and the shock of the truth kicked her in the gut.

She gasped for breath. "Beth?" she whispered.

The woman wasn't cowering now. She wasn't frightened by the eyes watching her or by Marstoke, hovering over her. She only stood and looked calmly out at the faces watching her.

Marstoke, however, was grandstanding. He stood straight and spoke loudly and clearly into the questioning murmurs of the audience. "Hestia Wright was once friends with this woman—and then she became her enemy. She stole more than money or opportunity from this dear lady. She got into a physical altercation with her and dashed her head against a stone hearth. She stole her very wits from her."

He took Beth's hand, nodded and gestured toward the crowd.

Beth stepped forward. "For several months after that fight, I was naught but a numbwit. I knew my name, but I'd forgotten how to read. I couldn't add numbers or tell them apart. I couldn't remember how to get to my room at the end of the day. Hestia Wright did that to me—and then she left me behind."

Hestia's heart wrenched. She wished suddenly, and with all of her heart, that Stoneacre was not here to hear this.

"But after a while, things began to come back. It went slowly, but I began to feel like myself again. To think like myself again." She glanced down. "And I hated Hestia Wright."

Marstoke stepped forward. "Now I urge you, as my most devoted followers, to pay tribute to this woman as the first among you. No one has played the Game so skillfully as she. She not only agreed to play a dangerous and cunning role, but she excelled at it."

There were dissatisfied mutters and murmurings from the gathered crowd.

Marstoke paid it no heed. "I heard about it when Hestia Wright first moved back to England. And I heard the news when the Queen of Courtesans was going to open a house—a place where any woman could come to her for help. So, I gave her a challenge. I sent her the half-wit she had so hated." He threw back his head and laughed. "And the foolish woman took her in."

Hestia held her breath steady. She would not cry. She would not give either of them a moment of triumph at her own expense.

"This woman played her role and lived in Hestia Wright's own house for years," Marstoke crowed.

She'd never seem him show such emotion.

"She has been a mouse in Hestia's house, burrowed in and scurrying about, finding what I need to know, lying to Hestia every day for *years*."

She fought not to be sick. She would not do it. How could she have been so blind? How many people had she endangered with her own inability to see?

"And there you have it, the last and greatest accusation laid at Hestia Wright's door. I think our case has been made."

A chair scraped against the floor. Hestia turned to find Stoneacre standing. "It's a one-sided trial, if you've allowed no one to speak in Hestia's defense," he called out.

The corner of Marstoke's mouth twitched. "Who would speak for her?" He looked out across his gathered people.

The silence held.

"I will," Stoneacre declared.

Marstoke laughed out right. "A few of the boys might like to hear about her talents in bed, but I doubt anything else you have to say would be of interest."

Someone shouted a rude affirmation and the marquess just raised a brow.

"Why not let me speak, Marstoke? Do you not want your followers to hear of the hundreds of women and children she's saved? How she lifted them out of misery and poverty and abuse and helped them to live better, safer and more useful lives? Or don't you want to remind them that you couldn't win her or keep her? Or of the times she's defeated you, foiled your scheming or blocked your treasonous plans?"

"I think you've made our case for us, my lord. We all know it would be expedient to eliminate her before we begin the next phase of our great project."

"What have you told them?" Hestia asked wearily. "That the opium will fund your new order? Help to rid the country of unearned privilege and primogeniture?"

Stoneacre turned to rake a scathing glance over the assembled crowd. "Idiots. You are all dumber than you appear, if you believe that. How do you think he came by his own power and wealth?"

"Lord Marstoke understands that some of us born without a silver spoon deserve a chance at better," someone called.

"Some of us born down the family line deserve a piece of the pie!"

"And yet, you all follow him because he has money and power," she said over her shoulder. "You bow down before him, run to do his bidding, leave your homes and betray your families because you believe he has it, and you want it." She shook her head. "But he doesn't. It's all a lie." She nodded toward Stoneacre. "He has committed treason, his blood is attainted and the work has begun to deprive him of his title. Stoneacre and other men in His Majesty's government have been dismantling Marstoke's empire. It's expensive to plot and scheme and play the Game, but his family funds are long gone. His estate sits an empty shell and his criminal enterprises have dried up." She turned and looked over the other shoulder. "Those opium profits are slated for his pockets, not for your uprising. Marstoke is chasing money, just like so many others."

The silence disappeared as the crowd erupted into shouted debate.

Marstoke's color heightened, but he kept calm. "Spill what lies you will, Hestia. It will not change what is to come."

But Hestia had noticed Beth, staring intently at the marquess. "No money? No title?" The woman took a step closer to him.

"You should know better than believe anything she says," Marstoke snarled. He turned to the crowd. "That's enough foolishness," he shouted. "Enough distraction. The woman is only trying to save her own skin. We know our mission here—and today it is to destroy her before she interferes with us again."

"Before she tells any more inconvenient truths," Stoneacre shouted.

"That's enough!" Marstoke roared suddenly—and the quiet

descended again. "She needs to die. I'm offering up the honor to you all. Who will grab favor and acclaim by killing Hestia Wright?"

A chorus of volunteers and arguments erupted again.

"No!" Hestia tried to stand, but her bonds brought the chair with her. She pulled it close and kept to her feet. "No!" She slammed the chair back down and fell into it. The crash echoed through the room.

"You do it, Marstoke," she called. "You complain about my crimes against you. You claim the new world will be different and that justice and progress will depend on merit? Prove yours, then! If I must die, then you should kill me with your own hand."

"She's right," someone said.

"Show us!" That one sounded like Eustace.

"Prove it!"

Marstoke stared disbelieving at her, as if he could not believe she'd defied him again.

She shrugged. One last time. And if she died today, she wanted her blood on his hands.

"No!" Stoneacre shouted behind her. "I'm the one who has done the work to empty your pockets. I testified before the Crown as to your treason! Let her go!" She could hear the rattle of furniture, as he struggled against his captors.

But suddenly, Beth left her position by the chair and stepped forward to the front of the dais. "I'll do it," she declared. "I've been waiting a long time for this day."

Beth watched Marstoke intently again, as if gauging his reaction, but Hestia saw that he only looked relieved.

"No! Marstoke should do it!" she yelled.

"A weapon," the marquess called. "Someone lend us a weapon!"

At least six men crowded up around her, offering up a selection of knives and pistols.

"No need," Beth said. She dropped her cloak and held out the dagger she gripped in her hand. "I brought my own."

"Enterprising girl," Marstoke began. He reached for her other hand to help her down the stairs, but Beth stepped past it.

She moved in close to the marquess. Touched his cheek. "You said

I would be your marchioness," she said. "Over and over you told me to hang on. Keep going. Keep acting a fool and telling lies and you would marry me when it was over. I would be your lady. But it wasn't ever true, was it?" She snorted. "You married nearly every skirt in the land —except me. It wasn't true and I've wasted my life."

She didn't wait for him to answer. Instead, she raised her hand and plunged her dagger into Marstoke's heart.

STONEACRE WAS ON HIS FEET, straining against the men who held him, when the girl stabbed Marstoke. The marquess, eyes bulging in disbelief, slumped slowly to the floor. All three of them went slack at the shock of it.

Stoneacre recovered first, wrenching free as chaos erupted in the room. He swung at the man on his left, the one more directly in the way of the path between him and Hestia.

But the guard stepped back. He exchanged a long, speaking glance with his counterpart, and then they both moved away, heading for the door at a trot.

They were not the only ones. People fought to get out, their numbers clogging the doorway. He saw a couple of people slip out the windows. Others stood still in shock, or cried or fought with each other. One slight and incredibly dirty man caught his attention because he marched against the crowd, moving toward the small crowd around Hestia with murder in his eye.

Stoneacre couldn't see her. The men around her were in a heated argument. On the stage above them, Marstoke lay still in a growing pool of blood. One of the hulking men who had stood at either end had grabbed Beth, holding her back pressed tight against his chest. She fought to get away, her limbs flailing as she screamed and cried. "It was all lies!" she shouted. "Pain and lies!"

"Hush," the behemoth holding her said. He dragged her while she fought tooth and nail to escape.

"All this time! And Hestia was nothing but kind to me," she sobbed.

"He never told me the truth of it. He never meant any of it." She let out a scream of rage toward Marstoke's slack body. "He's nothing but lies!"

The filthy man reached the group around Hestia and entered the heated debate of what they would do with her. Stoneacre moved around their perimeter and came in from the back. Hestia's chair had fallen over, or perhaps she had tipped it. The men were so busy arguing, they hadn't noticed Beth's dagger, flung from the stage and lying at the foot of the stairs. Hestia was moving toward it, dragging the chair with her.

He knelt beside her, his own knife drawn, meaning to cut her bonds, but she reared back, hitting his chin with the back of her head and spitting defiance while his jaw clapped shut hard enough to rattle his brainbox.

"Hestia," he ground out, his skull ringing. "Leave off!"

"Stoneacre?" She lifted her head and peered through her unbound hair. Her gown hung loose. A smear of dirt marred one perfect cheek—and still, she was the most beautiful thing he'd ever seen.

He cut her loose and she scrambled away from the chair. The world shifted back into balance when he took her into his arms. He held her tight while she trembled and clutched him back.

"You're here," she whispered. "And—he's dead. Did you see?" She looked dazed.

"I saw."

"And Beth—" Tears welled in her eyes. "Stoneacre, I didn't know! How could I not know?"

He gathered her closer—

"Let 'er go." The order rang out, harsh and loud.

He turned his head to see the dirt-covered man standing at the forefront of the angry group.

"The bitch owes me."

"Your claim's no better'n the rest of ours, Gordie." One of the men snapped, stepping up behind him. "You've had yer turn," he told Stoneacre. "Now move over and let the rest of us at 'er."

He pushed Hestia behind him. "She's mine." Simple truth, but it held a thousand meanings.

There was nothing more to be said.

The filthy bugger stepped forward and the rest of the crowd decided to let him take first crack.

"I'll be but a moment," Stoneacre told Hestia. "Wait here."

He stepped forward when Gordie growled and swung a raised fist.

Stoneacre ducked under it and punched him hard, direct to the kidney. The other man gasped and staggered a step away, but he rounded back and swung again. Stoneacre feinted and hit him dead on the jaw, hard enough to set bells ringing in his ears.

The man had clearly taken a beating before. He shook his head and cracked his neck, and, drawing in a couple of deep breaths, he straightened and rushed Stoneacre again.

He let him come. Blocking a blow, he pushed, raising the man's arm high and hit him right below his diaphragm. Gordie bent over, retching.

The crowd of his compatriots shouted advice. One of them tossed him a knife.

Stoneacre had left his blade next to the chair. Hestia should have picked it up, but the group of thugs stood between them and he didn't want to draw their attention back to her. He needed to finish this.

Gordie thrust at him. He dodged and had to continue to duck and weave for several more swings, dancing away to avoid the blade.

Then his moment came.

He blocked a vicious swipe and knocked the blade from Gordie's hand. And while the man was stretched wide and vulnerable, he raised a knee and slammed it into his stones.

Once. Twice.

Gordie crumpled.

The waiting men groaned. Stoneacre swept up the knife and turned to face them.

Several held up hands and backed away. But one smiled evilly and raised a flintlock pistol. His finger caressed the trigger.

Stoneacre braced himself. When the shot rang loud in the enclosed space, he flinched and winced—and then opened his eyes to see the other man clutching his neck while blood flowed through his fingers. He took a step and looked past the falling man to see Isaac, Hestia's butler, lower a rifle and give him a grim nod.

He didn't even ask how or why. He snatched up the pistol from the falling man's hand, then watched the rest of the group lose their enthusiasm for the fight. They started to melt away and he turned to grab Hestia up in his arms again.

But she was gone.

"Hestia?"

She was nowhere in sight.

"Where did she go?" Isaac asked.

Panic seized his soul. "She was right here!"

He called again.

The house was in chaos. Men fought or fled. One enterprising group was loading crates into a wagon. Stoneacre and Isaac sped through the house, searched through every crowd, every room.

But there was no sign of her.

CHAPTER 20

You might also wonder at my purpose. Why should I list out this man's foul deeds and expose you all to such ugliness?
--from the Journal of the Infamous Miss Hestia Wright

D amn Gordie, he had a blade and dangerous reach in his freakishly long arms.

Hestia scooped up the knife Stoneacre had dropped when she'd head-butted him. She took up the blood-stained dagger too, for good measure, and tucked it in a pocket. Then she crept forward, looking for an opening to slide the blade to Stoneacre and even up the odds.

There. There was her chance. She moved forward—and pain exploded in her head.

Darkness descended over her vision like a stage curtain.

SOMEONE POKED HER.

Hestia flinched and the nudge came again.

209

"Wake up. It's time, now."

She rolled her head. Saints, but her headache was back and worse than—suddenly she sat up straight. "Stoneacre!"

"No."

She stared wildly, uncomprehending, at the stranger across from her. "He was fighting Gordie! The dirty bastard had a blade! We have to go back!"

"No. Far too late."

She wanted to cry. To scream in frustration. Her gaze traveled wildly, taking in her surroundings. Another carriage—this one luxuriously appointed. Another headache. At least she was dressed this time. "Let me out, I'll go back on my own."

Something trickled down her neck. She reached up and her fingers came away bloody. Carefully, she explored the tight, pounding spot behind her ear and found a bump the size of a hen's egg.

"Sorry about that. It seemed the simplest way."

She shot the hulking man a sharp look. "To do what? Break my skull?"

"Get you out."

Suddenly, she realized who he was—one of the behemoths standing guard over Marstoke's stage play. "Listen. Just let me out. I'll make my own way back. I have to help Stoneacre."

"One way or t'other, that fight's long over. Your fancy lordship might'a beat Gordie, but there was a crowd waitin' to take 'im on." He sat back and folded his arms. "That place was coming apart at the seams. Nothing good was going to happen to you, there. So, I got you out."

"But not Stoneacre?"

"I don't owe him."

She waited.

He sighed. "My sister's girl moved to Manchester to take up a mill job. The mill owner said she was too pretty, too likely to cause trouble, and handed her off to a brothel. A bad one. You got her out. The girl's a maid at the British Museum now. Sweeps up and helps keep the displays neat. She's happy."

"Oh, yes. Sylvie. I remember her."

"I figured I owed you fer her. So, I got you out. I'll let you out here, though, and then yer on yer own."

"Here?" It was dark outside and rain battered against the carriage window, and she realized that they were passing over cobblestones instead of dirt road.

"Bath."

"So far," she said, dismayed.

"Yes. No use goin' back. The only ones left at that house by now are those that will never leave."

The carriage rolled to a stop. He reached out and opened the door from the inside. "Go on in. Stay there. Don't go back and don't go to the Red Fox. You just wait and let it all settle out. If your man made it out, he'll find you." He made a shooing motion. "Go on."

Dazed, her head aching, she slid out of the carriage. The door closed again. Rain pelted her while she watched it pull away. Slowly, she turned.

Amelia's house. She stood in front of Amelia's house.

How had he known? What else did she *not* know?

Shaking, she made her way to the stoop and knocked on the door. It opened quickly and Amelia's butler looked surprised, and then horrified, to find her there, wet and miserable.

"Miss Wright?"

"Just Hestia, please," she said through trembling lips.

He pulled her inside and then looked as if he didn't know what to do with her. "Thomas, fetch Lady Cartweld. Right away!"

Behind her, a footman rushed off. The butler sent for a blanket, but Amelia arrived first, with two noblemen on her heels.

"Hestia, darling! Oh, my word, you are bleeding." She waved a frantic hand. "Hot water, fresh towels. Someone ready a room upstairs!"

Her arm around Hestia, Amelia turned to her visitors. "I'm afraid I must ask you to call again some other time, gentlemen," she began.

"Wait!" Hestia ordered. "Men. We will need men."

One of the gentlemen struck a pose. "Of course. Anything you ladies need."

Hestia shook her head. "I need someone to watch the Red Fox. And the Queen's Crown. We need to keep watch for Stoneacre."

"Your footmen, gentlemen!" Amelia ordered. "Send them to me here. The more strapping, the better!" She steered Hestia toward the stairs. "You, my dear, are going nowhere until we get you clean and warm and dry and take care of that nasty lump." She looked back at the butler. "A bath, Wilkins! Right away."

Amelia took over completely and Hestia allowed it. She felt numb in body and spirit as she was stripped of her clothes and settled into a hot bath. A maid took her clothes away and Amelia raised a finger. "Soak. Relax. I'll be back in a thrice."

Alone.

The quiet settled in around her. So did the worry. Where was Stoneacre? Was he alive? *Of course he was,* she told herself sternly. That crowd of malcontents would be no match for him. But what would he be thinking? Feeling? Their time apart was over. He thought he wanted more, but they were about to go back to the real world—and to all of the real complications that world stand in the way of such a lovely idea.

The tears started then. Silent and streaming without number, they mixed with the bath water while her emotions reeled.

Everything was mixed up. She was free. Marstoke was gone. She should be relieved. But she couldn't fight the strange blend of grief and guilt when she thought of him—and of Beth.

She bit back a sob. She'd thought she would be happy. She wanted to be happy. Instead she felt furious and fearful and forlorn at the hole inside of her—and the knowledge that only one person could heal it.

And the knowledge that it likely wouldn't happen.

"Here, now. Enough of that." Amelia entered, bearing a tray of brandy and glasses. "Here. This will warm you from the inside." She handed Hestia a glass and nodded in approval when she tossed it back.

Hestia held the glass out in silent appeal for another. She sipped that one, while Amelia pulled a chair close, then poured one for herself. "Now. Talk. And start with Marstoke. Where is he?"

"Gone." Hestia drank again. "Dead."

Amelia sat back in surprise. "Well." She took a sip, too. "Or rather, well done. Tell me everything."

Hestia did. All of it. About Stoneacre, as well. Everything.

The water had gone cold before she finished, so she stood and wrapped herself in a thick robe while she continued to talk. Amelia came and carefully cleaned the cut behind her ear while she listened, then stood behind her and drew a comb through her tangled hair.

When Hestia had finally finished, she met her friend's gaze in the mirror. "I don't know what to do, now."

"Well, your choices are certainly wider than before," Amelia mused. "It is sad to say, but that girl has lifted a burden from you. Marstoke is gone. He won't be watching you, taunting you, or hurting women any longer. You won't have to dismantle a string of opium dens. There is no carting him to justice or worrying about him escaping captivity once again. No fervent preparation of evidence against him or the public suffering through a trial." She set the brush down. "Your long fight is over, Hestia. What do you *want* to do?"

Tears welled again, despite her best efforts to suppress them. She bit her lip and stared at her friend in the mirror.

"Ohhh." Amelia went and poured them both another drink. She sat in a nearby chair and pursed her lips. "Stoneacre. Does he want you, too?"

Hestia sighed. "I think he does. However—"

"There's a lot of how in that however," her friend said baldly. "I know you are no stranger to scandal, but it's been a while, and this one will be . . . beyond measure." She shook her head. "His family, too, will be an obstacle. You will be trading one sort of fight for another, vicious in its own way." She raised her brows. "Are you sure you wish to enter the fray?"

It was foolish in the extreme. Possibly hopeless. But she thought of going back to her old life, without him. Without his smile, and his charming help and his laugh and his stories and his unwavering belief in her. She thought of donning her mask again and soldiering on, alone, pretending she didn't need him.

"Yes."

Amelia nodded. "Well. If you are going to enter a fight like that, then we'd better start planning now, how you are going to win."

CHAPTER 21

My hope is to shine a light on the dark corners where such evil grows. To encourage you, dear reader, to cast it out of your own heart. Remember, when you are tempted to one small misdeed, to hold yourself above your fellow man, where such a step on a dark path might lead you.
--from the Journal of the Infamous Miss Hestia Wright

Several days later, Hestia stood before the doorway in Hanover Square. She breathed deeply. Once. Twice. Again. She was going into battle. Another sort of fight altogether, just as Amelia had said, but definitely a battle. Before she could lose her nerve, she raised her hand and knocked.

"Hestia Wright to see Lady Woodbury," she told the butler. "On a matter of some urgency."

Judging by the increased stiffness of his spine, the man had heard her name before. And the small, nervous glance he darted toward the parlor on the right told her that he hadn't heard it bandied about the servant's hall, either.

She took pity on him.

"I admit, my own cause would be better served if you would just announce me like any other caller. But if you are fearful of a reprimand, I will storm in unannounced while you flutter helplessly."

The butler didn't crack a smile, but she saw the twinkle in his eye. "I believe I will weather the storm of your call, madam. If you will stay here, I will inform my lady of your arrival."

He left the door cracked though, so she did not remain standing outside. She followed in his footsteps and once he announced her name, she stepped around him into the parlor.

The Marchioness of Woodbury abruptly stood, abandoning a small desk covered in correspondence. She shot her butler a hard look. "Thank you, that will be all, Sommes." The servant bowed and retreated, closing the door.

Stoneacre's mother stood very still and glared at her.

Hestia waited.

"I didn't expect you to arrive so soon," the marchioness said, her brow raised and her tone laced with scorn.

"I'm surprised you expected me at all."

Lady Woodbury waved a hand toward her desk. "My morning letters are full of accounts of you and my son in Bath. Laden with descriptions of the spectacle he made of himself in the Pump Room. Over you." She tossed her head. "I knew you would come, eventually."

"I fear your friends exaggerate, my lady. We were in the Pump Room, but there was no spectacle."

"The sight of a decent man escorting you in public is spectacle enough. Too much, when it comes to my son. Which, no doubt, leads us to why you are here." She took a step away from the desk. "I do not keep a large amount of money about the house, but I will talk to my husband and he will pay you what you require."

"Pay me?" Hestia tilted her head. "Blackmail? Is that why you think I am here?"

"Why else?"

Sighing, Hestia removed her gloves. She still had not been invited to sit. "I assure you, I have more than enough of my own money, my lady. I don't need yours, your husband's, or your son's, for that matter.

I am not here to blackmail your family. I am here because I care for your son."

Lady Woodbury lifted her chin. "Even worse."

"Is it?" Hestia asked quietly. "Is it worse that I love him? You would prefer that I meant to harm him?"

"Absolutely."

"Why?"

"Because you *will* harm him." Her jaw tight, she asked, "Has he offered for you?"

"No. I went away before he could have the chance to do so. I came here to speak with you."

The marchioness collapsed into a nearby chair. "Oh, thank heavens." She covered her eyes with a hand for a moment, then sat up and stared at Hestia with urgency. "You must not allow him to do it—and you must not accept him."

"Why not?"

"You *know* why not!"

"I would like to hear your reasons."

"Do you wish to be the ruin of him? You are a whore!"

"I was a whore, yes. It was a choice I made when it became clear that my family and friends had abandoned me. That Society would never look at me in any other way, no matter what I did. I chose to live, rather than die. To thrive rather than suffer forever for one tragically stupid mistake." She met the woman's gaze directly. "I had already suffered enough." She took the liberty to perch on the edge of a chair. "It was long ago."

"It doesn't matter that it was long ago. You lie with men for money."

"I did, although honestly, from the beginning my notoriety saved me from having to take many clients, or from taking any at all that could not or would not treat me with the utmost respect and generosity. Do you know," she mused, "that there were many times when, for the men, it was not about physical congress at all? Often they merely wanted a pretty woman on their arm. Or the masculine thrill of having been the one to win a woman that other men wanted. Sometimes, they only wished to talk, to spend time with someone who would listen. But yes, sometimes it was just about the bedsport." She gave the woman a malicious grin. "And I was good at that, too."

"You are shameless," the marchioness spat.

"Generally, yes," Hestia agreed. "But tell me honestly, my lady. Was your match with Lord Woodbury a romantic one? Or was it arranged by your families for their mutual benefit?"

The woman's mouth tightened.

"I see. So, you've spent your life lying with *one* man. For money. And social standing. And vast estates. And pretty gowns." She lifted a shoulder.

"I care for my husband."

"I'm sure he returns your regard. And yet, has he kept a mistress? So many aristocratic men do. I haven't actually asked Stoneacre, but I'd be surprised if he hasn't, at some time." She shrugged. "Being on the other end of the transaction hasn't made them unmarriageable, has it?"

The lady abandoned that argument and attacked with another. "It will be a scandal. Everyone will whisper about it. My son will be mocked in all of the broad sheets."

Hestia nodded. "That is likely. I've been featured in the scandal sheets, on and off, for years. It occasionally stings, but they've yet to draw blood."

"His friends will laugh at him!"

"Friends might laugh with him. The others won't be missed."

"He'll be ostracized!"

"Lady Woodbury, though you have not acknowledged me, I have attended many of the same events that you have, over the Seasons. I am welcome at court. I am received at Carlton House. Some of the highest members of the *ton* not only are kind to me, but they also support my work." Her mouth twitched. "Granted, there are high sticklers who will never receive me. Some enjoy snubbing me, I daresay. But as I said, they are not missed."

The marchioness's lip curled. "You don't have any idea what my son will miss."

Hestia cast a kind look at the other woman. "What is your son's favorite color, my lady?"

"What?" Lady Woodbury frowned. "What has that to do with anything?"

"It's the blue of a robin's egg. Do you know his favorite flower?"

The marchioness rolled her eyes. "He's a man. An earl. I'm sure he doesn't care enough about—"

"Lilacs. He says they remind him of home. Do you know what his favorite childhood toy was?"

The lady smiled triumphantly. "He was mad for books and his pony. He didn't play with childish things."

"He adored the two-masted schooner he received on his birthday, and loved sailing it in the lake."

Lady Woodbury looked startled. "Oh, yes . . ." She shook herself. "None of this has any significance," she said coldly.

"It does. Your son enjoys the work he does for the Privy Council, but I believe he wants more, now. He deserves to have someone in his life with whom he shares a rapport. Someone he can talk with, listen to and share his life with. Believe me, I fought against our developing feelings, but they are real and true and they would not be denied. We care for each other, my lady—and he deserves to have that. He shouldn't have to settle for a young girl who shares nothing in common and merely wants him for his title and status."

Lady Woodbury sniffed. "Well, if you know so much of my son, perhaps you'll know that he will not care to lose his family over this matter."

Hestia stilled. "Is that a real threat, my lady?"

"It is, if it must be."

She sighed. "That is what I feared—and it is truly a shame." Her brows lowered. "I find it *offensive*, even, that you would turn your back on your son for making a decision you do not agree with. Especially as he clearly did *not* do the same to your husband. He did not abandon his father—not even when your husband proved to be so catastrophically wrong."

The marchioness paled. "Stoneacre . . . told you?"

"He did. And make no mistake—this is not a threat. I will never tell a soul about it."

The woman looked as if she wanted to believe her.

"Just as I will never tell Stoneacre *our* secret."

The color rushed back into the woman's face. "I don't know what you are talking about."

"Yes. You do."

Lady Woodbury merely clutched the arms of her chair with white-knuckled fingers.

"I've seen it worrying at you every moment since I walked in."

"The notion is ridiculous. I do not even know you."

"But you knew my mother," Hestia said quietly. "Did you think that I would not remember?"

The lady sat frozen, not responding.

"You were her closest friend, her confidant. I was young, but I remember your visits well. How many hours did I sit, playing with my dolls at your feet, while the two of you shared childhood memories and made plans for the future?"

"I don't know what you mean," Lady Woodbury whispered. "That girl . . . that girl died, swept off by a sudden illness."

"That's what they told people, isn't it? But you knew." She sighed. "You knew I'd made a horrendous mistake in judgment. I believed in Captain Wilson's love for me. I believed I loved him. I was a young, headstrong fool and I defied my parents and ran off with him." She drew a deep breath. "You knew I was little more than a child. Did you know I was fooled? Tricked into a sham marriage and turned over to Marstoke on my wedding night? Did you know I was raped? Beaten? Held captive? You did, because my mother told you everything—and years later, she wrote to me. She told me how she felt, how difficult it was for her, when I finally got away and wrote to her, asking for help, asking to come home. How she wanted to come to me, fetch me home, but my father was adamantly against it and her friends counseled that she not do so."

She took a deep, shuddering breath. "You knew about that, too, because you were one of the people whispering in her ear, telling her to turn me away. To heed my father's anger. You told her I would never be accepted in Society. That I would drag my family down. You told her that it was easier to abandon me than to expose the lie they'd told."

Lady Woodbury said nothing, merely sat, still clutching the chair and staring straight ahead.

"Do not fear. I am not going to tell Stoneacre. Not ever. Not even if you threaten to cut him if we remain together." She sighed. "He would be angry for my sake and disappointed in you. And frankly, he's suffered enough disappointment at your family's hands."

The lady made a sound of protest. She looked furious.

Hestia only shook her head. "I will tell you, my lady, that it hurts to be estranged from one's family. It tore me asunder that I couldn't be with my mother in her final days." The corner of her mouth curled. "I couldn't care less for the scorn of most people, but it pains me when I walk into a room and my cousin, who holds my father's title now, looks through me as if I were invisible. We grew up together. I taught him to fish. I was there when he was thrown from his first pony. He and I danced my first waltz together. But I am dead to him, and it is a lance through my heart whenever we meet."

She stood. "I don't want that for Stoneacre. I love him, so deeply. I don't think it's possible to know him and not love him, actually." A smile crossed her face just at the thought. "He's a fine, strong, wonderful man. Kindness just comes naturally to him. He has the clearest vision of anyone I've ever known. He looks straight past the facades that people throw up and celebrates their hidden strengths."

She sighed. "I'm not entirely certain he will ask for my hand, but if he does, I will give it to him. And I urge you not to disavow him, but to get to know him instead. The real man, not the one you wish him to be."

She walked to the door and opened it a crack. "I want you to know, Lady Woodbury, that if Stoneacre is forced to make a choice between us, it won't be because of me."

With a nod, she turned and walked out.

CHAPTER 22

I urge you instead, to choose light over darkness. Care for yourself and for all the others in your sphere. Bring hope and happiness in your wake instead of fear and pain. If even one of you, gentle readers, takes this lesson to heart, then I will be reconciled to the exposure of my secrets and count my time well spent.

--from the Journal of the Infamous Miss Hestia Wright

Stoneacre had been frantic until he discovered that Hestia had been dragged out of the house outside Clevedon and dropped at Lady Cartweld's townhouse. Then he'd been furious that she'd left there without him.

He'd been forced to stay in Bath for two days, calling in help from the local revenue men and excise officers to break up and track down Marstoke's smuggling contacts. But finally the last of the opium had been confiscated and the men he could identify had been taken in, as well. As soon as he could, he set out with all speed for London.

He barely rested on the way, stopping only to change horses or sleep a couple of hours before pressing on. He meant to go straight to

Half Moon House, but Crawford was waiting for him at the Kensington tollgate.

"The Prince Regent is in a slavering fit, waiting for you to come and give your report," his man told him. "You are to proceed to Carlton House right away. He doesn't even wish you to go home and wash off the road dust."

"Was Hestia's report not enough?"

Crawford shook his head. "The Prince received your note, but nothing further. No one has seen Hestia in London, that I know of."

Seething with frustration, Stoneacre rode to Carlton House. It took hours to give his full account, to answer the Prince Regent's many questions and to endure his crowing with triumph, as if he'd been the one to rid the world of Marquess of Marstoke.

At last, though, the Prince was satisfied—and Stoneacre, tired and anxious, took a hack to Half Moon House.

"She's not here," Isaac said, on answering the door. "But she is safe and as well as can be expected."

"Where is she?"

"She has a special place. She goes there when things get hard to bear or when she needs a bit of peace."

Stoneacre recalled their discussion at Cross Bones, the place where she'd agreed to work with him and told him of the Bishop of Winchester's geese. She'd mentioned her own private place. "She's there?" he asked. "The place where you've laid to rest the ones you've lost?"

Surprise showed on Isaac's face as he nodded. "I think she's gone there to give you a chance to think about it all. To get back to your real world and see if your feelings have changed."

Stoneacre shot him a look and silently they communed over the utter daftness of such a notion.

But then Stoneacre frowned. "And Beth? Where is she?"

"We've hidden her away. She's safe, for now, but some of Marstoke's more belligerent fools are howling for her blood." He shrugged. "We may have to send her abroad."

Stoneacre didn't care, as long as Hestia never had to deal with her again. He sighed. "I need to see Hestia, Isaac."

The butler held his gaze for a long moment. He nodded. "I'll write down the directions."

Isaac went off and Stoneacre sank down onto the bench by the door. He leaned his head against the wall and might have fallen asleep, but he startled awake when someone settled in next to him.

"Oh, good afternoon to you, Molly. How have things been, here at the House?"

"Quiet—except for me. Things are happenin' fer me, sir."

"Oh?"

"Yes. Did you hear? I've a family now. Of sorts."

He lifted his head. "Do you?"

Her eyes widened. "Oh, I forgot! I'm not supposed to tell."

"I'll keep your secret. I promise."

"I knew you would, sir." She sighed. "Lady Diane cannot take me in, but she's settin' me up in a shop, right in the village near her home." She wiggled a bit. "Can you see it? Me? In a shop? I can scarcely wait." Her smile faded. "But I'm frightened, too."

"I don't blame you. It's a big change, to leave London and all. It's only natural to be a bit frightened of change."

He paused. Was that was why Hestia was avoiding him? Did she believe her life would have to change if they married?

"You know, you've had a good teacher, Molly. The best. All you have to do is think, whenever you are frightened—What would Hestia do?"

Molly nodded. "She'd learn how to keep those books, she would. And she would remember to talk to the customers without throwin' in a bit of a flirt."

"She would indeed," Stoneacre agreed. "And she wouldn't let fear keep her from her dream."

"No. She'd tackle it head on and beat it down until she'd made it hers," Molly said with a laugh.

"Yes, so she would. And so will you."

And so would he.

～

HESTIA SIGHED. How she loved it here. The river moved at a sedate pace, the lawns were green and springy beneath the feet and the trees were glorious overhead. In one corner of the acreage lay the grave-yard, fenced off, with each stone lovingly marked and tended. In another corner, a little folly had been built, a small, pillared structure with a stone roof to serve as shelter in the rain.

She preferred to sit beneath the cherry trees. They provided shade from the sun and just now, when spring was starting to turn to summer, pink petals wafted loose in the wind and drifted down to land softly across her skirts.

This was the place that brought her calm and peace.

Usually.

This time, though, she waited, her nerves on edge, a part of her unable to settle her mind enough to read her book.

Perhaps he wouldn't come.

No, he would.

She spent the morning careening between opinions, all the while holding tightly onto hope.

When he did come, the sound of the water masked his footsteps. She was unaware of him until he sank down onto her blanket and stretched out beside her.

She stared.

He breathed deeply and let it out on a sigh of satisfaction.

And the jagged blade of worry in her chest smoothed instantly away. She grinned at him and he smiled back and all was right with the world. For a moment, she could not see him through joy and relief and the first swell of tears.

"You were right," he said. "This place is pretty and peaceful."

"I am often right," she told him.

"A deplorable habit."

"You'll get used to it."

"Will I?" he asked. He took her hand and kissed the back of it. "I feared you ran away to this place because you didn't want me."

"No. That wasn't it."

"Isaac said you were giving me a chance to get over you. When I was done laughing, I took his directions and set out. I've had a number of disturbing thoughts on the way."

"Oh?"

"Yes. I know you for a fighter. So, at first, I worried that you perhaps thought I was not worth fighting for."

"I should think you would know better."

"I did quickly discard the notion—especially once I spoke to my mother."

That gave her pause.

"And I discovered you'd already been fighting for me." He shook his head. "I knew you were brave, Hestia, but damnation, even I would hesitate to take on my mother. And how on earth did you conquer her, I'd like to know?"

"Conquer her? I came out of there rather feeling she'd ravaged me."

"I don't think I wish to know the particulars," he said with a shudder. "But I went there expecting a row and instead found her as meek as a lamb."

"How . . . surprising."

"So, in any case, I knew that wasn't it. So I wondered if you believed that I wouldn't fight for *you*." He reached up and touched her cheek. "I know your family did not, all those years ago, but I promise you, I will always be there. You aren't alone, Hestia. I've *been* fighting for you—fighting myself and trying to stand back and let you come to your own conclusions about the inevitability of us."

"Inevitability," she mused. "I suppose it is true."

"It was the hardest damned thing I've ever done, but I'd suffer it all over again. And I will suffer worse in the future, if need be. And you must know, I'll always stand behind you and support you in your endeavors."

"I know. I knew it the moment you walked alone into that house to confront Marstoke and his minions. It was the single most brave and foolish thing I've ever seen."

"I meant to get you out of there or die trying."

She shuddered. "It was a near thing for both of us."

"It's over now." He shook his head. "Can you fathom it? He's gone and his evil ways with him. Riding to London, I wondered what on earth I would do with all of that time I've been spending, tearing down his empire. I made splendid plans as I rode. And then I talked to Molly about change—and it struck me. Perhaps you were worried I would ask you to change, should we come together."

"Come together?" she asked with a smile.

"Marry. I mean to marry you, Hestia Wright—but I was trying to ease into it."

"Ah." She laughed. "That sounds nice."

"The marrying? Or the easing?"

"Both."

He sat up a little straighter. "I want you to marry me. But there are conditions."

She straightened, too. "Conditions?"

"Yes. Expectations. For example, there's to be no easy, pampered life of a countess for you, my dear. I expect you will continue to run Half Moon House—and I expect I'll be helping you. I expect you'll allow me to use my considerable talents to help you find the rest of the women on your lists. I expect we'll eventually expand the work—perhaps we can buy a hotel or a factory to provide a safe place to employ the women who come to you for help."

She sighed, utterly charmed by each of those ideas. "That is a lot of expectations."

"I expect you'll meet them all with no problem."

"I expect I will." She frowned suddenly. "But what if I want the easy, pampered life of a countess?"

"Then you shall have it," he answered promptly. "For all of the two hours that such a wish would last."

She laughed. "That sounds about right." She leaned down, then, and kissed him, with warmth and soft, pleased leisure, feeling strong and sure in the knowledge that there would always, always be time for this, for the two of them, together. He dug his hands into her hair and kissed her back for a while, and then he pulled away and made a face at her.

"I suppose we shall have to delay the wedding until Rhys and Flightly return from their bridal trip."

"Yes," she said firmly. "I will want my son to give me away."

He nodded, looking glum.

"But I expect there is no need to delay the bedding," she whispered, caressing his strong jaw.

His eyes brightened. "I expect not." He drew her down to him.

And so they didn't.

AFTERWORD

Thank you so much for reading the Half Moon House Series! I hope that you have gasped and laughed and loved as much as I have on this adventure!

Want to know what happens after Hestia's Happily Ever After? Sign up for my newsletter and you can read the Half Moon House Series Epilogue for free!

This epilogue will not be available for sale. Unsubscribe options are available on every newsletter if you do not wish to continue receiving my news, contests and historical tidbits.

Click the cover to sign up and read!

ABOUT THE AUTHOR

USA Today Bestselling author Deb Marlowe adores History, England and Men in Boots. Clearly she was destined to write Historical Romance.

A Golden Heart winner and Rita nominee, Deb writes Regency Romance and Young Adult Fantasy Adventure.

A proud geek, history buff and story addict, she loves to talk with readers! Find her discussing books, movies, TV, recipes from Deb Marlowe's Regency Kitchen and her infamous Men in Boots on Facebook, Twitter, Instagram, and Pinterest.

Connect with Deb
www.DebMarlowe.com
Deb@DebMarlowe.com

ALSO BY DEB MARLOWE

The Half Moon House Series

The Novels

The Love List

The Leading Lady

The Lady's Legacy

The Lady's Lover

The Novellas

An Unexpected Encounter

A Slight Miscalculation

A Waltz in the Park

Liberty and the Pursuit of Happiness

Beyond a Reasonable Duke

Lady, It's Cold Outside

The Earl's Hired Bride

The Castle Keyvnor Pixies

Lady Tamsyn and the Pixie's Curse

Lord Locryn and the Pixie's Kiss

Writing as D.M. Marlowe:

The Eye of the Ninja Chronicles

Eye of the Ninja

Obsidian's Eye

The Fire in the Ice